Web

Web

J.P. Mercer

P.D. Publishing, Inc.
Clayton, North Carolina

ISBN-13: 978-1-933720-49-4
ISBN-10: 1-933720-49-2

9 8 7 6 5 4 3 2 1

Cover design by Linda Callaghan
Edited by: Verda Foster/Medora MacDougall

Published by:

P.D. Publishing, Inc.
P.O. Box 70
Clayton, NC 27528

http://www.pdpublishing.com

Acknowledgements

No book solely belongs to the author. It is touched by the skill and imagination of many as it travels a wondrous and enlightening path. My sincere thanks to P.D. Publishing, Linda and Barb, and Lynne Pierce, Andi Marquette, Verda Foster, and Medora MacDougall. Thanks to Linda Callaghan for creating the perfect cover. *Web* greedily absorbed the contributions of each of these very talented women.

My acknowledgement would not be complete without a special thanks to my two special friends who encourage me every step of the way. Sue and Lynne, if the words dim and the last words are written, you remain the constant and always dear to my heart.

Dedication

To all women who have a dream, a passion.
Never hear or accept the words "you can't".
You can.

"Your fee is substantial. In good faith, even before you completed the first stage of the project, half your fee, $2.5 million, has been transferred to your account in Switzerland. We...our investors feel that your requirement of the total amount being paid before the job is completed is, well, unreasonable and risky."

A cynical grunt of amusement at the expected demand could be heard on the other end of the phone.

Ah, how predictable and arrogant, but you've not disappointed me. Why is it that those who seek the death of another want to negotiate and dictate the terms as if conducting an everyday business deal?

The amusement quickly turned to annoyance at being disturbed. A voice destitute of emotion answered, "The conditions and fee for my service were explained to you very carefully. They are not negotiable. The balance of the amount is to be transferred as agreed, or our business is concluded." Apathetic eyes looked at the clock on the mantel of the stone fireplace. "That gives you less than an hour to complete the transaction. You were given the option to call this number one time. You've just used that option up."

Scalzon took an unhurried sip of her brandy. "When I hang up, this number will no longer be in service, and there will be no further communication whether the fee is paid or not."

Without waiting for an answer Scalzon closed the cell phone, dismantled it, and slipped the pieces in her jacket pocket to be discarded in various trash receptacles along the way to the station. Taking an unopened pay-as-you-go phone from the desk drawer, she carried it with her brandy to the table next to the easy chair by the fireplace. In a matter of minutes she'd removed the GPS tracking device and reprogrammed the cell with a new phone number that she'd easily pirated off the Internet. She knew that odds were that the stolen number wouldn't be discovered for at least a week or more. It didn't matter; she was careful and routinely changed phones and numbers every few days.

Picking up the crystal snifter from the table, she wrapped her fingers around it. Closing her eyes, she slowly passed the goblet under her nose. The aroma of the brandy, combined with the mood of Beethoven's "Moonlight Sonata" filling the room, delighted her and brought a look of pleasure to her androgynous face.

In an hour the train would depart the station for Zurich. Not for a second did Scalzon entertain the thought that the money — the entire amount required for her services — wouldn't be transferred into her numbered Swiss account. She regretted leaving Engadin so soon after arriving. The crisp clean air in Switzerland was invigorating, in contrast to the pollution she'd left behind in Washington, D.C., and Los Angeles. She'd looked forward to a few days to relax at her home in the village of Samedan and the stimulating effects and conditioning of hiking and climbing the still-snowy Bernina Massif.

Placing the snifter on the table, Scalzon walked to the desk and opened the laptop. After entering a series of numbers, she said while smiling, "It's so much easier when we get beyond all the posturing and demands. All they needed to know is that the price they so greedily palter buys the expertise of my service." Before turning off the laptop, she confirmed her flight out of Zurich for the States and sent a coded message to an arms dealer in Mexico.

After checking the passport and identification she had chosen, she placed them in the bag, along with the few essentials she would temporarily need until she arrived in Zurich. There she would buy what she needed to change her appearance before boarding the plane for the States the next morning. Picking up the pictures that lay on the table, she casually ran her finger across the face of one of the women before throwing them into the fireplace. "So very beautiful...much too beautiful to die."

The mountain air was crisp and cool as Scalzon stood on the platform at the station in Samedan listening to the train whistle echoing up the valley. She fingered the fob of the chain and slipped the watch out of her pocket and opened the hinged cover. *Good, right on time.* Just as she picked up her valise someone called out a name. Turning, she saw Hans, the postmaster. The small Samedan post office was housed in the train station. He had a few pieces of mail in his hand. "I saw you buying your ticket and forgot to give you your mail, Karl." Looking at the valise, he said, "You are going on another business trip so soon? We haven't seen you much this year."

"Unfortunately, yes. I have business to attend to, but I hope to be back soon."

"I can keep your mail if you'd like and you can pick it up when you return?" The postman thought he was addressing Karl Mercer, a middle-aged banker from Zurich who owned a small cottage outside the village that he used a few times a year.

Scalzon brushed one finger across the graying moustache, a gesture meant to discreetly check the disguise. "That would be kind of you, Hans. When I return, I'll bring you a pound of the special blend tobacco you like." The train pulled in, and people hurried to board.

Delighted the postmaster clapped his hands together. "Thank you. I'll look forward to it." Hans waved as he turned to go. "Have a good trip."

Arriving at the busy and crowded Zurich station, it was easy to slip into the Männer toilette, shed her disguise, and quickly morph into another. Before walking a few blocks to a small hotel, Scalzon shopped in several of the station's many shops and purchased a laptop, briefcase, a larger suitcase, and clothing. The last stop was at a pharmacy to purchase what she would need to prepare for the trip to the States.

The next morning, dressed in a pullover shirt and light olive-colored pants and jacket, the clean-shaven man boarded the plane at Zurich International Airport carrying his laptop and a briefcase. When the plane landed in California, sixteen hours later, the most sought-after assassin in the world disappeared into the crowds and sprawling city of Los Angeles.

PART ONE
Chapter One

Harry Sweeney arrived at Prufrock's Motel on the beach at Carpinteria. An old friend, Floyd Nolan, a retired homicide detective, owned the motel and the marina. It had been way too long since the chief of homicide had taken any time off or gone deep-sea fishing, and he was due. Life in Los Angeles County revolved around crime. Murder was the norm in L.A., not the exception, and it seemed that every time Harry planned to get a few days of fishing in, someone had the bad taste to turn up on a slab in the morgue.

The sun was beginning to sink into the Pacific when Harry pulled into the motel across from the marina. He'd rented a boat for a few days and planned to soak up some sun, throw out a line, and drink a few beers with his friend. After picking up his key, he unloaded his fishing gear from the truck and stowed it in the room, then went to meet Floyd to grab a beer and a sandwich at the tavern down the road.

Floyd was just locking up when Harry came around the corner. "Didn't think you were going to make it again, Harry."

Harry chuckled. "Neither did I. I kept expecting to see flashing lights in my rearview mirror and a cop pulling me over to haul my ass back to the precinct even before I got out of town. The fresh air feels good here. The pollution in L.A. has gotten so damn bad it's hard to get a decent breath of air."

"I keep telling you that you should get out of that hell hole and retire. Move on over here. I want to expand the bait shop and maybe add a few more docks. The place needs painting. Hell, Harry, I could use a partner."

Entering the pub, Harry looked around. A fire burned in a stone fireplace, and he could feel the warmth emanating from the room. The atmosphere was relaxed and easy. People were swapping fish stories while enjoying their food and drinks. Harry thought how nice it would be to chuck it all and retire and spend his days fishing instead of chasing down criminals and attending autopsies.

"I just might do that, Floyd. I just might do that."

By the time the sun came up Harry planned to be out on the Pacific trying out the new reel he'd bought. It felt like he'd just gotten to sleep when the phone rang and woke him. Annoyed, he rose up on one elbow, looked at the clock, and groaned. Dropping his head back down on the pillow, he thought about ignoring it, but his gut instinct told him that it would just keep on ringing. Without turning on the light, he grabbed the phone and bellowed, "This better be damn good."

The call was from California Attorney General Bob Redfern, who was a good friend. "You're as ornery as ever, Harry. Sorry to interrupt your fishing trip, but I have a favor to ask. I need you to look into a murder at Laguna Beach."

"How come I never hear from you unless you want something, Bob? This couldn't wait for a few days or at least until morning?"

Harry could hear the edge in the attorney general's voice. "I wish it could, Harry. I damn well wish it could."

"You know Laguna is out of my jurisdiction. How's Jay Brunelle going to like me sticking my nose into her county and her murder?"

"I never asked her. I told her you'd be on loan as a consultant on this investigation, but you know Brunelle. I still got an earful. That one has a mouth on her. Let me tell you, she can cuss with the best."

Harry chuckled. He liked the feisty ex-Air Force pilot, but he would never tell her that. "She's a good cop. I don't blame her. I'd do the same. Who went and got themselves murdered that has you all in an uproar? Must be someone pretty important."

"Triple murder, and it's more a situation of who might be arrested for them. Sasha Sheppard, Ingrid Sheppard's younger sister, was found at the crime scene with what could be self-inflicted wounds on her wrists. She was whacked out of her head on something. At this point, we don't know if it was murder, then an attempt to commit suicide, or if Sheppard is a victim, too. Before we jump to conclusions and charge the President's sister with a triple homicide, we damn well need to be sure."

"President Sheppard's sister? Holy shit. I suppose the news hounds are all over this. Hell, why wouldn't they be? Christ, they monitor every frequency we have, and they have better snitches and resources than we do and deeper pockets."

"An old friend of mine, the publisher of the *Washington Post*, faxed me copies of pictures of the crime scene and the bodies. The pictures will be on the front pages of special late editions of the *Post* and the *Washington Times* in a few hours. CNN has already broken the story. It's curious, and I ask myself why CNN or any of the local station didn't get the pictures. I've been told the newspapers are not sharing until after the papers hit the streets.

CNN is pissed the pictures were sent gratis to the papers instead of them. They would have paid a bundle for them."

Mentally asking the same question, Harry threw the covers back and sat at the side of the bed. "Did they have pictures of Sasha Sheppard?"

"Several. She was covered with blood and appeared to be unconscious. In one of the pictures she was lying next to one of the bodies. It's not a pretty sight, Harry. No one knows who took the pictures or how they ended up on the desk of the publisher, but it sure in hell has the White House in an uproar. And they're pointing their finger at the Laguna Police Department. I don't need to tell you that Brunelle is livid."

Harry grunted. "No, you don't. Jay is probably lopping heads off as we speak. I take it you're telling me that President Sheppard has seen the pictures?"

"I sent the pictures to her as soon as I saw them. I met Ingrid and her partner Marty at Pepperdine Law School. We've been friends ever since. It's a hell of a thing and couldn't have happened at a worse time. She's been leading in the polls by such a margin she was sure to win by a landslide. This could jeopardize her reelection."

"She's done a damn good job. It would be a shame if she lost because of something like this."

"If I were asked to name one honest politician in Washington, I'd have to say Ingrid Sheppard. In my opinion she gives this country the leadership that's been sorely needed for a long time. I need your input on this, Harry. I need indisputable evidence and to know without a doubt that Sasha Sheppard is innocent — or that she's responsible for these murders."

Many thoughts were running through Harry's cop mind. Ingrid Sheppard was the first woman to serve as President of the United States. And she was a lesbian. When she moved into the White House with her wife, the political right had rallied and gone on a witch-hunt, chanting that the country and family values were in the hands of an amoral deviant, condemning her to an eternity in hell. In her three-plus years in office, Ingrid was well on the way to cleaning out corrupt politicians in Washington and reducing the enormous deficit of the previous administration. Her honest and open administration was slowly changing the world's view of the United States to a positive one. Still, the extreme right and advocates of conservative ideology and family values were always looking for something to crucify Ingrid with to assure that the heathen would not be elected to a second term. Because she was gay, they'd played the morality card to the hilt, but surprisingly enough, this time the country wasn't buying.

"Sorry to interrupt your trip, but I need you on this, Harry. I'll be in touch."

Before Harry hung up he could hear the thrashing of helicopter blades. When he lifted a slat on the blinds to look out, he saw the bright lights of a police chopper as it landed on the highway in front of the motel. Cursing, he threw on his clothes, pushed his ID into his back pocket, and grabbed his Beretta, shoving it into his shoulder holster.

"They'd find me if I put an anchor around my neck and sank myself out in the middle of the fucking ocean."

Ever since ditching a plane in the Iraqi desert, the gruff chief of homicide had liked having his feet planted solidly on the ground. Bleary-eyed, he looked down at the string of lights that pierced the night as the police chopper followed the Pacific Coast Highway toward Orange County and Laguna Beach. Day or night, the traffic on the winding highway never let up. When the chopper set down in the driveway of a multi-million dollar beach home, the light of day was just beginning to break through the remnant of darkness that hovered on the edge of the horizon. A scowling Jay Brunelle, chief of the Laguna Police Department, met Harry as he stepped out of the chopper.

"Nothing personal, Harry, but I was a bit put out when Bob Redfern called and told me he was sending you both here to help with this investigation. Orange County has some damn competent investigators. I know. I trained them."

"It's good to see you, too, Jay. And in fine form, as usual."

The hard expression on Jay's face relaxed a bit, and her eyes warmed as she looked at Harry. "Sorry. It's been a zoo. Given it was Sasha Sheppard who was taken from the house in an ambulance, I can use all the help I can get. Did Redfern fill you in on how many bodies we found here?"

"He did. He said it wasn't pretty."

"No, it sure in the hell isn't. I've seen plenty of killings, both as a cop and when I was in the Middle East, and these women were butchered. Senselessly butchered. I'll never understand the demented mind that could do something like this. I'm afraid Laguna Beach is going to have to brace itself for the frenzy and circus that's on its way."

Knowing that it was going to be a long day, Jay looked toward the sanguine horizon, then at the line of reporters her officers were fending off at the entrance to the driveway down on the highway. A few of the reporters were shoving and had pushed through the barrier, but they froze in their tracks when they heard her bellow, "Damn it. Push them back and if they don't stay there — arrest their asses!" Under her breath she mumbled, "Or just shoot the bastards."

Harry chuckled as he removed the wrapper from a piece of nicotine gum and placed it in his mouth. Jay Brunelle was a spirited woman, and one hell of a cop, just like her dad Lucas. He followed her to a CSI van where he acquired covers for his shoes, a hairnet, and a pair of latex gloves. It was the usual procedure before entering a crime scene, but it struck a familiar note when an investigator handed him a plastic bag to deposit chewing gum, cigarette butts, and even his own spit so as not to contaminate the crime scene. Harry slipped the covers over his shoes and pulled on the hairnet. "Jay — you said both of us?"

Jay handed Harry a cup of black coffee, but before she could answer, two red-faced homicide investigators approached them. "What the fuck is going on, Chief? That son-of-a-bitch from L.A. kicked everyone out of the house and off the beach. Then he told us no one was to enter or cross the perimeter or step on the beach until he says so! Does he have the authority to do that?"

As Jay tried to calm her detectives, Harry smirked and used his tongue to push the nicotine gum between his teeth and his cheek. He gulped down what was left of his coffee, pulled on his gloves, then started toward the house. He shot over his shoulder, "That S.O.B.'s name is Han Kiong, but most just call him Hank. He's the chief medical examiner of L.A. County and the best damn forensic crime scene investigator in the country. Take my word for it, Orange County is lucky to have him."

Jay held back a smile as her detectives watched Harry walk toward the house. Harry could be pushy and annoying, but he was fair beneath the gruff exterior, and he had the best investigative instincts and nose for crime of anyone she'd ever worked with — except her father.

Harry entered the house, then looked around. The carpet was white and soiled with several bloody footprints. As he walked through the house, he cursed, "Hell, no wonder Hank kicked them all out. They've probably tramped through all the evidence in the whole house."

Harry could recognize death at any stage. The stink of dead flesh and the metallic smell of blood reached his nostrils long before he reached the bedroom containing the bodies of two of the murdered women. The room had been decorated in contrasting shades of white. Now, it looked as if someone had taken a can of paint and deliberately desecrated and defiled a perfect white canvas.

The scene was grotesque. It looked like something wild or crazed had been set loose to do the killing. Blood was splattered everywhere, across the walls, the carpet, and the furniture. One victim was lying supine on the bed, her hands and feet tied to the bedposts. The white sheets and the scarves that had been used to bind her were saturated with blood. Another half-dressed woman was lying on the floor next to the bed. From the wounds on her body, it looked like she'd been stabbed repeatedly. A trail of blood indicated that she might have tried to crawl toward the victim on the bed.

Harry's gaze moved to a large bloodstain, then to another trail of blood that led out the open French doors. Walking carefully through the room, he stepped out onto the deck and saw a slightly-built Asian man bent over the partially clothed body of another of the murdered women. The corpse lay face-down. Floodlights had been set up, but the natural light was beginning to brighten the scene as Harry silently watched Hank work, taking pictures from every possible angle that he would retake when it was fully light.

Harry could see the silhouette of a boat bobbing out on the Pacific and wished like hell he was in Carpinteria heading out to fish. As he watched the surf break across the shore, a sandpiper skittered along the railing, unmindful of the woman's body on the deck. It was in moments like this that Harry cursed himself for not retiring. He'd had a bellyful of death and the handiwork of man.

Hank meticulously worked his way around the body, bagging any possible evidence, focusing on the areas he'd marked with numbered yellow tent-table flags. Harry always admired the way Hank worked and the respect he showed the dead.

After a bit Hank pushed his glasses up on his nose with the back of his gloved wrist, straightened his back, and said, "We need to quit meeting like this, Harry. I thought you went fishing." He offered a wry smile, then pointed out the bloody handprints on the railing and the blood on the deck. "The handprints are probably the victim's. The blood on the deck and the footprints are smudged. The evidence has been contaminated. Most likely the footprints belong to the victim, whoever did the killing, and the officers who answered the call." Hank shook his head. "The chief's investigators were in the house when I arrived, so they were probably out here, too."

Harry stuck another piece of nicotine gum into his mouth, hoping it would help quell the feeling that was threatening to bring up the cup of black coffee he'd downed outside. "Bob Redfern called you, too, I see."

"Yep, he did. He didn't tell me anything, just asked if I could get here as fast as I could. Jay Brunelle and her investigators are pissed that we're here."

Harry shrugged, then nodded toward the body. "Looks like she tried to run, but didn't get too far."

"As bad as she was wounded, and at the rate she was losing blood, it couldn't have taken too much effort for the killer to catch up to her and take her down, then finish her off. I'll know more when I examine the bodies. Did Redfern tell you that there was a woman found in the house when the police arrived? She was rushed out of here in an ambulance before I got here. Don't know if she was a victim or a suspect. I heard that the paramedics said the woman was lucky to be alive, given the amount of blood she'd lost."

Harry thought about the picture that had been sent to the papers. It wasn't going to go well for Sasha Sheppard. Whether out of a growing distrust or jealousy of those who have great wealth, people had no sympathy for the well-to-do and were ready to believe the worst.

"What time do you think this went down?"

Unclipping the Blackberry that was hanging from his vest in a plastic baggie, Hank looked at his notes. "The 911 call came in at four-fifteen AM. Rigor is just beginning on the two victims in the house. At this temperature, we can narrow it down to about four hours ago. The two in the house were killed first, then this one." Hank looked at the oversized watch on his wrist — five after six. "Sometime after midnight and before four-fifteen."

Squatting down beside the woman, Harry noted that she was barefoot and had on a pair of slacks and a bra. She had three deep wounds in her back. Hank kneeled and motioned to Harry, and they carefully turned her body over. The woman's throat had been cut.

Something about this murder started to gnaw at Harry's gut. He forced back the black coffee rising in his throat, spit the nicotine gum into his hand, wrapped it in the paper he'd saved, then put it into his pocket. Reaching into his breast pocket, Harry took out a stub of a cigar. He stuck it into his mouth and started to chew on it.

"Damn, you think a woman could have done this?" He caught himself. "Hell, that was a stupid question. I've seen worse done by women."

Before he rose, compassion for the woman who died such a horrible death compelled Hank to reach out to close her eyes. "Are you going to tell me who was arrested, Harry?"

"What makes you think I know?"

"Must be someone important for Jay Brunelle to agree to us sticking our noses into her case and me keeping her investigators out." Hank pushed his wire-rimmed glasses up on his nose. "And only an act of God or something mighty important could get you to cancel your fishing trip."

A balmy breeze off the Pacific helped ease the nagging weariness between Leah's shoulders as she left the ER of South Coast Medical Center. With the top of her Jeep down, she drove along the coastal highway toward home. Leah Stanhope, chief of emergency medicine, glanced at her watch. She'd promised Sidney she'd try to be home early, but a pileup on the coastal highway made a long day in the busy ER even longer. The accident had filled SCMC's emergency department with a busload of severely injured people, and the staff was already shorthanded. Then Sidney left her a message, saying that a crisis had come up with a case and she, too, would be late getting home.

Leah reached into her pocket to be sure she had the earrings she'd picked up at the jewelers before going on duty. They were a gift for Sidney for their anniversary. Sidney, always on the fast track, had been working tirelessly for months preparing the defense in a murder case. That, coupled with Leah's own demanding schedule, meant that days could go by when they didn't see each other. Tonight was supposed to be special. She wanted to surprise Sidney with the gift, a bottle of wine, and a much-needed night of pampering for them both.

Her weariness vanished when Leah pulled into the garage and saw Sidney's car. She picked up the shopping bag, hopped out of the Jeep, and headed for the kitchen door. When she stuck her head through the door of their bedroom a little after three AM, their anniversary had been officially over for three hours. Leaning against the doorway, Leah smiled. Her partner was propped up on her pillows asleep, a folder opened on her lap. Still, Sidney must have sensed Leah was there, because she stretched and opened her eyes. "Hey, you're home."

"Hey, sweetheart, sorry about the time. Did you get my message?"

Sidney had been so exhausted doing damage control that she hadn't listened to her messages. A major witness in a murder case she was working on was having second thoughts about testifying and had up and disappeared. She would have to ask for a continuance and approach the case from another angle.

"I've been home a while. Sorry. I was so tired when I got in I didn't listen to my messages. I took a shower and went straight to bed. I intended to work on..." She looked down at the papers on her lap. "...A file, but I must have fallen asleep. Another emergency?"

"A loaded tour bus, head-on with an eighteen wheeler. Multiple casualties and injuries." Smiling, Leah looked down at her soiled, wrinkled scrubs. "I should go shower. I didn't change before I left the hospital. I was too anxious to get home."

Sidney watched her lover strip out of her scrubs and go into the bathroom. When she heard the water running, she turned out the light, slipped her glasses off, and set them and her papers on the nightstand. Sliding down in bed, she put her head on the pillow and closed her eyes just to rest them. She must have dozed because the next thing she knew was the feel of Leah's hand covering her eyes.

"Uh-uh, no peeking. Not yet." Leah had set the shopping bag on the floor beside the bed. Bending down, she took out a bottle of Sidney's favorite wine and placed it on the night table next to two crystal wineglasses. Then she reached back into the bag to retrieve the gift. She brushed her lips across Sidney's. "Open your eyes, darling."

Sidney opened her eyes to see Leah wearing a big red ribbon draped over one shoulder and across her bare breast. In her hand she held a small blue velvet box tied with another red ribbon. Her voice was husky, and her gray eyes had deepened to obsidian, something Sidney was quite familiar with.

"Happy anniversary, sweetheart. You have a choice. Which present do you want to enjoy first?"

Sidney's heart was a lump in her throat as she looked at the velvet box in Leah's hand. Guilt washed over her. She loved this woman with her whole heart, and she'd forgotten their anniversary. They'd been together for ten years, and Leah was everything she'd ever wanted in a partner.

Oh, Leah, I can see the desire in your eyes and on your face. You want to make love tonight. I don't deserve you.

Sidney took the velvet box from Leah's hands and placed it on the nightstand. She felt Leah tremble as she ran her hand over her firm thigh, then across the gentle arch of her hip and upward until she reached the ribbon that cradled Leah's breast. Sidney cupped it and brushed her thumb across the hardened nipple before untying the ribbon. As it fluttered to the floor, Sidney pulled the covers back and said, "I choose..." Her tongue reached out to caress a swollen nipple, "...you."

Chapter Two

The elevator doors opened, and Sidney DeRoche stepped out into the reception area of DeRoche Law Offices. In one hand she carried her briefcase, in the other a copy of the late edition of the *Washington Post* that she'd hurriedly bought at the newsstand on the main floor of her office building. Avril Savoy, her law partner, their office manager, Jason, and the smell of freshly brewed coffee greeted her as she walked down the hall toward her office.

Jason trailed behind Sidney with a stack of files. Energetic and a stickler for neatness and detail, he had chosen to leave the Sheppard Law Firm when Sidney did to join her in her new law practice. "Good morning, Sid." He looked at his watch. "You're running a few minutes late."

"I know, traffic was terrible and if you must know, I slept in. Is that coffee I smell?"

Jason rolled his eyes. "Your partner made a pot."

Avril shot Jason a look. The day didn't officially start until the two began their morning ritual bickering over who made the worst coffee.

"Come on, Sid. When he makes it, it's so strong you have to spoon it out of the pot. It's undrinkable. If he values his fingers, he will not touch the coffeepot — ever. Right, Jason?"

Jason grinned, wriggled his fingers in front of his face in a suggestive manner, and then disappeared down the hall toward the conference rooms. Avril's words followed him, "One of these days, Jason..."

Avril poured two cups of coffee and followed Sidney into her office. "On second thought, I should have let him make it. Strong might have been good this morning. I think you're going to need it."

Sidney set her briefcase and the still-folded newspaper on her desk, then looked quizzically at Avril. Concern caused a questioning eyebrow to rise. Avril usually took everything in stride, but this morning the edge in her voice said something was up. Avril placed a steaming cup of coffee on the desk in front of Sidney, then asked, "Did you watch the morning news or listen to it on the drive in?"

Sidney blushed. She and Leah had made love again after she opened her earrings, and it seemed like she had just gotten to sleep when the alarm went off. As it was, she turned it off and overslept.

When she woke, Leah was gone. "No, I didn't this morning. What did I miss?"

Avril reached for the newspaper and unfolded it so that the front page was in full view. Sidney's breath caught. A picture of Sasha Sheppard, a face from her past, was staring up at her. Dominating the rest of the full-page coverage were gruesome pictures of three dead women, along with a close-up of an unconscious Sasha Sheppard, on a gurney, being loaded into an ambulance. The headlines screamed the Sheppard name in bold print, saying that President Sheppard's sister had been found at a murder scene, covered with blood. The killings had taken place in Laguna Beach, the story said, at the home of Lauren Serantis, the CEO and founder of Serantis Pharmaceuticals.

Sidney had seen enough crime scene pictures to know these were taken close-up. They looked like official evidence photos. She wondered how they happened to be splashed across the front page of the morning news and within hours of the crime.

Sidney was stunned, but almost immediately her thoughts were of her best friend and Sasha's sister, Ingrid. Before she could reach for the phone, Avril handed her a file, then sat back in a leather chair and sipped her coffee, all the while looking expectantly at Sidney over the rim of her cup.

Avril knew her business partner better than most. She could see the well-hidden emotion on Sidney's face as she flipped through the file of crime scene photos. After a few minutes, she turned her chair around to look out the expanse of windows that faced the harbor and the blue-gray water of the Pacific. When she turned back a few moments later, she looked at Avril, an unreadable expression on her face.

"When did this arrive?"

"It was delivered by a special courier shortly after I got in this morning."

"You've read it?"

"Yes, I have."

"Well, then, you know Ingrid authorized it to be sent and that she feels there's a good possibility Sasha will be charged with these murders."

Sidney stood up, took off her jacket, and then picked up one of the papers in the file. "They took Sasha to SCMC. Her Uncle Isaac is there with her. DeRoche Law Firm is now officially counsel..."

"Avril, please contact Grant. We need him on this. Tell him to dig as far back as the womb and start with the dead women. I want to know how these pictures made it on the front page of the paper and who took them. While I sort through this, please call the hospital, talk to Isaac, and check on Sasha's condition. He will know not to let anyone question her."

Sidney buzzed for Jason. "Jason, please take everything off my calendar. Assign all my appointments and pending case files to Merrill." She looked at Avril. "I suppose you've already organized a research team?"

"Yes, ma'am. And I've already called Grant. He's made a few calls. The pictures arrived anonymously at the newspapers. He said he was going to follow up with the courier service to find out where the package originated."

Sidney nodded, not surprised that Avril had anticipated her response so well and that the wheels of the defense were already in motion.

"Jason, the research team will be arriving. Please arrange for food and beverages for lunch and dinner and stock the refrigerators. It's going to be a long day and a longer night."

"Already done. The war room is set up and ready."

Avril tucked away her cell phone and took a drink of her coffee. "I've talked to Isaac. I told him I'd come to the hospital as soon as I talked to you."

"Good. How's he holding up?"

"His voice is shaky, but he's thinking like a lawyer. He was concerned that the story in the paper sensationalized the fact that Sasha was covered in blood. He says it didn't mention that the blood was most likely her own or even that Sasha had been wounded."

Sidney stared at Avril. *Blood? Wounded?* She paled as the facts began to sink in. This wasn't just another client. It was her ex-lover. Sasha had been injured and was in the hospital. "Is...is she all right?"

"She's unconscious, and her condition is listed as critical. Isaac is aware that Ingrid had the file sent to you, and he's made sure that no one except hospital personnel has been allowed near Sasha."

Avril could see the emotion behind Sidney's eyes and the slight trembling of her hands. Representing Sasha was going to be difficult for Sidney, she knew, and she knew why.

"Sid, considering what we can see in the pictures of the crime scene and the murdered women, if Sasha is charged with the murders, the court will deny bail and... The attorney of record will be important."

"I know. We can deal with that. We really don't know anything at this point, and we don't know that she'll be charged. But if she is, she's still innocent until proven guilty."

Sidney looked again at the pictures spread across her desk. Avril could see the wheels turning in her head.

"We need to find out everything we can about these women. I don't believe in coincidence. Even if I did, it's just too much of one that someone had access to the crime scene to this extent and that fast and that these pictures made it to a major newspaper. Something is not right, and I suspect Ingrid feels it, too. Please tell Isaac...tell him we'll devote every resource to this. I'm going to call Ingrid."

Sidney shook her head. The pictures of Sasha, disheveled and strapped on a gurney, were a stark contrast to the beautiful and vibrant woman she remembered. She looked up at Avril. "You were that sure that I'd get involved?"

Avril looked back for a long moment. "I knew without question you would, Sid. Because Ingrid is like a sister to you and Isaac is a dear friend and because..."

Avril didn't finish what she had been going to say. Instead she got up from her chair, headed toward the door, then paused and turned to ask, "You're sure about this?"

Sidney didn't answer; her gaze went back to the pictures of Sasha. Avril slipped quietly out the door.

The slender woman lying under a sheet on the hospital gurney began to twitch, then shake. Her eyes flew open and rapidly moved back and forth. In her delusional state, Sasha could hear bloodcurdling screams coming out of the fog. Waves of nausea washed over her as she desperately clawed at her arms to free them of their bonds.

Struggling to overcome her fear, Sasha desperately thrashed and crawled off the thin mattress. In her mind she was at the beach house, seeing a distortion of shadows and images that terrified her. Strangely enough, though, she was running toward the darkness and not away from it. She managed to get off the gurney, but her legs were too weak to support her and she fell to the floor. She could see blood everywhere — on the sheets, on the floor. Blood covered her hands.

Drenched in sweat, Sasha shook violently as her stomach muscles clenched in agonizing spasms. She retched over and over as she desperately tried to wipe the blood off her hands. She could see vague images of Lauren's face twisted in pain; she could hear

Lauren's voice screaming her name over and over. A thick fog shrouded her mind. She couldn't remember.

Oh God, why can't I remember? Please, I need to remember!

Too weak to crawl, Sasha curled into a fetal position until she felt arms fold gently around her, lifting her off the floor. She heard her uncle's voice calling her name just before she fell back into the darkness.

Before Avril left for the hospital, she called Isaac to ask if he needed anything. His voice was weary as he told her that Sasha was still being treated in the ER and that her condition was critical. When she arrived at the hospital, she went straight to the ER. After she showed her ID, she was directed to the exam room where Isaac stood watching Leah and a nurse working on Sasha.

Avril was not surprised to see Leah. She would have heard about Sasha's admittance when she arrived at the hospital that morning. Given Sasha's status and the fact that she was the chief of emergency services, Leah would scrutinize every aspect of her care while she was in her ER.

Avril's gaze took in the disarray in the room. Discarded tubing, a half-empty bag of blood, and a bag of IV fluids lay in the sink. A bloody sheet was on the floor. "What happened, Isaac?"

Isaac's voice shook as he explained. "Sasha was unconscious when they brought her in. They'd stopped the bleeding and were infusing a unit of blood to replace what she'd lost from the wounds on her wrists. The nurse went to the desk to check on her lab work. I stepped out into the hall to call Ingrid. While we were gone, Sasha woke up, hallucinating. She somehow managed to get off the gurney and tear out her IVs. She ripped open the sutures in her wrists before she passed out. I found her on the floor."

Isaac's shoulders were bent, and his lip quivered. "She's so pale, and she's lost so much blood. Doctor Stanhope is resuturing the wounds and infusing another unit of blood. The doctor said she might need a third. My God, I wish her parents were here! They're on their way home from a cruise. But I don't know...they haven't seen her in months."

Isaac's face reflected a deep sadness. "I just wish they'd been here more for Sasha. Maybe if I had been..."

Avril put her hand on his arm. "Sidney told me that you've always been there for Sasha. What matters is that you're here for her today."

Isaac's worried eyes watched Sasha as Leah worked. "She's been doing well these past few years. Her business has prospered, and she's seemed content for the first time in her life. She's learned how to let go of the anger and jealousy that was so destructive when she was younger. Her aunt and I have spent time with her and..." Isaac's voice faltered, "We...we liked Lauren. My God, it's so hard to believe she's...dead."

Sasha's eyes were open, and she was staring at the ceiling, seemingly unaware of any pain or what was going on around her. When Leah finished tying off the last stitch, Isaac bent and kissed his niece on the cheek. "Sasha, it's Uncle Isaac. Avril Savoy is with me. She's a friend of Sidney's."

Lethargic and appearing to be in a stupor, Sasha slowly blinked her eyes. Avril moved closer to stand next to the gurney. "I work with Sidney DeRoche. Do you remember Sidney, Sasha?"

Sasha responded to Sidney's name. "Sidney? ... Where...where is Lauren?" Sasha's eyelids fluttered, then closed, and Leah quickly glanced at the monitors to check her vital signs. Sasha's heart rate and blood pressure were improving with the IV fluid replacement and the blood she was getting, but they still were a concern. A few minutes later the ward secretary handed Leah the results of Sasha's hemoglobin and hematocrit. Leah frowned and wrote an order for another unit of blood.

Avril had seen the subtle change and stiffness in Leah's posture when Sasha moaned something that sounded like Sidney's name. Leah kept her eyes on Sasha and the machines as she spoke briefly to Isaac and Avril. "She's too weak to answer questions. She doesn't even know where she is. It will have to wait."

Isaac looked gaunt; he was trembling with exhaustion. Concerned, Avril suggested, "Isaac, why don't you go to the cafeteria and get something to eat? Rest a few minutes. You look like you're about to collapse. I'll be here with Sasha."

Fatigue showed in Isaac's eyes. "I believe I will, thank you. I do need to call my office and contact Ingrid. She's on her way back to the States from Korea. I'm sure that right now Air Force One is breaking the sound barrier." Isaac sadly shook his head. "Excuse me."

Avril sat on a chair watching as Leah and the nurses tended to their patient. At times, Sasha would jerk, and her eyes would fly open. They looked glazed and wild, like those of a wounded animal. Avril noticed the hospital gown that Sasha had on and jotted down a note, reminding herself to ask where the clothes were that Sasha had been wearing when she was brought in.

The nurses left the room. Avril waited until Leah finished entering notes in a chart before she said anything. She'd always envied the relationship between Sidney and Leah. They were good together. They'd been successful in balancing very stressful and demanding careers and were each other's best friend. They were also still in love with each other.

"Leah, can I say something — something personal?"

After making an adjustment to one of the machines, Leah said, "It's not necessary. I think I know what you're going to say."

"Sidney and Ingrid have been friends a long time. Who else would Ingrid turn to for help but her best friend who is also the best criminal attorney in the country? What was between Sasha and Sidney ended long before she met you. You know that."

Leah kept her eyes on the monitors on the wall above the gurney, but Avril sensed more was mulling around in her mind. Finally, she spoke. "You don't owe me an explanation and neither does Sidney. If it were my sister, I'd want Sidney and you in my corner, too."

The door to the exam room opened, and Jay Brunelle and a scowling Harry Sweeney entered the room. Before Jay could say a word, Harry said, "We'd like to question your patient here, doc."

Avril was quick to get up, putting herself between them and Sasha. "Please, let's step out into the hall."

"I..." Jay looked over at Harry, trying to hide the irritation she felt. "We came to see how Ms. Sheppard is. And if possible ask her a few questions."

"Please, can we step outside?"

Avril held the door open while Jay and Harry reluctantly turned and walked past her into the hallway. Avril looked from Jay to Harry. "You're a ways from the big city, Harry."

Harry nodded toward the room, mumbling around the unlit cigar in his mouth. "Is she able to answer a few questions?"

"I'm afraid that Ms. Sheppard has been through a traumatic experience and is not up to answering any of your questions at this time."

Jay spoke before Harry could say anything more. "Please don't think we're insensitive to that, Avril. We hope Ms. Sheppard will be all right. We have three dead women and speaking with her could be of help in finding who did this. Is the DeRoche Law Firm representing Ms. Sheppard?"

"Sidney and I are personal friends of the family, Jay. We're not aware that Sasha needs legal counsel, but if she does, yes, we are her legal counsel and do represent Sasha. Is she being charged with something?"

Harry opened his mouth to say something, but Jay cut him off. "No, no charges have been filed against anyone. We were hoping Ms. Sheppard might be able to help us determine what happened at Lauren Serantis' beach house."

Avril was about to respond when an overhead voice cut through the ER, echoing threateningly off the sterile walls and tile floors and repeating the words, "Code blue, ER three." People dressed in scrubs of various colors came running from everywhere, pushing them out of the way. Through the open door of the exam room they could see Leah manually bagging Sasha. A moment later the three of them were ushered out of the ER to the waiting room. Isaac came running down the hall from the direction of the cafeteria. "Is it Sasha? My God, is it Sasha that coded?"

Avril put her hand on Isaac's arm. "We don't know what happened. We were standing outside the room when the code was called."

Isaac stumbled and leaned unsteadily against the wall. He looked as if he were about ready to collapse. Avril held onto his arm and led him toward a chair. "Please, sit down, Isaac. Leah will come out and tell us what's going on as soon as she can." After getting him a glass of water and making sure he'd be all right for a few minutes, Avril walked down the hall, looking for a private place to call Sidney.

When the phone rang, Sidney saw Avril's cell number on the caller ID and quickly answered it. "Is everything all right? Are you with Sasha?"

"Right now I'm standing in the hallway outside the ER. Sasha just coded. I think she's in pretty bad shape, Sid. Jay Brunelle and Harry Sweeney are in the waiting room with Isaac. Isaac doesn't look too good himself."

"She coded! Who's the attending?"

Avril took a deep breath. "Leah."

For a moment an odd feeling briefly swept over Sidney. "I'm on my way. I'll be there as soon as I can."

Sidney made her way to the parking garage under the building, grateful that she was able to get to her car without running into any reporters. She also knew that wouldn't be the case much longer. Even though the building had monitored security cameras and the entrances in and out of the garage had coded security gates, more than once during a case she'd been waylaid by reporters and photographers who had managed to get into the building or into the garage.

The ramp that led onto the coastal highway was a short distance from the garage's rear exit. Within minutes Sidney was heading toward the hospital. The traffic, as usual, was bumper to bumper, filled with impatient drivers leaning incessantly on their horns. As Sidney inched along, she delved into her past. She thought about Ingrid and about Sasha. Once, a long time ago, the intriguing Sasha had been all she could think about.

The traffic noise faded as Sidney recalled Pepperdine Law School, how she met her best friend, Ingrid, and about her affair with Ingrid's kid sister. It had been years, but the heartache of their breakup still hurt as if it were yesterday.

Chapter Three

Sixteen Years Earlier

For the aspiring students of law at Pepperdine University, the Robert J. Traynor California Moot Court Competition was the culmination, the brass ring. The mock trial drew the crème de la crème from many prestigious law firms around the country who came to scout and evaluate up and coming talent. Sidney was vying for the last spot on the team that would represent Pepperdine in the competition. So was Ingrid Sheppard. The position would go to the student who won the decision in a mock trial in Pepperdine's Mendenhall Appellate Courtroom.

As far back as Sidney could remember she had known what she wanted to be when she grew up — a lawyer. When she was a freshman in high school, she persuaded a classmate to let her take her place on a field trip to Pepperdine. It cost Sidney a month's worth of doing someone else's homework and her $30 in savings — but it was worth it. The minute Sidney stepped off the bus, she knew she was going to attend Pepperdine, no matter what it took. She received her bachelor's degree in criminal justice there in three years. Her hard work and a 4.0 grade average earned her a coveted Sheppard Law Scholarship and enabled her to attend the university's law school. Her goal was to graduate with honors and to participate in and win the moot court competition.

After weeks of grueling rounds of elimination debates, it was Sidney for the defense against Ingrid Sheppard for the prosecution. The name Sheppard was synonymous with that of Pepperdine, well known for the family's charitable donations as well as for the generosity of the all-inclusive Sheppard Scholarship.

The day Sidney learned that Ingrid Sheppard was to be her opponent, her heart and her hopes of winning the competition sank. Ingrid was not only a Sheppard and wealthy, but she came from a long line of successful lawyers and politicians who boasted Pepperdine University as their alma mater. Sidney thought she didn't have a chance. A Sheppard had never lost at Pepperdine.

Sidney was uncharacteristically nervous the afternoon she and Ingrid were to appear in front of the competition committee to receive the case files for the trial. She had never met Ingrid Sheppard, but she knew that she was being compared to a young

John F. Kennedy. She was charismatic, brilliant, and beautiful, and she was being groomed to be a name in future political arenas. Sidney dressed hurriedly. It had never bothered her to shop the thrift stores for her clothes. But as she stood looking in the mirror at her blouse and her one good pair of slacks, she vowed to buy a decent suit on sale to wear for the competition.

Looking at her watch, Sidney walked through the thick mahogany doors of Mendenhall. She was early and glad to be the first to arrive. She felt most alive when she stepped into a courtroom. A chill of excitement quickened her breath and sent a shiver down her spine. An autonomic response raised goosebumps along her arms. She stood in front of the judge's bench and looked at the great seal of jurisdiction and the flags of the federal and state governments on the wall behind. Then she closed her eyes and took a deep breath, inhaling the rich smell of polished wood and leather. She could almost sense those who had stood in the hall before her. Sidney closed her eyes and visualized standing in front of a jury. Her heart was pounding, and she wrapped her arms around herself, trying to imagine how it would actually feel. Ingrid Sheppard or not, she silently vowed that she was going to fight to win this competition.

When Sidney heard the soft clearing of someone's throat, she turned around. Ingrid Sheppard stood looking at her with a sheepish grin, aware that she had interrupted a very personal moment. Annoyed, Sidney was about to say something about sneaking up on people when she noticed how Ingrid was dressed and laughed. Ingrid raised a questioning brow as Sidney took in the sweaty Pepperdine T-shirt and shorts.

"Uh, I just came from soccer practice. I didn't have time to change."

"Please, I...it's...I'm not laughing at you. I'm laughing at myself. I spent all morning fretting about what to wear here today to meet you." She stuck her hand out and said, "I'm Sidney DeRoche, your opponent in the competition."

Ingrid took the extended hand and looked into Sidney's eyes, seeing exactly what she had expected: a competent woman determined to win. Ingrid had checked out every participant in the competition and calculated the odds of anyone besting her. After every round, she calculated the odds again. The one name that consistently came up was Sidney Anne DeRoche. It came as no surprise that Sidney was the one to face her for the last spot on Pepperdine's team. Of all, Sidney had the best chance of winning. They stood sizing each other up, but before either had a chance to say anything else, the committee representatives entered the room and both women concentrated on listening to the rules for the final competition.

Mendenhall Appellate Courtroom was standing room only for the mock trial, filled with people curious to see if Ingrid was a chip off the family block or just a pretty face. The well-presented arguments and heated exchanges ended up drawing praise from many spectators as well as from the faculty and attending attorneys, including Ingrid's uncle, Isaac Sheppard. Years later, talking about watching the competition, he would say that the interaction between the two women was the most stimulating and the best he'd seen at Mendenhall. That he'd felt he was watching exceptional and finely honed minds, advanced beyond their schooling, disciplined and skilled in the art of attack and counterattack.

It hadn't taken long for Sidney to realize that Ingrid was a formidable opponent. Each matched the other point for point. If Ingrid drew blood, Sidney regrouped and adjusted her strategy. The battle was one for the books. Both presentations were brilliant, and it was obvious to Sidney, and to anyone else watching the interaction, that no one had bought Ingrid Sheppard's way into Pepperdine. Each woman challenged and kept the other on her toes. Both prepared well into the night for each day in court. One was always a step ahead of the other, and on more than one occasion the two women ended up standing toe to toe, in each other's face, arguing a point.

Isaac, priding himself on having a good eye for talent, decided well before the decision was announced that he would offer Sidney a position at the Sheppard Law Firm when she passed the bar. He was proud of both his niece and of Sidney and felt both were destined to have auspicious careers.

As it happened, Ingrid won the decision by a slim margin, securing her position for the Traynor Competition. Although disappointed, Sidney accepted the defeat with grace, knowing that she had been beaten fair and square and by someone who had gained her high regard and respect. Years later when Sidney spoke to the graduating class of Pepperdine, she was asked how she felt about losing the decision to Ingrid Sheppard. She just smiled and pointed out that the person who beat her became the first woman President of the United States.

One afternoon a few days after the competition was over, Sidney was sitting alone studying in the atrium overlooking the Pacific

Ocean when she heard someone say hello. She looked up to see Ingrid standing in front of her.

"Can I buy you a cup of coffee?"

"Uh..."

Ingrid grinned, her brown eyes expressing her amusement as she sat down in the chair next to Sidney.

"I do believe I caught Sidney DeRoche at a loss for words. Will wonders never cease?"

Sidney felt the warmth creeping up her neck. "Well, I guess you have. Not a distinguishing attribute for an aspiring 'mouthpiece', now is it?"

Ingrid chuckled and leaned back in her chair to study Sidney for a moment before she spoke. "My honest opinion. I think the majority of attorneys talk just to hear themselves talk. You give them a little knowledge, and some think they own the world."

Ingrid leaned toward Sidney and made direct eye contact. "Tell the truth. You don't like me, do you? You think I'm an arrogant, spoiled, rich bitch whose family is paying her way through law school so that I can uphold the Sheppard tradition of lawyers and have a cushy office with a diploma hanging on the wall. Or is it that I'm a lesbian?"

Sidney stared at her. She had had no idea that Ingrid was gay. She admired Ingrid's candor and directness. After a moment Sidney answered, never looking away from Ingrid's questioning eyes.

"You're right. When I first met you, I did think you were riding on your family's money, but my opinion changed during the trial. You're a remarkable woman. You beat me with your knowledge and skill. And, for the record, I'm not homophobic. I didn't know that you're a lesbian."

"Can I ask you a personal question?"

Sidney knew what was coming and nodded.

"Are you family?"

Sidney hesitated. In light of Pepperdine's entrenched religious affiliations and conservative politics, she wondered if it was wise to answer the question. No one would question Ingrid Sheppard's sexual orientation or take away the only means to her dream, but she had her scholarship to be concerned about.

Ingrid took Sidney's hesitation as a signal to mind her own business. She stood to leave. Sidney caught Ingrid's hand and stood up. "What say we go have that cup of coffee and get better acquainted?"

That day a bond of friendship formed between Sidney and Ingrid. They became the shining stars of Pepperdine, destined to make their marks in whatever areas of law they chose. Ingrid took Sidney under her wing, and Sidney spent all of her free time with Ingrid and her lover Marty. Coming from old money and a long line of successful attorneys and politicians, Ingrid was naturally accepted in circles that afforded her all the advantages of knowing those with influence and connections. When an opportunity arose, Ingrid always made a point of including and introducing Sidney to people who could be advantageous to her career.

By their last year at Pepperdine, Sidney had met most of Ingrid's family except her younger sister Sasha. Ingrid spoke often about her, mostly out of concern, or when she was spitting nails and angry with her. Sasha had her share of the Sheppard brains Sidney deduced, but was the extreme opposite of Ingrid. She had a wild streak and had been kicked out of several prestigious schools because of her rebellious antics.

The weekend before their graduation ceremonies, Ingrid and Marty invited her to the family beach house in Dana Point. It was a beautiful spring day, and they were going to have a clambake and invite a few classmates over. The three had gone to breakfast at a quaint little place a few miles down the beach, then spent some time exploring a few shops.

When they returned to the beach house, Ingrid and Marty went upstairs to clean up and take a nap. Sidney went out on the deck to relax in a lounge chair. She was just about to doze off when she heard sounds coming from the open window of Ingrid's upstairs bedroom. Ingrid and Marty were having a pillow fight. Then, as suddenly as the laughter started, it stopped. Everything was quiet — except for a few moans and groans. She woke up a while later, when Ingrid called to her from the kitchen.

"Hey, Sid, we're going to the market to pick up the stuff for the party tonight. We need beer and ice. Do you want to take a drive?"

Sidney raised her hand and waved, opting to stay behind to take advantage of the quiet and seclusion of the beach and private cove. "You two go ahead. You both have a lot more energy than I do. Probably that restful 'nap' you took."

Ingrid laughed and threw Sidney a beach towel. "Take a swim and get yourself a girlfriend. You might be able to work out all that frustration. All work and no play."

"If I could find one like Marty, I would. Now leave me to my celibate misery."

It had been a long, hard semester preparing for finals and studying for the bar exam. As weary as Sidney felt, the sun glistening off the clear blue waters and the waves washing across the sand were too enticing. Stripping her clothes off, she walked barefoot across the grass and down the few stairs to the warm sand and dove into the water. She swam to the small dock that the family's sailboat was moored to. The cool water was invigorating, and the swim eased the tension headache she'd developed during the last marathon all-night study session.

After climbing up the ladder to the warm dock she lay on her stomach, resting her head on her arms. Feeling totally relaxed for the first time in weeks, she reveled in the feel of the sun on her naked body. She slipped into a half-asleep dream state, basking in the peacefulness until she heard a splash and felt cool water on her bare backside.

Opening her eyes, she saw a naked and stunning young woman holding onto a skim board and treading water alongside the dock. The way the girl's gaze raked over her nudity, expressing an appreciation of a woman's body, had Sidney blushing and left no doubt about the young woman's sexual proclivities. The girl's intense brown eyes made her heart skip a beat.

"You stay much longer out here, and you'll burn that sweet little tush of yours."

Squinting against the sun, Sidney instinctively reached for a towel, then remembered she didn't have one. "Hasn't anyone ever told you that it's impolite to sneak up on a person when she's lying naked on a private dock trying to enjoy herself?"

The girl laughed and deliberately focused on Sidney's ass. "Sorry, I just couldn't help myself. You have the sweetest...no, the most gorgeous ass I've had the pleasure to behold. And you should never be lying naked alone."

Hear me groan. It's been so long that I can't even remember when someone last commented on my ass. God, and she's just a kid. A mouthy one, but still a kid.

"And you've seen just how many...sweet little asses?" Self-consciously Sidney tucked her arms around her breasts, wishing that the girl would go away. "No, on second thought, don't answer that. It wasn't a question I should be asking a kid."

The girl laughed. The desire in her eyes was that of a woman who knew well the touch of another woman. "And you're all grown up and so much older. I don't suppose you'd like me to climb up there and show you that I'm not such a kid, now would you?"

For less than a second, Sidney was tempted. "No, I wouldn't like it. If you don't mind, I'd like to go back to being — alone."

The lingering look the younger woman gave Sidney sent a shiver along her sun-heated skin, and she was glad the younger woman couldn't see the hardening of her nipples. "Go home."

The girl laughed and splashed water on Sidney again, then she pushed off and slid onto the board. "Don't say I didn't offer my services or warn you. You're getting burned."

Sidney stared as the young woman disappeared into the sun. There was no doubt in Sidney's mind that the brash, self-assured young woman could probably teach her a few things about sex or that she had more than a few notches on her bedpost. *God, she's gorgeous! If only she wasn't so cocky, and so young...*

Chapter Four

Present Day

Sidney already had a splitting headache, and the people leaning on their horns all around her wasn't helping it, nor were they helping to move traffic along the PCH. She looked at her watch. The usual fifteen-minute drive to the hospital had turned into thirty, thanks to an annoying backup of traffic slowly moving past an accident. She could never understand why people slowed down to gawk at wrecks or followed ambulances or fire trucks. Society in general was preoccupied with the macabre, she decided, and the curious were essentially slowing down to give thanks that it wasn't them bleeding in a twisted pile of metal.

The exit to the hospital was just ahead. Given who Sasha was, the sensationalism of the murders, and the fact that Sasha's picture and name were plastered all over the news, Sidney knew a horde of reporters would be converging on the hospital. As a precaution, she took the exit past the one to the hospital, drove along a road that circled behind the hospital to the employee parking lot, and entered the hospital through a back service entrance. Working her way through the maze of halls, she reached the door to a hall that led to the ER. She pushed through it and saw Avril talking to Jay Brunelle and a grouchy looking Harry Sweeney.

Sidney could make out the conversation as she approached. Jay Brunelle was diplomatically trying to wheedle information out of Avril, who appeared to be her usual composed and calm self. Harry was stalking back and forth, impatiently chewing on an unlit cigar and glaring at the closed doors of the ER.

Sidney glanced toward the doors, too. Just knowing Leah was behind those doors fighting for Sasha's life evoked mixed feelings. If it had to be anyone, Sidney was glad it was Leah. She was the best. That didn't relieve the uneasiness Sidney felt in the pit of her stomach.

This would be the first time she'd seen Sasha since she ended their affair. The image of a naked Sasha in the pool of their home with two other women had been burned into her memory, causing emotional wounds that still ran deep. Sidney's uneasiness skyrocketed when Leah came out of the ER and approached the group standing outside the door.

Before anyone could say anything, Harry took the cigar out of his mouth. "Did she make it, Doc? It's very important that we talk to Ms. Sheppard."

Jay shot him a dirty look, then looked at Leah.

"Leah, this is Harry Sweeney, chief of homicide of L.A. County. Please, pay no mind to his bad manners. We were here when Ms. Sheppard coded. Our first concern, of course, is that she has survived."

Sidney approached and stood next to Leah, reassuringly touching her lightly on the back, needing the contact. When he saw her, Harry almost lost the intimidating scowl on his face and almost smiled. He had a deep in the gut dislike and distrust for most lawyers, but Sidney was one of the few he respected and actually liked.

After briefly making eye contact with Sidney, Leah nodded toward Harry, then looked at Isaac. Sidney held her breath, waiting to hear what Leah had to say. "Mr. Sheppard, your niece made it through the code. She's alive, but in critical condition."

Sidney kept her expression impassive, but relief washed over her, and her fingers trembled against Leah's back. Isaac took in a breath. "Doctor, can I go in and be with her?"

"Please keep it short. Any stimulus could trigger another episode. When her condition is stable, she'll be transferred to intensive care."

As Isaac hurried through the doors of the ER, Harry took the cigar out of his mouth. "Glad to hear she made it. What were the extent of her injuries, and when do you think we can talk to her?"

Sidney looked at Harry with an expression that said, "Really, Harry, you know that Leah is not going to answer your questions." But she knew that Harry would try anyway. Ignoring him, she directed her reply to Jay. "I'm sure you and Harry know that Leah cannot give you that information. Sasha has a right to her privacy, and her medical information is confidential."

When Leah looked at Jay, Sidney felt the subtle relaxing of tension in her partner's back. "Jay, I'm sorry. Sidney's right. Until Sasha Sheppard, or whoever has her power of attorney, authorizes the release of information or until I see a court order, her medical condition is confidential. All I can tell you is what I said, that her condition is serious. As far as how soon she'll be able to answer your questions, I don't know at this point. Considering who she is, I'd think that you'd all want everything done by the book."

Harry's irritation was evident in his faded blue eyes and in his voice. "Ms. Sheppard may be the only one that can clear up a few things for us. Like what was she doing in the beach house while three women were being murdered?"

Sidney was an expert in turning an accusing question to her advantage. "Harry, you know that even if Sasha was found at the beach house that doesn't mean she was there when the murders took place, or if she was that it makes her responsible or implicates her in the deaths of those women. Do you have witnesses that put Sasha in the beach house when the murders took place or evidence indicating that Sasha isn't a victim just as the other women were?"

Straight to the point and most disarming, as usual, Sidney. Jay spoke before Harry could start a losing argument with Sidney. "Are you and Ms. Savoy here in an official capacity to represent Ms. Sheppard?"

Sidney could feel the underlying tension radiating between Jay and her. It was obvious how Jay still felt about Leah. Jay's eyes betrayed her when she looked at Leah, prompting a rare feeling of insecurity on Sidney's part that put her slightly on edge whenever she and Leah ran into the woman. Hoping her poker face was holding true, she looked at Jay and answered. "As far as I know, unless you're prepared to tell me differently, Sasha has not been charged with anything. Please, let me clarify our positions here. DeRoche Law Firm does represent Ms. Sheppard's interests, and both Avril and I are friends of the family, which I'm sure Avril has already told you. We're here out of concern. But, if the need arises, we *will* protect Sasha's rights. Ms. Sheppard's condition is serious, and until it improves I'm afraid I'll have to ask you to direct all your questions to Avril or to me."

Without waiting for a response, Sidney took the offensive, putting Jay on the spot.

"I also have a few concerns I'd like to express, Jay. I'm curious about the photos that were taken at the scene. Those pictures had to be taken by someone who had access to the crime scene. Do you know how they got into the hands of the press? Sasha's family would like to receive an official explanation and to know who is responsible." *I also want to review the 911 call and how long it took your officers to arrive at the scene and for Sasha to arrive at the hospital. Something about this whole thing stinks and if you're half the cop I think you are, you know it, too.*

Jay felt the heat creeping up her neck. She was well aware that Sidney was putting her on the defensive in order to evade further probing on their part. In truth, she was asking questions that any rookie public defender would ask, and for good reason, but somehow, when Sidney DeRoche did the asking, the questions became all the more intimidating. It didn't help that Jay was asking herself the same questions. Who had access to the crime scene? When were the pictures taken? They were obviously taken before her homicide investigators and LBPD's CSI arrived and before the paramedics arrived to transport Sasha Sheppard to the hospital. But, were they shot before or after her officer responded to the 911 call?

The crime scene had been a circus from the moment she arrived at the beach house. Her detectives, who had spoken to the responding officers, had briefed her, but she hadn't had a chance to read the officers' report. She planned to do that as soon as she returned to her office — and then to call them in and quiz them further.

If Sasha Sheppard is implicated in these murders, those pictures could well turn out to haunt the department and to be the case's Achilles heel. Someone who had access to the crime scene took those pictures, but who, when, and why?

Jay studied Sidney's face. Sidney's determination was evident. If Jay's officers were responsible for those pictures, she was going to find out why. A gut feeling warned Jay not to push. Sidney and Avril were not just at the hospital because they were friends of the family. They were there because the Sheppard family and the President of the United States had decided to call in the big guns.

"I honestly don't know who took those pictures, Sidney, or how they made it to the press, but I can promise you this. I have every intention of finding out who did. Look, we know that Ms. Sheppard has been through a harrowing experience, and we're concerned with her recovery. We're just hoping that she can tell us what happened at the beach house. Three women are dead, and anything she can tell us that helps find who is responsible will be greatly appreciated." *Which better be real damn soon.* "I don't need to tell you the hysteria that will grip this town knowing that we have a murderer running around out there." Harry was irritated at the ass-kissing, she could tell, but he had enough sense to keep his mouth shut.

Jay shifted her gaze to Leah, who was standing with her arms crossed over her chest watching Sidney. It was the stance that Leah unconsciously took whenever she had something on her mind. Something in Leah's gray eyes made Jay wonder what was going on in her head.

Too bad I didn't take the time to read Leah's eyes and heed her heartache before she left me. She begged me not to reenlist after my tour overseas was up. I didn't listen, and it cost me what I cherished most in this world — her.

Jay wanted to reach out and push an errant lock of hair out of Leah's tired looking eyes, just as she'd done so many times when they were together. As hard as it was, she forced her eyes off the doctor and back to Sidney, noting the knowing look behind her glacial stare.

Sidney responded to her request with practiced composure and a semblance of detachment. "I believe you when you say you don't know who took the pictures, Jay. And I do understand your situation. As soon as Ms. Sheppard is up to it, we'll let you know when you can speak with her." *If Sasha is charged with these murders, however, that will never happen.*

Jay's cell rang, and she stepped aside to answer it. The fine lines around her eyes deepened, and a concerned expression crossed her face as she listened. "I'm just leaving the hospital. I'll be there in a few minutes." *Damn it! Now we have the murder weapon, and they're telling me the only prints found on it are Sasha Sheppard's. How in the hell do they know they're her prints? I need to get back to the precinct before this gets leaked to the press, too. If it already hasn't.*

Jay slipped the cell into her pocket, then said to Sidney, "Thank you. I hope she makes it through this. I'd appreciate it if you'd let me know just as soon as she's able to speak with me." As Jay hurried down the hall, Harry stuck the stump of the cigar back in his mouth and followed her toward the back entrance of the hospital where the chief had parked her SUV.

Sidney and Avril looked questioningly at each other. Whatever the phone call was about had made Jay nervous. Something was up. Sidney pulled a document from the side pocket of her briefcase and handed it to Leah. "This informs the hospital that DeRoche Law has accepted a retainer to represent Sasha. There is also an order restricting access to her medical records with the exception of approved medical personnel, her family, and her attorneys."

Leah glanced briefly at the paper without making eye contact with Sidney. "I have already been informed. Avril told me." She opened the chart she was holding and in an impersonal tone started to update Sidney on Sasha's condition. "Your client has been in and out of consciousness, definitely drugged and overdosed on something, and she's lost a lot of blood from the deep wounds on her wrists."

The controlled edge in Leah's voice worried Sidney. "Were they self-inflicted?"

"Hard to say. If they were, she was serious about killing herself."

"Was she using cocaine?" Sidney asked.

"None has shown up on our preliminary tests. Even if she was, cocaine isn't what knocked her into this stupor. She's been traumatized, I believe — psychologically as well as by her wounds. I'll know more when I see her toxicology report and other lab work. When she's up to it, she should have a psych evaluation. I'd recommend Dee Matula. In situations like this, she's the best. You can go in. I'll let you know more after I check the lab reports." Leah closed the chart and turned to leave.

"Leah, wait. What happened to cause her to code? Was it loss of blood?"

"Not entirely. Her heart went into ventricular tachycardia. Possibly caused by the combination of drugs in her system and the loss of blood."

Sidney felt an emotional distance coming from Leah. When Leah turned and started to walk toward the nurse's station, Sidney caught up to her and grabbed her hand, pulling her aside. "I'm sorry, this was all just thrown at you. Do you think you can get someone to cover for you so we can talk? I would like to explain..."

The expression in Leah's eyes softened a little. "I have to sign off on a few charts, and I want to look at your client's lab results. Then I'll write the orders for her to be transferred to ICU when she's stable. I can let you know when I can get away."

Sidney squeezed Leah's hand, kissed her lightly on the lips, and watched as Leah disappeared through the double doors that led to the lab. Leah knew all about her past relationship with Sasha. She had told Leah everything before they became lovers. She had wanted her past with Sasha out in the open.

When she looked into Leah's eyes, there wasn't a doubt in her mind that Leah felt uncomfortable about her taking on Sasha as a client. Their careers were an important part of their lives. Each supported the other in issues that arose, and in this case Sidney felt she should have been the one to tell Leah about Sasha, instead of it being dumped on Leah the way it had been.

Sidney's headache had worsened, and her stomach was in knots. It had been a long time since she'd felt so conflicted. It looked to be an even bet that the sister of the President of the United States could be charged with the grisly murders of three women. She couldn't help but think that it was all too coincidental, all too convenient, and that it couldn't have happened at a worse time for Ingrid.

Avril's voice from behind and an arm around her waist interrupted her thoughts.

"Sid, you okay? Is everything all right between you and Leah?"

Avril hadn't approved of Sasha from the start. She thought the wealthy and beautiful young woman was a selfish, spoiled player who used people up then discarded them after draining them to feed her unquenchable thirst for the fast life. When the relationship fell apart, Sidney had thought her broken heart would never trust or love again. Avril was the friend who had held her hand while she struggled to pick up the pieces of her life after the split. Who had watched the hell she went through.

Nodding, Sidney said, "I'm fine. Let's go in."

As they walked through the doors of the ER, Sidney felt her mouth go dry and her legs begin to shake slightly. It had been years since she'd seen Sasha. In the exam room, Isaac was standing next to the gurney, wiping Sasha's forehead with a damp cloth. Sidney forced herself to go and stand beside him. She felt a tightening in her chest when she looked down at the face of the woman she had loved and wanted with an indescribable desire and passion. Sasha's sunken eyes were closed in her ghostly pale face. Sidney was surprised by the concern and tenderness that she felt toward her.

Next to her Isaac swayed and leaned against the bed. Sidney put her arm around the man who had taught and mentored her, then wished her well when she left his firm to go out on her own. "Isaac, you're exhausted. Let me have someone take you home to rest. I promise we'll be here with Sasha. We think the best thing for now is to have her moved to the Krause Suite on the fourth floor and to arrange for private nursing around the clock."

Isaac's eyes filled with tears as he looked at Sasha. "Sasha, if you can hear me, it's Isaac. I love you, sweetheart."

At the sound of Isaac's voice, there was rapid eye movement behind Sasha's closed eyelids. Avril moved to stand next to them, aware that Sidney was struggling with her emotions. "Isaac, Sidney's right. Go home and rest. Someone will be with Sasha at all times."

Isaac nodded. "Before you came, she looked at me, but she wasn't seeing me. It was as if she was seeing something that scared her to death."

Without taking her eyes off Sasha, Sidney said, "Maybe it was death she was seeing."

"Please help her, Sidney. She was happy with Lauren. She would never have hurt her or those other women. I know she could never do that."

Squeezing Isaac's hand in reassurance, Sidney said, "We will. I promise we will."

At the sound of Sidney voice, Sasha's heart rate had escalated and set the monitoring machine off at the nurse's station. One of the ER doctors and a nurse rushed in. After checking Sasha over and administering the medication that Leah had ordered, the doctor turned to Isaac. "Are you family?"

When Isaac nodded yes, the doctor continued. "She's okay, but her condition is fragile. Right now, stimulation of the simplest kind, voice recognition or reference to what happened to her could trigger an adverse response. Her mind is a jumbled mess, and she's hallucinating. If we want to avoid putting her on a ventilator, we'll need to keep her calm until her condition improves."

Isaac was too shaken to respond. Sidney spoke. "I'm Sidney DeRoche, a friend of the family, and this is Avril Savoy. We're also Sasha's attorneys."

The doctor nodded. "We were informed."

The administrator acted fast or was it Leah? "Please hold off on the transfer to the intensive care. Arrangements will be made for Sasha to be transferred to the Krause Suite."

The doctor nodded again and jotted down a few notes in the chart. Before he left the room he said, "I'll tell Doctor Stanhope."

Isaac called his driver and arranged to be picked up at the ER entrance, then said to Sidney and Avril. "I'll be back shortly." He ran a shaky hand through his graying hair. "I need to call my brother and Helena, and Ingrid. They asked me to keep them updated on Sasha's condition. How can I...thank you both for being here."

After Isaac left, Sidney stared at the fragile figure lying on the gurney. "Avril, will you stay with her? I'm going to admitting and make the arrangements."

"I won't move a muscle out of this room. Before you go, can I make a suggestion? You know this is just the beginning. We're in for the long haul. You should think about going home with Leah tonight. The team is doing their thing. I'll stay here and if anything happens, I'll call you immediately."

Sidney knew Avril had felt the same tension coming from Leah that she had. "You're right, I do need to be home tonight. I should try to explain...I'll be back early in the morning." Sidney looked down at Sasha. "Let's hope she's out of the woods by then and that her condition improves. Right now, it's imperative that we don't let Sweeney or Brunelle or any reporters anywhere near her. Jay is going to be under the gun with this one. We probably won't have to wait long to find out if Sasha is the number one suspect. All we can do is wait and see. It does make me uneasy that we don't know what they have other than the fact that Sasha was found at the scene. I hope Grant can find something — fast. Those damn pictures in the papers sure don't help."

Sidney's gaze lingered on Sasha's face a moment longer, then she walked out of the room and headed toward the doctors' dictating room. She'd used the room at times, waiting for Leah, because it was private and usually empty. As she sat down, her emotions had her trembling. She tried to rationally analyze the reaction she was having to seeing her ex-lover again and in the condition she was in. As she opened her cell to call Jason, she prayed that she'd made the right decision by agreeing to represent Sasha. Weighing the seriousness of the situation and the fact that Ingrid was her best friend, it still seemed to be the only decision she could have made.

"Jason, this is Sidney. Please ask Grant to arrange for around-the-clock security, and 24/7 private nursing for Sasha. She'll be admitted to the Krause Suite on the fourth floor of SCMC. And all the nurses need to be trained in critical care and have top VIP clearance."

"I'm on it as we speak."

"Let me talk to Grant, please."

"Grant just left. He said he wanted to check on something. You should be able to get him on his cell phone. Is there anything I can help you with?"

Sidney took a tired breath. "Call Grant, and if he hasn't already, ask him to run a complete security update on our building. He'll know what we need. An electronic sweep, a total security update, including all modes of communication into and out of the building."

"I'll call him now. Anything else?"

"No, thanks." Sidney hung up and sat heavily back in the chair.

Chapter Five

As Jay sped toward the crime lab, Harry took what was left of the shredded stub of cigar out of his mouth and pitched it out the window. "You want to tell me what the call was all about?"

"That's littering, Harry. And besides it's a disgusting habit. The damn things can kill you just as easy that way, too." Jay inhaled deeply. "They found the murder weapon that killed the women, and they're saying the only prints on it were Sasha Sheppard's."

"And they know that, how?"

"Don't know yet. Maybe Sheppard has an arrest record and was fingerprinted."

"Looks like this case is being handed to you on a silver platter, Brunelle." Harry pulled another cigar from his jacket pocket and stuck it in his mouth. He scratched his two-day-old beard, then cocked his head and looked at Jay's profile. The muscles of her jaw were clenched tight. "Mighty nice of the killer to leave the weapon behind and with Sheppard's fingerprints on it."

Yeah, Harry, mighty damn convenient.

"Tell me, Chief, do you get the feeling that Sheppard is being served up like a sacrificial lamb?"

"What I can tell you would fit in a thimble. Nothing about this case feels right." Jay hit the steering wheel with the palm of her hand. "Damn, and to make things worse, Sasha Sheppard is the President's sister and now Leah...Sidney DeRoche is involved."

Harry sensed that more was eating at Jay than just this case. She was a good cop, just like her father had been. Lucas had been killed when he'd walked into a hold-up in progress at a coffee shop he stopped at every morning, shot by a drugged-out junkie waving a gun and a fistful of stolen bills. It had happened a week before Jay was due home from her last tour of duty in the Middle East.

When Harry's reserve unit was called up after Desert Storm, during the ongoing military operations and flyovers, Lucas asked him to look Jay up. One of the first women to fly combat missions in the Middle East, she was with the First Fighter Wing out of Langley, assigned to patrol the Saudi-Kuwait-Iraq border areas. Harry promised he would.

As it turned out, it was Lucas' little girl who came to his rescue when his plane was shot down by Iraqi forces during a routine surveillance flyover. He got out and parachuted safely to the ground, but the Iraqi Guard was hot on his tail. When Jay heard that he'd gone down and was on the run from the Guard, who most likely would skin him and display his head, she insisted on being part of the rescue mission.

Pinned down and out of ammo, except for one last round he always kept in the chest pocket of his flight jacket, Harry thought it was over. The Iraqi troops were almost on him as he slipped the round in the chamber of the .45. He looked toward the sky to see death swoop out of the blinding Iraqi sun, guns blazing. Jay came in so low that the Apache A-H 64 shook the floor of the desert. She fought off the rebels like a demon until a rescue chopper could land to pick him up. It was the most courageous and skillful demonstration of combat flying he'd ever seen.

After he was aboard the chopper and they'd lifted off, Jay gave him a two-finger salute off her helmet, then flew shotgun until the rescue chopper landed safely on the carrier. He always wondered how she managed to talk the Army into lending her one of their Apaches. Whenever he asked her, she'd wink and say she traded a few favors and her F-16 for it.

Lucas Brunelle had loved all his children, but he had a special bond with Jay. His only concern was that she be happy. It was Lucas who told Harry that Jay was gay. He also told him that she had been in a relationship with a woman who was a doctor but that the relationship ended during her second tour of duty.

Harry had recognized Leah when he saw her at the hospital. She had been at Lucas' funeral services. It was a good bet that she was the doctor Jay had been with. A blind person could see that Jay hadn't gotten over her.

Talking to Jay about her love life would be awkward, but it was what Lucas would do if he were there. Harry moved the cigar to the other side of his mouth. "The doctor at the hospital, she the one you were with?" Jay continued to stare straight ahead. "You've been alone awhile now, Jay. You seeing anyone?"

Her voice tight but controlled, Jay answered. "Tell me, Harry, you've been alone a long time, too. You never remarried after Elizabeth died. No one would have faulted you if you had. Why haven't you found someone?"

Harry turned his eyes back to the road. Elizabeth had been his first and only love. He knew from the first moment he laid eyes on the eighteen-year-old fiery redhead that he would only love one woman in this lifetime, and that was Lizzy. They had thirty-two years together before cancer took her, and his crotchety old heart still missed her every day. "Are you telling me politely to mind my own business?" After a few minutes he said, "And to answer your question, because no one could ever take her place."

As Jay drove past the offices of the Laguna Forensic Lab, she saw a group of people gathered outside the front door, undoubtedly reporters. Irritated, she cursed. "Damn reporters, they'll be camped out on every doorstep in town! They probably knew that Sheppard's prints were found on the murder weapon before I did." Harry just grunted and continued to chew on his unlit cigar. He was used to high-profile cases and the attention that a sensational murder attracted from the media.

In no mood to deal with the questions of the press, Jay drove around the block and down the alley, then pulled into the parking lot of a building a few doors down from the lab. They walked a short distance without running into anyone. Jay used her key card to open the door to the back entrance.

It wasn't unusual to see the lanky chief of police there, but today her presence went unnoticed. The murders, and the fact that the murder weapon had been recovered, had the lab in a flurry of activity. Jay's long stride quickly covered the distance down the hall as she scoured the rooms, looking for the on-loan medical examiner from L.A. He was probably processing evidence from the crime scene in one of the labs.

The uneasy feeling that had been shadowing Jay ever since she received the call about the murders and was told that Sasha Sheppard was found at the scene was stronger than ever. Why was the evidence incriminating Sasha falling so easily into their hands, like a gift? She could hear her father's voice saying, "When a case is too easy and has too many unanswered questions, look beyond what is obvious. Question what you see. More importantly, question what you don't see."

All the coffee Harry had consumed sent him looking for the men's room. Jay continued her search for Hank. It was a relief not to have Harry hounding her for a few minutes. Despite the fact that Sasha had been unconscious, he had grouched and bellyached all the way from the hospital about not being able to question her. Even if Sasha had been able to talk, she knew, they would never have gotten past the two watchdogs, Sidney and Avril.

Opening the last door at the end of the hall, Jay found Hank hunched over a microscope. On the counter, tagged and placed protectively in a cardboard box, was what Jay assumed was the murder weapon. Without looking up, Hank acknowledged her. "Hi, Chief. Did you decide to leave Harry along the roadside?"

Jay shook her head. Hank never failed to impress her. The medical examiner had an uncanny ability "to know things". As she spoke to him, her eyes never left the knife, covered with dried blood. "Wish I'd thought of it. He'll be along."

She eyed the large take-out container of Starbucks sitting in front of Hank. "You both drink too much coffee. How do either of you sleep at night?"

On cue, Hank reached for his cup of cold coffee. "There's no such thing as sleep in L.A. County, Chief. Not in this business."

Even though Laguna's crime statistics were a far cry from L.A.'s, Jay could relate. "What do you have so far?"

"Give me a few minutes." Hank placed one of the slides he'd prepared between the stage clips and turned the revolving nosepiece to choose the lens he wanted. He adjusted the fine focus and studied the smear on the slide. Changing the slide several times, he repeated the procedure, each time carefully entering his notes in a leather notebook that he would transfer into his laptop later. Jay patiently sat on a stool at the end of the counter watching, knowing that he'd have something to tell her soon enough. A few minutes later she heard the door open and glanced over her shoulder to see Harry.

Hank took off his glasses and rubbed the bridge of his nose, then said, "I'm glad you're here, Harry. I'll only have to say this once." He motioned toward the knife. "It's a ten-inch boning knife, and it's the murder weapon. The knife is one missing from a set on the counter top in the Serantis' kitchen. I found it in the wastebasket in the bathroom off the master bedroom. I was able to match the blood from all three murdered women to the blood I found on it." Hank slipped his glasses back on and picked up his notebook.

"I also found blood from a fourth, unidentified person. Preliminary finding is that the two inside the house died first, then the woman on the deck. The trace you did on Lauren Serantis' credit card showed that dinner and wine for four people was charged at a restaurant at 10:15 last night. What they ate corresponds with what I found in the stomachs of the three victims. Two had curried chicken salad with broccoli, another a portobello mushroom salad. A fourth person had salmon. Factoring in the small amount of alcohol I found in each woman's system, and using a variable metabolism rate for each, I was able to approximate a time of death. I'll be more precise after I do a more thorough examination on the bodies."

"You didn't find any drugs in their systems?"

"Just the wine. And not much."

Her mind was quickly processing everything Hank said. No drugs and only a small amount of alcohol. "Hank, you said you identified the blood of a fourth person. Does our DA know about this?"

"Ramey was here when I arrived, chomping at the bit as I did the prelim and analyzed the blood on the knife. The prints I found on the knife were Sasha Sheppard's. The blood from the unidentified person on the knife, and on other evidence I gathered at the murder scene, is the same type as hers. But until we have a sample of her blood we won't know if the unidentified blood I found is hers or not."

Hank took his glasses off and said, "Never knew Ramey to be so efficient. He knew every member of the President's family is required to have blood type as well as fingerprints and DNA on file. It surprised me that I got high-level security clearance to the FBI database so quickly."

Harry mumbled around the stump of cigar in his mouth, "Hard for me to believe Ramey would know his ass from a hole in the ground."

"True. One thing that Ramey didn't mention was that the FBI file says Sasha is predominately left-handed. The prints on the murder weapon are from her right hand. If a person slashes both their own wrists you would expect to find prints from both hands, but the predominant hand probably slashes first. Therefore, left-hand prints should be smudged under the right-hand prints."

"I'm going over to see Ramey," Jay said. Her voice conveyed the seriousness of her thoughts. She looked at Harry, who had stopped chewing on his cigar, the deepening wrinkles of his face reflecting his own thoughts. "You want to tag along, Harry?"

"Hell no, I never liked that tight-ass bastard. I'd as soon..." Harry took the cigar out of his mouth and stuck it in his jacket pocket. "Watch your back with that slimy S.O.B., Jay. I don't trust him. Anyway, I want to grab something to eat, then head back to the beach house. I'd like to take another look around. You want to come along, Hank? We can drive back to L.A. together and get an early start tomorrow."

Hank had been securing and tagging the remaining bags of evidence and looked up. "If we don't have to stop at some greasy spoon. Your pores ooze the cholesterol you put in your body. You're the only person I know who thinks that French fries dripping with grease should be at the top of the food pyramid. But I did tell the Chief here that I wanted to go over the crime scene

one more time before I officially turn it over to her investigators."
With a hint of a smile, Hank said, "I'm sure by now they've
expressed their concerns."

The lab phone rang, and Hank answered. The couriers had
arrived to transport the evidence. A few minutes later the evidence
Hank had gathered was loaded and safely on its way to the lab in
L.A., where Hank would sort through it all again before sending it
to the FBI forensic lab in Quantico, Virginia. Hank took off his
glasses and carefully folded the stems, then put the glasses in his
shirt pocket. He stood with his hands folded in front of him. "We
can go now, Harry."

The energy in District Attorney Ramey's office vibrated off the
walls. Every phone was ringing, and people were running about
shouting orders to whoever was closest to fetch a file or research
something on the computers. When the door opened and the
California attorney general stormed into the room, everything
came to an abrupt halt. A few people scurried into their offices in
fear of being in the way of the wrath that was evident on Bob
Redfern's face.

He wasn't jumping for joy that the prime suspect was the
President's sister. And he was far beyond angry that Ramey hadn't
informed him about the murder weapon being found and Sasha's
fingerprints being the only ones on it. Ramey was an impulsive
glory-seeking asshole. Bob Redfern wanted to make sure Ramey
didn't jump the gun and charge Sasha Sheppard prematurely with
the murders. They needed to build a case first and that would take
more than fingerprints.

*That stupid son-of-a-bitch. He fucking better have more than
just Sasha's fingerprints on the murder weapon before he goes
running off half-cocked, or they'll be digging a hole for him and
filing a murder charge against me!*

Redfern was well aware of Ramey's politics. A staunch
conservative, he had openly opposed Ingrid Sheppard when
President-Elect Brady Lawrence was shot and Vice President-Elect
Sheppard was sworn in as President. Redfern was leery of Ramey's
motives and despised the arrogance that he'd heard in Ramey's
voice a half-hour ago on television. Without consulting with him,
Ramey had called a press conference to announce that they'd
found the murder weapon and expected an arrest soon. He did
everything but say out loud that Sasha Sheppard was the number
one suspect.

Tight with anger, the attorney general stalked toward Ramey's secretary. Knowing what was coming, she looked toward Ramey's office. Before she could get a word out, Redfern walked around her desk and, without knocking, barged into Ramey's office and slammed the door shut. A few minutes later, raised voices and a heated argument could be heard throughout the offices.

Jay arrived as the two men were going at it tooth and nail. Ramey's secretary, purse in hand, was wisely leaving for the night but stopped when she saw her coming in.

"This office is not a good place to be right now, Jay. Bob Redfern is in the little prick's office, and he's ripping him a new one. Which is why you're here, I suspect. Come back tomorrow. The poor bastard's heart can't take the stress of both of you kicking his ass in one day."

Jay looked at her watch. It was getting late, and her head was pounding. She hoped that Redfern would do what she had always wanted to do and slam his fist into Ramey's big mouth. All the man did was make it more difficult for her to do her job.

Marsha was right. There was no sense in approaching Ramey until after Redfern got through with him, and there was no point in getting Ramey's back up against her this early in the investigation. There would be plenty of time for that later. She would talk to him in the morning. They needed time to investigate before Ramey did anything stupid. "Thanks. I'll walk you out."

Jay stopped briefly at her office to pick up the responding officers' reports and leave a message for both officers to call her as soon as they got her message, then drove toward home down Gull's Way. She hadn't eaten all day, and when she drove past Mallory's Bar and Grill she thought about stopping. She wasn't all that hungry; too many things about this case were gnawing at her. *Maybe a walk to Mallory's will clear my head.*

Mallory's Bar and Grill was the neighborhood tavern and catered mostly to the locals. Weeknights, other than during football season, were usually quiet, and the tavern was within walking distance of Jay's house. Mallory Flynn was a long time friend of the family and, in Jay's opinion, she made the best Manhattan clam chowder in all of California.

Because Jay was Italian, learning to cook and appreciate a good meal had been mandatory while she was growing up, just as learning to recite the rosary was. Maria Brunelle, her mama, always said that the success of any dish was in its secrets. Every time Jay tried to charm the secret of the chowder out of Mallory,

Mallory would smile, kiss Jay on the cheek, and then say, "If I give my secret away, my favorite customer will quit coming in and do her own cooking."

Tonight the last thing on the chief's mind was food. Any idea she had of getting an uninterrupted night's sleep was wishful thinking at this stage of the game. It had been one long day, and the reports to review in her briefcase promised an even longer night. Every day until the book on this case was closed would be a three-ring circus. Not yet having talked to the officers who responded to the 911 call was sticking in her craw.

When she'd picked up their reports at the station, she'd also pulled their files and made a copy. She remembered talking to both a few months back after a junkie's complaint of unnecessary force. That alone didn't raise a flag, but when an informant reported to her that he'd heard the two officers were on the take, she'd asked Internal Affairs to open an investigation. The junkie had overdosed, and the informant had recanted his story, saying his source was unreliable.

Jay pulled into the garage beneath her older mission-style house and sat thinking as she tapped her thumbs against the steering wheel.

It isn't unusual for officers who work the night shift not to pick up messages during the day. But they damn well better return my call when they report back on duty tonight.

She exited her truck, took off her jacket and hung it up, then removed her shoulder holster and locked her weapon in the safe built into the cement foundation wall of the garage. Grabbing an old sweater off a hook, she set the alarm and used the remote on her key ring to close the heavy garage door.

The fog was beginning to roll in as Jay walked down the street past several well-kept older homes that looked much like her own. Evening brought a cool wind off the ocean that Jay always welcomed. Tonight, it carried a chill, and Jay pulled the collar of her sweater up. By the time she reached the corner all she could see through the heavy fog was Mallory's neon sign across the street and a soft orange halo around the old streetlights.

Usually, the fog and the familiar sound of the fog horn comforted Jay, but tonight she had an eerie feeling that raised the hair on the back of her neck and sent a shiver down her spine. As she crossed the street, the sound of her boots seemed to echo off the pavement, but when she stopped to listen, all she could hear was a dog barking off in the distance.

When Jay opened the door to Mallory's, the smell of simmering chowder made her mouth water and her traitorous stomach growled. Mallory looked up from what she was doing and smiled, then pointed to a stool at the end of the bar. She ladled a serving of chowder into an oversize bowl, drew a mug of beer from the tap, and set the meal in front of Jay.

"You look like hell, Brunelle. I've been watching it on the news. Hard to believe that President Sheppard's sister could be involved in something like that. Matter of fact, looking at those pictures in the newspaper, it's hard to believe that a woman would be capable of doing that to another woman, no matter the rage. Takes a whole lot of strength to do the damage that was done to those women. But then again, I've seen a ninety-pound woman hopped up on drugs take down several guards trying to restrain her."

Jay listened to what Mallory was saying. Mallory knew women, the worst of the lot. She spent twenty years as a corrections officer at Chowchilla Women's Prison in central California. Jay blew on her first spoonful of chowder, then tasted it. She thought about what Mallory had just said and made a mental note. Although they hadn't seen the wounds on Sasha's wrist or been able to review the doctor's notes, she had a question she wanted to ask Hank. "Slow evening, Mallory? The streets seem unusually quiet out there tonight."

Mallory had gone back to drying and stacking glasses, but Jay could tell something was on her mind. "It's been dead. Just a few regulars and a woman who sat at the table over by the window for a few hours. Never drank anything but bottled water. Left a hefty tip, though." A concerned looked crossed Mallory's face. "Strange thing, she kept looking down the street toward your place like she was waiting for something or someone. Only stayed a little while after getting a call on her cell phone. Never said a word, just listened. A bit after that she got up and put a bill on the table and left."

The spoonful of chowder that Jay was about to put into her mouth hung in midair. A second later she lowered the spoon back into the bowl, concentrating on the glasses Mallory was washing.

"Did she drink out of the bottle or a glass?"

"The bottle."

"And the bill that was on the table?"

Mallory shook her head. "If it's a print you're after, it wouldn't do you any good. She wore leather gloves. Never took them off all the time she was here."

Jay took the cell phone from her pocket to call for a patrol car to cruise the neighborhood and to keep an eye on the tavern and on Mallory, who lived upstairs. The phone rang just as she was about to dial. She looked at the caller ID — unknown caller. Odd, since very few had her personal cell phone number and those that did were programmed in.

"Chief Brunelle here."

A woman's voice that sounded vaguely familiar said, "Two of your officers were found dead. The same officers that responded to the 911 call at the Serantis' beach house."

Jay's heart started to pound. "Who are you? How do you know this?"

The phone went dead. Jay stared at the phone a moment before she pushed the number for the precinct. The night commander answered, and after Jay identified herself. Before she could say anything else, he said, "Chief, I had the phone in my hand to call you. I just received a call from the highway patrol saying that two of our officers have been killed in an accident up the coast along Big Sur at Bixby Bridge. They said the bodies were burnt pretty bad, but the license plate on the vehicle belongs to Dale Davis and the ID's on the bodies confirm it was Davis and his partner, Chuck James."

Her heart raced, and Jay felt as if the wind had been knocked out of her. "Ted, check their personnel records. I'll need to know who to notify. If I'm not mistaken, neither was married. Before you do that, though, check to see if they reported off for their shift tonight and pull the duty report. I want to know if they were assigned to the area of the Serantis' beach house last night."

"Sure thing, Chief. Hang on a minute."

Jay gritted her teeth. Who was the woman who had access to her unlisted number? And how did she know about the accident before her own department did? Why the warning? Jay looked at Mallory. "Do you think you could recognize this woman if you saw her again?"

"Yeah, I think so."

"Chief — nope, neither called off tonight. Oh, and Chief. I checked the area they were assigned. Hell, they were way off their beat when they radioed in that they were close and would take the call."

"Ted, assign a car to keep an eye on my house. Have them check in with Mallory at Mallory's Tavern down the street. And keep this information to yourself for now. Don't discuss it with anyone. Anything that comes in tonight about these officers or the

Serantis case, no matter what time it is, I want to know. Call me on my cell."

What the hell is going on? Jay took a few seconds, then stood. "Mallory, take care. If you see that woman again, or anything that looks out of place or suspicious, call the precinct, then me. You have my cell number?"

Nodding, Mallory said, "Watch your back, Jay."

Jay went home to pick up her weapon before heading to the helipad and the department's helicopter. She wanted to take a look at the bodies and accident site where the officers were killed.

The fog along the coastline was too dense to land anywhere near the bridge, so Jay flew inland to Monterey. An officer in a patrol car picked her up and took her to the police station. After reading over the accident report, she asked, "Can I get a copy of this?"

The officer copied the information and handed it to Jay. "I added the name and address where the car was towed on this copy. It's not in the one I gave to your detective."

Jay's head snapped up. "My detective?"

The intensity of Jay's words and stare unnerved the officer, and she stammered, "A...a woman. She had a Laguna Beach Police Department ID. She also viewed the bodies."

"Do you remember her name?"

The officer fumbled for the sign in clipboard. "A Detective Taylor."

"What did she look like?"

"Blonde hair, 135 pounds. About five ten. Good looking enough for a second look. Chief, is there something wrong?"

There sure in the hell is, but nothing I want to share right now.

"It just surprises me that Detective Taylor was here already. I left her a message after we got the call. She's been vacationing in the area."

Puzzled, the officer looked questioningly at Jay, then asked, "Do you want to see the bodies?"

Nodding, Jay followed the officer back to the patrol car. On the ride to the morgue, Jay's mind was racing. Who was this woman who seemed to be a step ahead of her? The death of the two patrol officers left more unanswered questions. It was a growing puzzle, and none of the pieces fit. The evidence, or rather what little they had, seemed to peg Sasha Sheppard as the killer, but in her gut, Jay wasn't so sure. It was circumstantial and flimsy at best.

After viewing what was left of the bodies, Jay declined a ride from the officer. She borrowed a car from the department, then drove the thirty-eight miles alone to the accident scene. She mentally clicked off what she knew.

The officers who had answered the 911 call were miles out of their assigned area.

Someone with access to the crime scene had taken pictures that were sent to the newspapers. The pictures could have been taken before the 911 call was made, or after the officers arrived, but they had to have been taken before the detectives, the crime scene investigators, and Hank arrived.

She couldn't question the officers now because they were dead.

Who had called in the 911? And what part in all this did this unknown woman play?

Something about the woman's voice bothered Jay, like she'd heard it before.

Jay slowed. Bixby Bridge was a few miles ahead. The curve coming up on the west side of the bridge was where the CHP's report said the accident happened. Jay knew the spot. It was a narrow sightseeing turnoff with a road that led down to the beach. Even if one was familiar with the road, if the bridge were shrouded with fog it would be difficult to see and easy to end up on the rocks below. Tonight was one of those nights. A dense layer of fog covered the road and hung between the mountain and the ocean, making it slow going and hard to see. She wondered why she had bothered coming. She wouldn't be able to see anything until dawn pulled the breeze off the Pacific, pushing the fog further inland.

When she drove down the access road that led to the beach, she could see the outline of a lone vehicle parked in one of the spaces. Pulling over, she sat a few minutes. The bodies had been removed, and the car towed. It was unlikely that a reporter would be hanging around. Even the investigators would wait to go over the site until morning and the lifting of the fog.

A keen sense of knowing when something didn't feel right had Jay slipping her hand inside her jacket and wrapping her fingers around her weapon. She took the pistol out of her shoulder holster and opened the car door. Waves crashing against the rocks drowned out the click of the car door as she gently pushed it shut. Cautiously approaching it from the rear, Jay slowly worked her way toward the SUV until she could see through the windows with her flashlight. It was empty. Walking to the front of the car she touched the hood — it was still warm.

Jay moved a few feet down the beach, then crouched, trying to see through the fog. Nothing was moving except the tide and the fog rolling across the sand.

"Holster your weapon, Brunelle."

The voice from behind was close. Close enough to encourage her not to try anything. It was the same voice she'd heard earlier on the phone telling her that her officers had been killed. Jay quickly ran through her options. *If whoever it is wanted to kill me, I'd be dead already.* Slowly, she holstered the Beretta, then asked, "Mind if I stand up and turn around?"

"Please do."

Jay stood and turned. Standing less than ten feet away was a figure dressed in black, wearing a baseball cap. The bill of the cap was pulled down low, obscuring the features, but Jay knew it was a woman.

"We think alike, Chief. Seems we both wanted to see the bodies and where the accident took place. Bad night for it."

"Who in the hell are you and what authority do you have to be poking around? The ID you showed in Monterey, where did you get it?"

The woman remained silent for a few moments before she said, "I'll tell you this much, because I'm sure our paths will cross again. I used to work for...a certain government agency. Unofficially, I'm looking into these murders by request of Ingrid Sheppard. It would be best if you keep that to yourself."

As Jay listened, the knot tightening in her gut told her the woman was, or had been, a government spook, but that wasn't the only reason this woman made her uneasy.

"Until this case is over, Chief, I suggest you be extremely cautious."

Who the hell are you? Jay felt her irritation toward this woman rising. As the woman moved closer to the parked SUV, Jay noticed she limped. Before she got into the car, Jay called out and asked. "What do I call you?"

Without turning back around the woman said, "The name is Liberty Starr. Be careful, Chief. Deception comes with many faces. If I could get the drop on you, so easily, so could someone else."

Before Jay could express what she thought of the woman's arrogance, the mysterious stranger was in the vehicle and driving up the road, leaving Jay with a strong feeling that she'd met Liberty Starr somewhere before.

Chapter Six

When Sasha's condition and vital signs were stable, she was moved to the Krause Suite on the fourth floor of the hospital. Sidney followed, then stood quietly in Sasha's room watching Leah do an assessment and check the calculations and rate of the antiarrhythmic medication that was infusing into Sasha's arm.

Glancing at Sidney, Leah said, "She'll be under for a while. You should go home. You look beat. "

Concerned by the indifference in the tone of Leah's words, Sidney took a step closer and put her hand on Leah's arm. "So do you. Can you get away and come home with me?"

The hopeful look on her partner's face softened the feelings Leah was unaware were showing. "Moser and Dobbs are covering tonight. If they get slammed, they can call me, but I still have some work to finish up. Why don't you go on, and I'll see you at home."

"I'd like to wait for you." *I'm not going home without you.*

"It may take a while."

"That's fine. Call me when you're ready to go."

Two hours, and several interruptions later, Leah called Sidney and told her she was at a point where she could leave and would meet her outside the back entrance of the ER. Sidney was waiting when Leah dragged through the doors. One look told Sidney that Leah was exhausted.

When Leah's gaze met Sidney's worried eyes, she chided herself for being so touchy and short with Sidney earlier. "Have you eaten anything?"

"No, I'm not very hungry. If you are, we can pick up Chinese, or I can make something when we get home." Sidney took Leah's hand. "I just want to spend some time with you. Why don't you leave the Jeep here and drive with me? I told Avril I'd be here early. I can drive you back in the morning..." Sidney looked at her watch. "Well, I guess that's in a few hours."

Nodding, Leah followed Sidney to her car. They got in, and Leah pushed her seat back, stretched out her long legs, rested her head on the seat back, and closed her eyes. Sidney wanted to wait until they got home before getting into a discussion about Sasha, but the uncomfortable silence was unbearable.

"Leah, I..."

With her eyes still closed, Leah said, "It's okay. You don't need to say or explain anything. My reaction to you representing your ex-lover is my problem, not yours. I'll deal with it."

Sidney pulled into a grocery store parking lot, released her seat belt, then turned to face Leah. "It's not only me representing her. You're treating her. Darling, I love you with all my heart. If you have a problem with it, then it's our problem." Sidney reached down and unbuckled Leah's seat belt. "Sweetheart, please, look at me."

When Leah opened her eyes and turned toward her, Sidney took her face in both of her hands and kissed her lightly on the lips. "Have you ever doubted my love for you? Have I ever given you a reason to?"

Leah met Sidney's gaze. "No, baby, you haven't. I…I guess I'm just feeling…I don't know…stupid…jealous. Even in the condition Sasha Sheppard is in she's still a beautiful woman. I hate the thought of her ever having touched you or her hurting you the way she did. I'm sorry. Can you understand?"

Sidney traced her thumb gently along Leah's lower lip. "You, my love, are the most gorgeous, caring, and loving woman I've ever known."

Sidney replaced her thumb with her lips, taking Leah into her arms and kissing her with all the passion she felt in her heart. Leah responded with a hunger and desire of her own, pushing Sidney back against the seat and delivering a demanding kiss. She slipped a hand under Sidney's jacket and cupped her breast. Her thumb caressed a taut nipple while the other hand went around Sidney's waist.

When the kiss ended, both women were breathless.

"My God, Sid, I want you so much right now." When Leah moved her long legs to get closer to Sidney, she bumped her knee on the console. "Ouch…sweetheart, I love your car, but what say we hurry home?"

Sidney caught Leah's mouth for another kiss, then took a shaky breath and put her seatbelt back on. "Buckle up, darling. This is going to be one quick trip home."

Sidney felt the comfort of Leah's warm body under her. Leah was her anchor. When everything was hectic and rushing at her at a maddening pace, she focused on Leah and their life together and everything righted itself and she felt calm inside. Knowing that at the end of the day she would be going home to Leah made the work and long hours bearable.

The musky redolence of their lovemaking lingered on Leah's abdomen where her head lay. Brushing her cheek against Leah's pubic hair, she kissed the soft skin of Leah's groin.

"I love you so much. I don't know what I'd do without you. Why do you put up with all this? Put up with me and the chaos my job brings into our lives?"

Leah's stomach muscles tightened with arousal as Sidney's fingers circled her pulsating clit. She ran her fingers through Sidney's hair, trying to think. "For the same reason you put up with me and live with a doctor. I love you, Sid. Never forget that. I'll always be here when you need me."

Sidney positioned herself between Leah's legs, pushing them farther apart, then slid her hands along Leah's slender hips to cup her buttocks. The heady smell of Leah's desire deepened the sensual pleasure she felt as she nuzzled then kissed the baby soft skin of Leah's inner thighs. She was so close to Leah's swollen and throbbing need that she could feel the heat. When the tip of her tongue tasted the juices there, Sidney's own desire surged through her veins, raged in her lower belly, and then radiated down her thighs.

Breathless, Sidney said, "Darling, what...what would you say if I told you that I needed you — to come for me, so very much." Sidney's tongue made love to Leah's clit. Mesmerized, she gazed at the protruding dusky engorged flesh.

"God, you're so beautiful." With her thumbs Sidney spread the swollen lips of Leah's labia, ran her tongue through the musky wetness, and then took Leah's clit again in her mouth and gently raked her teeth across the sensitive flesh.

Leah jerked. She felt like she was going to burst. Sidney's tongue was teasing her relentlessly. Her hands reached for the railing of the headboard as her hips started to move to the relentless rhythm Sidney kept with her mouth and tongue.

Driven by the need she felt inside, Sidney wanted to drive away any doubts Leah might have about her love for her. She could feel her own wetness and desire as she moved against the sheets beneath her. She heard Leah cry out, "Oh God, please, baby, do it. Don't stop now."

Every muscle in Leah's body tightened as her body strained for release. Her hips bucked against Sidney's mouth. Sidney's own orgasm was close as she felt the smooth, silken flesh tighten around her fingers. Leah's hands tangled in Sidney's hair as they both came. Leah's thighs closed around Sidney's head and unbelievably soft skin quivered around Sidney's fingers. Sidney knew she could stay exactly where she was forever.

Spent and breathless, Sidney collapsed across Leah's thighs until Leah pulled her into her trembling arms. A few moments later Leah caught her breath and tightened her hold protectively around Sidney.

What are you afraid of, my darling? Why do I have this feeling that this case and Sasha are going to change our lives?

Leah's arms were still wrapped around Sidney when her cell phone rang a few hours later. She struggled to get her eyes open, then looked at the clock and groaned. The intimacy that she and Sidney had shared was wonderful and so very needed. But it was going to make for a very long day.

Leah gently untangled herself and eased Sidney's head onto the pillow, then pulled the covers up over Sidney's naked body. As Leah reached for the phone, Sidney muttered something, then turned on her side and pulled the covers over her head.

Leah's voice was hoarse with the passion of their lovemaking and lack of sleep when she answered, "Doc..." Leah cleared her dry throat. "Doctor Stanhope." Leah listened for a few moments, then, as she swung her long legs over the side of the bed, Sidney's cell started to ring. A moment later a hand came out from under the covers, blindly searching the top of the nightstand. The phone disappeared under the covers. "Sid, it's Avril. I'm still at the hospital. Sasha had a seizure and coded again a few minutes ago."

Sidney threw off the covers and sat up in bed. "My God, is she...?"

"I don't know, Sid. The room is full of people working on her, and no one has told us anything yet."

"I'm on my way. Call me if she...if...if... Is Isaac there...has anyone called Ingrid?"

"Yes, Isaac is here, and so is Ingrid. She and Marty arrived just after you left last night."

"What? And no one thought to call me! I would have come right back to the hospital!"

"I knew you'd be pissed. It wasn't my decision, Sid. Believe me, Ingrid's arrival has caused quite a stir here at the hospital. The Secret Service has taken over the entire fourth floor and the one below it. The hospital has been moving people for hours. It isn't often that the President of the United States just pops in to be with her sister who may be charged with a triple murder. The reporters outside are literally salivating."

Sidney could hear Ingrid's voice in the background asking for the phone. The next thing she heard was Ingrid saying, "It was my decision, Sid, not Avril's. I knew you'd be here early, and there wasn't anything you could do here. Sasha just now coded."

"Oh, Ingrid. Honey, I'm so sorry. You should have called me. I'm on my way." Sidney hung up without waiting for Ingrid to answer. Leah was in the shower, and Sidney joined her and started to soap up. "Leah, your call, was it about Sasha?"

"Yes, it was. You know that she coded?"

"That was Avril on the phone. She told me. Ingrid is at the hospital. I spoke to her. Did they say she was going to make it?"

"They didn't know. They're still running the code. I'll know more when I get there. Sasha's heart went into another potentially fatal arrhythmia. Her central nervous system is irritated, and she seized. It doesn't surprise me, given her lab results."

"I was so anxious for us to get home I didn't ask. What did her labs show?"

"A small amount of alcohol, a hefty dose of Ketamine, and, strangely enough, Rohypnol."

Sidney stopped washing. She couldn't have heard right. "What did you say? Rohypnol and Ketamine, but definitely no cocaine? That doesn't make sense."

"I agree. The combination of drugs in her system seems unlikely. I've seen people in the ER that have been slipped Roofies. Rohypnol is not a drug that someone takes on their own. Ketamine — Special K — is cheap, easy to get, and a favorite of a much younger crowd."

Leah rinsed off, got out of the shower, and grabbed a towel. "Honey, I need to go. I'll take the Triumph. Remember, I left the Jeep at the hospital." Before Leah hurried into the bedroom to throw her clothes on, she kissed Sidney quickly on the lips and said, "Making love with you is always very special, lady. I love you. I'll see you when you get to the hospital."

Leah was gone before Sidney could say anything. As she hurried to shower and dress, she kept going over what Leah had said about the drugs found in Sasha's system. It was still on her mind as she drove through patchy fog along the coastal highway toward the hospital.

The closer Sidney got to the hospital, the heavier the traffic became. Now that Ingrid was at the hospital, the media and onlookers were out in full force. Sidney wondered if she would even be able to get through. Traffic slowed to a snail's pace, but finally Sidney could see the roadblocks ahead going into SCMC and the Secret Service checking cars. Reaching for her cell, she punched in Avril's number.

"Sid, where are you?"

"The traffic is terrible, but I'm almost to the roadblock."

Sidney could hear Avril telling Ingrid what she said. "Sid, Ingrid wants to talk to you."

"I'm sorry, Sid, I didn't think. I should've sent a car for you."

"Is she...is Sasha still...?"

"They're still working on her, but she's alive."

"Leah left a few minutes before me on the bike. Is she in with Sasha?"

"Yes, she's keeping us informed of Sasha's condition. I don't know what we'd do if you and Leah weren't here. I'm so grateful to you both..." Ingrid's s voice quavered. "God, this so hard."

"I know, but she'll pull through. I just know it. Can you clear the way for me at the road block?"

"I'll take care of it right now."

People were standing along the highway blocking traffic. Cars and news vans lined both sides of PCH for a good five miles in each direction. With less than a half-block to go, she was about to park the car and run the rest of the way when she saw the police cars clearing the traffic in front of her. When they reached her, they escorted her through the roadblock to the front entrance of the hospital. An agent opened her car door and took her keys. "I'll park your car, Ms. DeRoche."

When Sidney entered the lobby, a woman approached who Sidney presumed to be a Secret Service agent. "Ms. DeRoche, I'm Liberty Starr. President Sheppard is waiting for you upstairs." The woman was tall and slender with shoulder-length hair the same dark blonde color as her own. The gray tailored suit and shoes she wore struck Sidney as being too expensive for a government agent. "Do you know how her sister is?"

The woman answered cordially, but the glacial reserve never left her eyes. "I'm sorry. I don't."

As Sidney followed the woman onto the elevator, she noticed that she limped. She thought it odd, given the potentially physical nature of an agent's job. When the elevator doors opened, Ingrid was standing waiting. Moisture welled in Ingrid's eyes when she looked at Sidney and said, "I'm so glad you're here."

Sidney stepped off the elevator and put her arms around Ingrid and held her. "How is she?"

"She's alive, but Leah told us she's far from being out of the woods and that she could code again. I don't know what I would've done if...if we'd lost her."

Her best friend's pain tore at Sidney's heart. "I haven't been there for her these past few years. I should have..."

"Ingrid, you've always been there for Sasha. Both you and Marty have loved and supported her. You can't blame yourself for this."

"The last time we helped her into a treatment program, she promised she was done with the drugs and the crowd she was running with. Marty and I believed she meant it when she said it, but she did what she always does and checked herself out of rehab. The next time we heard from her, she was halfway across the world on a yacht with some woman."

Ingrid reached for a handkerchief in her pocket. "I...I was at such a loss on how to reach her, I gave up trying. She's my kid sister, and I just gave up, but I love her, Sid."

Ingrid had been emotional when her twins were born, but Sidney had never seen her so upset. "Honey, I know you do. Sasha loves you, too."

"I really am so glad you're here and Leah. She's in with Sasha, and so are Avril and Marty. We need to talk." Ingrid took Sidney's hand. "There's a room down the hall."

Ingrid requested that Liberty join them, then led the way down the hall to one of the suites. After closing the door, she went to a table where a coffee urn had been set up. "Please sit. Coffee?"

Liberty walked across the room and stood for a moment looking intently at the fog clearing over the Pacific Ocean before drawing the curtains. Ingrid noticed Sidney watching Liberty with a questioning look. Ingrid handed Liberty a cup of coffee. "Sid, this is Liberty Starr."

"So she said."

Liberty took the coffee and went to sit across the room.

"Still like it black, Sid?"

"Please. Are the girls with you?"

"No, we thought it best to leave them at home. They're with Marty's parents. I didn't want Marty to come, but she wouldn't listen. She can be one stubborn woman." Ingrid handed Sidney a cup of coffee, then sat down. "Do you think she did it? Could Sasha have murdered these women? I've seen the pictures. My sister has always been wild, but..." Ingrid shuddered. "You know that better than most, but to kill somebody? I just can't...I can't believe she's capable of that kind of violence."

Sidney glanced over at Liberty, who sat expressionless and who Ingrid apparently trusted to hear very personal and sensitive information. It was Liberty's eyes that made Sidney shiver. She had all the earmarks of a Secret Service agent, but there was a cold edge about her that made Sidney uncomfortable. In spite of the limp, Sidney had no doubt that Liberty Starr could handle herself and take care of any trouble that came her way.

"Sid, if..." With a look of pain on her face, Ingrid squeezed her eyes shut... "If she's charged, who do you think will prosecute the case?"

"Britt LaHood. Ramey will go with her. She's one of the toughest prosecutors I've ever gone up against. The last time we met was particularly ugly, and Britt lost. She's aggressive and will use any trick and will go unmercifully for the jugular and for the kill."

Ingrid nodded thoughtfully. "I've heard about her."

"You know we're going to do everything we can to defend Sasha, don't you?"

The profound worry in Ingrid's voice was unmistakable. "I don't doubt that for a moment, Sid. I just hope it isn't necessary."

Sidney got up and went to sit beside Ingrid and held her hand. She prayed she would never have to defend Sasha for murder. The possibility of it sickened her. But, if it came to that, they would be ready. Preparing for a trial of such magnitude would take priority over everything else — including a personal life. The team would go without sleep, eat on the run, and see very little of their families until it was over. Both Sidney and Ingrid knew about Ramey's opinion of women, particularly about Ingrid. As she held Ingrid's hand, Sidney had an uneasy feeling that this was the calm before the storm and that all hell was about to break loose. "You said that Leah is in with Sasha?"

Ingrid nodded. "I'm sorry I haven't asked this. Is Leah all right with all this?"

Sidney studied the deep lines on Ingrid's face that weren't there the last time she saw her. "We've talked about it. Yes, she is. What aren't you telling me? You look like hell."

Ingrid ran her fingers through her dark hair and took a deep breath before answering. "Thanks, I feel like hell. I'm worried about Marty. I didn't want her to come with me."

Sidney looked puzzled. "Ingrid, you never could have kept Marty away from here. You know that. She travels with you a lot. Is there something wrong?"

Ingrid slowly leaned back against the couch. "There was an attempt on my life a few weeks ago. Someone took a shot at me."

Sidney felt the air leave her lungs. She stared at Ingrid, unable to believe what she'd just heard. When she caught her breath, she said, "My God, Ingrid. Who...why...?"

The lines on Ingrid's face deepened even more as she shook her head. "Take your pick. Pro-family activists, right-wing fanatics...without question, any ultra-conservative or extremist anti-gay group. Then we have the 'good old boys' in Washington, whose political masculinity is threatened and who don't give a damn if women remain uneducated, barefoot, and pregnant as long as they stay out of politics. My plan to cut our oil consumption by fifty percent over the next four years has a whole lot of powerful people in a panic, believe me." Looking weary and very troubled, Ingrid sighed. "Throw in the usual nut case and we have quite a list, I'm afraid."

Sidney buried her face in her hands for a moment, trying to calm her pounding heart. Her eyes filled with tears when she looked at Ingrid.

"You've been able to keep something like an attempt on your life quiet and from the press? Why didn't you call me? I could have done something. I—"

"Sid, I'm the President, remember? Surrounded by an army of Secret Service agents? I didn't call, because I didn't want to worry you."

Sidney stood up and started to pace. "Why do I get the feeling there's more?"

"There is. Sit. You make me nervous when you pace. You always pace when you're upset."

Sidney reluctantly sat back down.

"Even in school when we first faced off against each other in that mock trial you could read me better than anyone." Ingrid managed a wry smile. "There are powerful people that don't want me in the White House for a second term. As unbelievable and as inconceivable as it sounds, there are those who would think nothing of having those women killed and framing my sister for their murders to get to me."

Ingrid glanced at Liberty, then back at her friend. "Sid, what I'm going to tell you now is in confidence and only known by a few trusted people. Liberty was an agent who worked deep cover with an antiterrorist group for President Kincaide. That group no longer exists, and Liberty is no longer associated with any government agency. It took some doing to convince her to come out of retirement, but she did, and she's here strictly because I asked for her help. In my heart, I don't believe Sasha killed anyone or that she tried to kill herself. Uncle Isaac told me Sasha has been doing well and that she'd settled down and was happy with one of the women who was killed. I've asked Liberty to protect Sasha and to find out who did kill those women. I believe it quite possible that the failed assassination attempt on my life and these murders could be connected in some way."

The implications had Sidney's mind reeling. "This is all so...so... We've discussed this many times, when we studied and debated the Warren Report. You've always said that if an assassin targets someone it would be impossible for anyone, including the Secret Service, to prevent it. No offense to Ms. Starr, but how is one woman going to protect Sasha and stop an assassin that might come after her, or you, if all the resources of the Secret Service can't?"

Sidney never felt as helpless as she waited for some kind of a response from Ingrid.

Liberty stood and set her cup down on the table. She buttoned her jacket and walked toward the door, then stopped before she opened it and turned around. Her gray eyes had darkened to almost black.

"The President is right, Ms. DeRoche. If an assassin wants to kill you, odds are they will. At this point we don't know if the murders are connected to the attempt on the President's life. I question why an assassin would go to such elaborate means to devise a plan that includes murdering three women to incriminate the President's sister. To prevent her reelection? It would be cleaner and more efficient to simply kill the President outright."

Sidney simply stared, then asked. "How...how can Ingrid and Sasha be protected? We just can't wait for—"

"To stop an assassin you have to think like an assassin. You have to be more cunning, more calculating, and more deadly. To walk in the assassin's footsteps. To see and feel what the assassin does as he plans another person's death. The only person that would have a snowball's chance in hell of stopping an assassination would be another assassin who was even more ruthless and more cunning."

Sidney gaped at this woman whose voice and cold eyes sliced effortlessly through the air. Liberty opened the door. "You both have things to discuss. It was nice to meet you, Ms. DeRoche."

When the door closed, Sidney let out the breath she'd been unconsciously holding. "My God, what was that all about? She's not...I mean...is she?"

"It's a long story. I've told you everything I can. I will say this; President Kincaide trusted Liberty with his life, and I trust her to protect my sister's life. I need you to think about the risk you could be taking by continuing to represent Sasha, and you need to discuss it with Leah. It could be dangerous for you. I'll understand if you choose not to. Uncle Isaac has several top-notch trial lawyers associated with his firm that—"

"You can just stop right there, Ingrid. Leah and I have discussed my representing Sasha, and she understands and respects my decision." Sidney took both of Ingrid's hands in hers. "Your hands are ice cold."

Ingrid's voice shook. "I should be in more control of my emotions right now, but I'm scared to death for Sasha and I'm worried about the safety of my family. I don't know what I'd do if anything happened to hurt them or if I didn't know you were in Sasha's corner."

"Well, you don't have to worry about that. My entire staff, Avril, and I are in her corner and so is Leah."

Chapter Seven

Sidney stayed at the hospital until Leah informed them that the crisis had passed and Sasha was again holding her own. Avril had gone back to the office earlier and was in the war room sorting through the information that the research team had gathered. She looked up, anxious, when Sidney walked in.

"How is she, Sid?"

"Stable. She's still disoriented and doesn't know anyone or where she is. Leah thinks if she makes it through the next forty-eight hours she'll be over the worst of it. It's heartbreaking what this is doing to the family. They're devastated, and I've never seen Ingrid look so beaten up."

"I know. She did look exhausted. I can't even imagine how I'd feel if it were my sister."

"What's been going on here?"

"As expected, we've been bombarded with calls from the newspapers, reporters, networks, you name it."

"How's Jason handling it?"

"Like he does it every day. Which he usually does. Want a cup, Sid?" Avril gestured toward the coffee.

"Yes, the stronger, the better. We're going to need Jason's high octane." Sidney took off her coat, pulled a chair out from under the table, and looked at the papers Avril had spread out. "Before we get started I want to let you know what Ingrid told me today."

When Sidney finished, Avril said, "God, no wonder Ingrid looks exhausted. Besides running a country, she has to worry about being assassinated, the safety of her family, and if someone is setting up her sister for a lethal injection to get to her."

"Bastards." Sidney closed her eyes, trying to get her anger under control. A moment later she said, "Ingrid knows we're here for her and her family, and she knows that we'll do everything we can to defend Sasha if she's charged with these murders."

She looked at the reports spread out on the long table. "What do we have here?"

"Everything the team has gathered so far, and they're still at it. I had to threaten them to get them to take a break."

Sidney and Avril had hired the best hackers money could buy Anything and everything could be obtained, they knew, when you had the best in the business on retainer, and that included hackers with extraordinary skills in accessing and plucking out of cyberspace information that was supposedly guarded by unbreakable security programs. Skilled intruders, they entered secured areas and left without a trace.

Sidney put on her reading glasses, reached for one of the stacks of papers, and started to read. Sasha's history wasn't difficult to obtain. The Sheppard name was synonymous with position and old money. The beautiful and spirited Sasha, as the daughter of real estate magnate Cyril D. Sheppard and also the troubled kid sister of rising political star Ingrid Sheppard, had always been a media target. Her escapades sold copy.

"Well, this is interesting. A trace of Sasha and Lauren Serantis' credit cards places them at a restaurant early in the evening on the night of the murders. Then later, just Sasha's credit card shows a charge at the Club Palais du Plaisir."

Sidney scanned the list of exclusive members of the club that Grant had somehow managed to get his hands on. "This list Grant sent in reads like a who's who of southern California's influential and very wealthy women. We know several. A movie star, a couple of attorneys, and a judge. Even a senator."

Avril looked at her copy of the list. "I see Taylor Kent's name. Did I tell you that when we had lunch with her last week, she hit on me when you went to the ladies' room?"

"I warned you. Did she get to first base?"

"In her dreams. That one is a player."

"Did you notice that none of the murdered women's names are on this list? Neither is Sasha's. At one time, years ago, but she's not on this list now."

"Sure did."

Sidney knew that the underground club was beyond the eyes of propriety and catered to a subculture of women with certain preferences and tastes. Anything desired could be obtained — for a price. And that price could be a favor asked at some time in the future. Palais du Plaisir was an elusive shadow, well connected and untouchable.

A knock on the door sounded. Janine, one of the investigative hackers, came in and put several pictures and more reports on the desk. "Billie and I just pulled these. Thought you'd want to see them right away."

"Thanks. If there's anything you need, let Jason know."

Janine was already halfway out the door. "Will do."

"Janine."

"Yes, boss?"

"I think that color green you have in your hair is beginning to grow on me."

Backing out the door, Janine grinned and rolled her eyes, then closed the door and stuck her tongue out.

"How many times have I asked her not to call me boss?" Sidney spread the pictures out across the long table. They were of the slain women: Lauren Serantis, Constance Williams, and Kim Lang. This information hadn't yet been released. They knew Lauren Serantis' name, and the team had been able to uncover the names of the other women. Constance and Kim were lovers and had been together for thirteen years. In one picture, they were on a sailboat, a sleek thirty-eight-foot Islander. Constance was at the wheel, her hair blowing in the wind. She was smiling and had one hand on Kim's arms, which were wrapped around Constance's waist. Kim was standing behind Constance, her head resting against her partner's back. Sidney shook her head. How much in love and how happy they looked. And now both were dead.

Constance Williams had been a corporate attorney and, it appeared, a very good one. She had represented Serantis Pharmaceuticals and was also Lauren Serantis' personal attorney. Kim Lang had been a well-known art dealer and owned several galleries.

The next picture was of Lauren Serantis, the woman who had been Sasha's lover. The photograph had been taken for an interview in *Fortune* Magazine. Sidney read through the article. The FDA had approved a new wonder drug developed by Serantis Pharmaceuticals, sending the stock of the company off the charts. In the picture, a barefoot, casually dressed Lauren was walking along the sand toward whomever was taking the photo. Lauren's smile lit her face, and she had the most beautiful, expressive eyes.

All three women had been in their mid-to-late forties. All had been successful and attractive. They certainly didn't look like players, but Sidney knew that looks could be deceiving. Did they all share secrets? Secrets which, if exposed, could be used to portray Sasha as a rich, self-indulgent playgirl? The team had to peel away the layers and dig deeper. If there was anything to be found, they had to find it. It was only a matter of time before Sasha's troubled past, her involvement with women, and her history of drug use would be exposed for the world to see.

Avril picked up a picture of Sasha. "She's still very beautiful."

Slipping off her glasses, Sidney rubbed her temples, rested her head back against the chair, and closed her eyes. Maybe it was the emotion of the day. She felt the same anger and hurt stirring in her chest when it came to Sasha. Still, it had been years. Sasha had hurt her, but it was unfathomable to think that she was capable of murder. Everything they'd heard indicated that Sasha had changed, that she'd settled down in a monogamous relationship with Lauren Serantis. She had moved in with Lauren four years ago, reestablished her consulting business, and by all accounts seemed to be on the straight and narrow. If true, that positive fact could be overshadowed by Sasha's rebellious past, her history of womanizing, and her many attempts to get her cocaine habit under control.

They continued to work well past midnight, pausing only to call the hospital to check on Sasha, who continued to hold her own. When they finally took a break, Avril stretched out on the couch. Sidney wanted to stretch her legs and went down to the main floor of the office building to the 24-hour coffee shop. She stopped at the newsstand. The early edition of the local paper was just being delivered. She glanced at the headlines, and any vestige of grogginess she felt vanished. She grabbed a paper and hurried back to the elevators, repeatedly jabbing at the up button until the elevator doors opened. Upstairs she scribbled a quick note for the dozing Avril. Foregoing a shower and change of clothes, she grabbed her car keys and headed for the stairs, too impatient to wait again for the elevator.

Ingrid hadn't called, so she hadn't been told nor had she seen the papers yet. As Sidney sped toward the hospital, she prayed that continued to be true. She wanted to be with Ingrid and Marty when they heard the news. When Sidney entered their suite, Ingrid was sitting at the desk and Marty was coming out of the bedroom, dressed in her robe.

Suppressing a yawn, Marty greeted her. "Good morning, I guess, or it soon will be." Marty looked at Sidney's wrinkled clothes. "Looks like you worked all night, too." The look on Sidney's face concerned Marty. "You're here early. Is something wrong?"

Sidney held the newspaper out to Ingrid. When she opened it, big bold letters screamed: "Three Counts of First-Degree Murder. The State of California Will Ask the Death Penalty for the President's Sister."

The article quoted District Attorney Marcus Ramey as saying that Sasha's fingerprints and blood type had been found on the knife that killed all three women. It went on to say that when the state of California convicted Sasha Sheppard, he would ask for the most severe punishment. The heinous nature of this crime demanded nothing less than the death penalty.

Ingrid threw the newspaper down on the desk. It knocked a cup of coffee over onto the files she'd been working on.

"Damn it. I'm the President and I'm not informed of this before it hits the papers? That bastard! Marcus Ramey was a prick in college, and he's a prick now! I swear to God, he'd better have the evidence to back up these charges. If I find he's manipulated anything to use my sister to get to me, he'll regret the day he was born! As God is my witness, I swear he will!"

A shaking and angry Ingrid grabbed a handful of tissues and started to wipe up the coffee that was staining the papers spread out on the desk.

Marty picked up the newspaper, read it, then looked at Ingrid and Sidney, shock stamped on her face. They had anticipated that Sasha might be charged, but they hadn't anticipated it would be so soon. Seeing it in print was horrifying.

"Fingerprints and blood type? That's all he has? What judge would issue an arrest warrant this soon on that kind of evidence? It doesn't make sense."

Ingrid slammed her hand on the desk. "A God damn judge in someone's pocket, that's who!" It was a rare day when Ingrid lost her temper. She was usually the epitome of calm and reason.

Sidney felt just as angry as Ingrid did. She also knew that Marty was right. Ramey was banking a hell of a lot on just Sasha's fingerprints and a matching blood type. If that was all he had, he had made a move that could cost him dearly. This was insane — and just might give them grounds for dismissal of the charges. First-degree murder was going to be hard to prove given the nature of the crime and Sasha's condition when they brought her into the hospital.

Frustrated, Ingrid threw the coffee-soaked tissue into the wastebasket. "This shouldn't have hit me as hard as it did. The charges are nothing we didn't expect, but it's so damned hard to accept." Sidney could hear the catch of emotion in Ingrid's voice. "That sneaky bastard Ramey didn't have the guts to call and tell me himself, and his family owns this damn paper. I'll bet Ramey snuck this by Bob Redfern, too."

There was a light knock on the door. Ingrid's assistant poked her head in and said that the attorney general of California was on the phone and that it was important that he talk to her. Ingrid took the call, and when she hung up she said, "Bob was calling to tell me that the warrant for Sasha's arrest has been issued. Ramey called a news conference for this morning. As I expected, Bob didn't know about the charges until his office called and told him a few minutes ago. Ramey kept it under wraps. He wanted an exclusive for that rag of a paper. Dangling the death penalty. That SOB. Sid, we both know he'll play this to the hilt hoping I'll withdraw from the race and that it'll open the door to the governor's office for him. If he's involved, if it's the last thing I do, I promise..."

Marty went to Ingrid's side and took her in her arms.

"I'm sorry for losing my temper, baby. I'm frustrated, Marty, but I swear I intend to get to the bottom of this."

"It's all right, honey. Let's all try to calm down so we can think. Ramey has a warrant. We can't prevent Sasha from being arrested, but we need to block her from being taken from the hospital. That shouldn't be too difficult, considering her condition. If bail is granted, we'll post whatever bond is required, and we'll guarantee that Sasha will surrender herself when her condition improves."

"Marty's right, Ingrid," said Sidney. "We expected this. I'm going to contest the evidence and ask for a dismissal of the charges immediately. We'll make damn sure an honest judge is sitting the bench. I can also make it pretty uncomfortable for Ramey by submitting a complaint to the California Grand Jury asking for an investigation. We won't let him get by with this."

Running a hand through her hair, Ingrid took in a deep breath. "You're both thinking better than I am. You're right, Sid, we're not going to let Ramey get away with this." Ingrid drew Marty closer and pressed her face against her hair. "I love you, lady. Thank you for being here."

Ingrid picked up the coffee-stained papers that her Uncle Isaac had prepared and handed them to Sidney. "Sorry. I'll have another copy printed out." As Sidney accepted the wet papers, Ingrid explained, "Isaac and I share joint power of attorney for the entire Sheppard family, for good reasons. One of which is to be able to act quickly in any situation concerning the family. Sasha is incapacitated and not capable of entering her own plea. Anticipating the worst, Isaac drew up papers authorizing the DeRoche Law Firm to officially represent Sasha and to enter a plea of not guilty at an arraignment."

Ingrid continued, "If you can't get a dismissal, we're in agreement that asking for a delay, for any reason, could reflect poorly upon Sasha's innocence. We need to manage this carefully. Those pictures were damaging, and Sasha's past history will also go against her. We all know how public opinion can be manipulated. Too many cases have been decided by how the defendant was tried by the media."

Listening intently as Ingrid and Marty talked reaffirmed what Sidney had known from the first day in the courtroom at Pepperdine, that Ingrid had a razor sharp legal mind. And that Marty was just as competent. Public opinion and the media did sway many a jury. It had already begun. Three prominent women being murdered in a tranquil seaside community was sensational enough, but the sister of the President being charged with their murders was mind-boggling. Curiosity seekers, news vans, and television crews already lined the streets. Hordes of reporters and hungry tabloid vultures loaded down with cameras, hoping to get an exclusive story or picture, would dog their lives. Laguna Beach had been thrown into the eye of a storm and into the focus of not only the country, but also the world.

Things had already taken on a frantic air, spurred by the media-feeding frenzy. Reporters would be asking questions and prying into the lives of Sasha and the women who were murdered. Without question, every sordid detail of Sasha's life would be exposed. It was imperative that Sidney talk with Sasha as soon as it was possible, to find out what had happened in Lauren Serantis' beach house.

As Ingrid talked, she calmed down. She asked Marty and Sidney to sit, then took the chair opposite and pulled it close to them.

"Sid, I met with Leah last night to discuss Sasha's condition and to request that she consider staying on as Sasha's attending physician. I've given this considerable thought, but I need your honest opinion. I know we've discussed Leah taking care of Sasha while she was in her ER. Do you have any objections or qualms about Leah continuing?"

Ingrid took Sidney's hands in her own, her voice softening as she conveyed her concern. "I know that Sasha being thrown back into your life has dredged up memories well left in the past, and it's not what you would have chosen. You know I'm grateful to you. I know how attorney Sidney DeRoche will answer my question. I'm asking my best — my dearest friend — how she would answer."

With a simple phone call, Ingrid could well summon a team of specialists from anywhere in the world to attend to Sasha, but Sidney knew Ingrid trusted Leah and that Leah was as skilled and competent as any. A little part of Sidney wanted to protest, but it went unvoiced. She agreed with Ingrid's reasoning. The fewer the people who had access to Sasha and the confidential information concerning her medical history the better. Leah was the best choice all around.

Making direct eye contact with Ingrid, Sidney chose her words carefully. "So much is at stake here. Avril and I can and will fight for Sasha's life in a court of law, but you're the target of someone who wants you dead." Sidney squeezed Ingrid's hands. "Since you took the office of the President of the United States, you have made a difference in our country and this world. What's happening to you and Sasha is too important to allow personal feelings to affect what we have to do. Leah and I love each other. We share a life, but Leah makes her own decisions."

The phone in the suite rang. Ingrid answered and listened for a moment before she spoke. "Thank you, Leah. Is she coherent enough to talk with us, or with Sidney? In your opinion, is her condition stable enough to handle being told about the murders and that she's been charged with those murders?"

Ingrid pinched the bridge of her nose. Her lower lip trembled as she listened. "Well, unfortunately, whether she's strong enough or not, talking to Sasha can't be put off any longer. She's been charged with murder. If it were up to the district attorney, she'd already be in shackles and being hauled off to the prison ward at L.A. County Medical Center. Sidney is going to do everything she can to keep Sasha at SCMC, at least until her condition improves."

As Ingrid talked to Leah, the pain in her voice and on her face broke Sidney's heart. Marty's eyes were moist with tears.

"Leah, being married to a trial lawyer I'm sure you know that in a capital case, bail is not a matter of right. Sidney and Avril will have to dispute any evidence or hard presumption of guilt at an arraignment. And, as hard as it is for me to say, the district attorney is going to do everything he can to not let that happen. In our favor, he's too damn overconfident about making his case against Sasha. We need to find out everything we can about what went on in that beach house so Sidney and Avril can build a defense. If this charge sticks, they'll have to convince a judge to grant bail. It's going to take Sasha's help to do that."

The phone in Ingrid's hand shook slightly. She was saying all the right words, but Sidney knew that Ingrid was scared to death. "Hold on a moment, Leah, I want to speak to Sid." She turned to look at Sidney. "Sasha is awake and somewhat lucid — and she's asking questions. This would be a good time to talk with her. I'm not sure how she'll react. Do you want me to go with you?"

"Other than the one time she woke up delirious, when I was in the room, she hasn't seen me in a long time. I think it might be a good idea if you went in with me, then give us some time alone. Can Leah stand by, just in case we need her?"

"Leah, did you hear that? Can you come up...good, we'll wait for you."

Marty went to get dressed, and Ingrid paced the floor. Sidney sat quietly thinking about the imminent face-to-face with Sasha. It had been a long time since she'd felt so compelled to ask the question, "Are you guilty?"

All three were waiting when a light tap sounded on the door. Ingrid went to open it, knowing it was Leah. When Leah stepped into the room, her gaze immediately found Sidney and she smiled. Just looking at Leah and seeing the love in her eyes eased the butterflies Sidney had in her stomach. She walked over and put her arms around her waist and kissed her. "You're sure a sight for sore eyes, doc. I've missed you."

"Is that so?"

"Yep, that's so."

The smile that brightened Leah's face wrapped around Sidney's heart. Holding onto Leah's hand, Sidney turned toward Ingrid and Marty. "Can we have just a few minutes?"

Marty took an anxious Ingrid's hand and tugged her toward the door. "Darling, waiting a few more minutes to talk to Sasha isn't going to hurt." Knowingly, Marty smiled at Sidney and Leah. "We'll meet you outside Sasha's room."

Not taking her eyes off Leah, Sidney said, "Thank you. We'll be out in a few minutes."

When the door closed, Leah wrapped her arms around Sidney and pulled her close and returned her kiss. "You feel mighty good." Leah leaned back and looked at Sidney with concern. "You look tired, baby. Will you be able to get some rest today?"

Sidney was tired. And it just wasn't because of working all night. That was the norm while preparing for a case. It was this case, and it was already taking its toll. "Honey, come sit with me for a minute. I want to ask you something." Sidney held onto Leah's hand and led her over to the couch. "Ingrid told me she asked you to stay on as Sasha's physician. Have you decided? If there's any doubt or you feel—"

Leah pressed her finger lightly against Sidney's lips. "Sweetheart, I know why you're asking, and I'll be honest with you. I'd like to think that I was the only woman you've ever loved. I admit, I get a bit jealous. But, we both have loved before. That's in the past. I made the decision to stay on as Sasha's physician because I know what's at stake here — not only for Ingrid, but

Sasha as well. I also know how difficult it will be for you and that you are going to put everything you have into defending Sasha. I believe, as you do, in what Ingrid is trying to do for this country, and I love you with all my heart. If I can help by staying on as Sasha's doctor, then that's what I'll do."

Love and pride filled Sidney's heart. "I love you, Doctor Stanhope. Do you think there's a chance you might kiss me right now?"

Leah tenderly brushed the back of her fingers against Sidney's cheek, then leaned her forehead against Sidney's. "Counselor, I think there might be a very good chance of that."

Chapter Eight

Sasha opened her eyes, her heart pounding. She'd been dreaming, horrible pictures flashing rapidly through her mind, merging one into another before dissolving into a kaleidoscope of disjointed, distorted images.

When she'd been awake earlier, a nurse told her that she was in the hospital and she was going to be all right but the nurse hadn't said why or how long she'd been there. And she couldn't remember. It was as if her memories were caught in a web; as hard as she fought to remember, her subconscious mind fought harder not to. The last thing she could remember, in fact, was going to the restaurant with Lauren and being joined by Lauren's lawyer and her partner. But, where was Lauren now? she wondered. It wasn't like her not to be there. A feeling of dread washed over her, and her mind danced nervously away from the question.

There'd been an early morning phone call, hadn't there? A little before 6 AM? It had woken them both up. Lauren had gotten out of bed to take the call in her study, and Sasha had fallen back asleep. When she woke later that morning, Lauren was gone.

She'd just put on a pot of coffee when Lauren called from the lab, apologizing for having to leave so early, then asking if Sasha would mind changing their plans to stay in that evening. Constance, Lauren's attorney, needed a file that Lauren had at home. Lauren had made arrangements to meet Constance at a restaurant halfway between the house and Constance's office.

Pressing her fingers against her temple, Sasha remembered fixing a salad for lunch and then working in her studio when she heard Lauren come in, go straight into her study, and close the door. Lauren never came home early. Even when a new Serantis Pharmaceutical wonder drug wasn't about to be released. It was odd, too, that Lauren didn't stop in the studio to spend a few minutes with her first like she always did.

Sasha attributed it to the fact that Serantis Pharmaceutical was days away from releasing the new drug, a metallo-enzyme compound which would dissolve life-threatening clots of myocardial infarction and pulmonary embolism. The drug would significantly lower the rate of deaths after an occlusion. She debated going and asking Lauren if everything was all right. She was worried. The past few months Lauren had been working long hours at the lab and was near exhaustion. And recently — she'd been unusually quiet and distracted the last few weeks.

Eventually she went to Lauren's study, Sasha remembered, but before she could knock, she heard Lauren on the phone. Her voice was raised in anger, but Sasha couldn't make out what she was saying. Deciding not to disturb her, she went to their bedroom, undressed, and went out to do a few laps in the pool. She'd fallen asleep lying in the sun on the chaise, waking when she felt Lauren's cool hands on her bare back.

"Darling, you're starting to burn." Lauren sat next to her, pouring sunscreen on her hands to apply to her reddened skin. When Lauren's hands moved over her back, she groaned. "Hmm, your hands feel good. It's been a while."

"I know. I'm sorry. I've been a bear to live with." Lauren's hands caressed Sasha's back and buttocks, then down the backs of her legs. Brushing her lips across the sensitive skin of Sasha's lower back, Lauren said, "You have such beautiful skin, my love. I don't know how I've managed to stay away from touching it for so long. I promise I'll make it up to you as soon as...how would you like to take the boat out and sail to all those places you've been wanting to show me? We can go any place your heart desires and anywhere the wind blows us."

Hearing the fatigue in Lauren's voice, Sasha had rolled over. Lauren had looked exhausted, but Sasha had been more concerned about the worry in her eyes.

"That would be a dream come true, Lauren, to have you all to myself with no one else around for miles. You look tired, sweetheart. Why don't we cancel our plans to go out tonight? Call Constance and have her drop by the house. I'd much rather stay home and just spend a quiet evening with you. I'll fix dinner while you rest, then maybe we can work on that promise."

Lauren smiled, her dark eyes softening. "Darling, believe me, there's nothing I'd like better, but it's best we meet Constance at the restaurant to give her the file. It's important she has it tonight."

Sasha remembered wondering why Lauren hadn't arranged for Constance to pick up the file earlier at work, or why Lauren didn't want Constance to stop by the house to pick it up.

Before they left to meet Constance, Lauren had taken a file from the wall safe hidden in the floor of the master closet. Then they drove to a little Italian restaurant on the coast highway Sasha had never been to. Then...she drew a blank. Try as she might, she had no memory beyond Constance and Kim joining them at the restaurant and ordering drinks.

Sasha trembled. A flash of Lauren's face distorted in pain sent a cold shiver throughout her body. She managed to reach the water on the bed stand. Her mouth was dry, but the water made her nauseated. She closed her eyes, picturing Lauren and how Lauren had caught her eye the night they met.

It had been Lauren's birthday. Friends had taken her out to dinner and then to the exclusive Club Palais du Plaisir. Lauren had never been to the club, she told Sasha later, but she was having a good time, so she agreed to go along.

Sasha had been there, in withdrawal, fighting the need to use, and bored with the same indulgent women she bedded most nights. She was about to leave when Lauren came in with her friends. With her dark hair and Mediterranean looks, she'd caught everyone's eye, including hers. Before she reached her table, half the women in the room were drooling, aching to pounce. Sasha had stood at the bar, watching as a steady stream of women had propositioned and tried to seduce Lauren. Offering a night of sex or drugs or whatever pleasure would appeal, promising anything and everything to entice the beautiful Lauren.

The smile never left Lauren's face. A smile that said she was not uncomfortable, but amused. That she wasn't hungry or buying. The music and the energy in the club soon reached a frenzied pitch. The air reeked of sex and pulsated to the grinding, gyrating bodies of very beautiful and very wealthy women — women who were dressed in an eclectic display of dress, from collars and leather to gothic and punk. Even those in one-of-a-kind designer evening gowns and diamonds were reveling in unrestrained indulgence.

When her friends headed for one of the more private rooms, Lauren stayed behind. Sasha found Lauren fascinating. She reminded her of Sidney in many ways. Both were attractive women, Sidney as blonde as Lauren was dark, but both had a look of confidence, a special aura. No woman since Sidney had caught her interest as much.

Sasha had been intently watching Lauren when her body brutally reminded her of its gnawing need. She hadn't used since the day before, determined to prove this time that she could kick her cocaine habit on her own.

The room had been suddenly too hot and the music too loud and too irritating. She hadn't eaten, and alcohol was making her nauseated. She'd avoided a tray of complimentary pick candy the first time it was passed around, but the next time the bartender had winked, slipped a packet of cocaine off the tray, and slid it under her glass. Her hand had shaken as she fingered the small package. She could have easily opened it and taken the hit right where she was standing. No one would have noticed or, if they did, even cared. Everyone was high, everyone but Lauren and her. She crumpled the packet into her fist and went out the side door that led to where her car was parked. The cool night air blew through her hair and chilled the sweat on her body, but failed to cool the fires of hell that were gnawing at every nerve. She leaned against the fender of her Jaguar with her eyes closed, still clutching the packet of cocaine in her fist, when she heard a voice.

"You can get help."

When she had opened her eyes, Lauren was standing there looking at her with compassionate eyes. Sasha hadn't realized she was crying until Lauren brushed the tears from her face. "You're going to have to use some of that or be even sicker."

Her hands shook as she struggled to get the packet opened. After she sniffed up the white powder and felt the shaking ease, she lowered her eyes in shame.

"Would you like to go somewhere for coffee?"

"I don't...think I can drive."

"I'll drive."

Lauren had helped her into her car, and they drove to an all-night diner. Hanging onto Lauren's arm, she managed to get into the diner and to eat a few spoons full of soup. They talked until daybreak — rather, Lauren talked quietly and Sasha listened. When Lauren drove her back to her car, she wrote her home phone number on the back of her business card and handed it to her. "When you have this thing beaten, call me. Maybe we could have dinner."

Finally kicking her cocaine habit wasn't going to be easy. Sasha had been in many different treatment programs over the years. She would be fine for a while, then she'd relapse, telling herself it was only recreational and she could stop any time. She had refused to admit, even to herself, that she was an addict — not even after Sidney left her the first time and Sasha committed herself to a treatment program.

Ingrid and Marty saw her through another treatment program after Sidney left her the last time, then another and another. Each time, she would vow to stay clean, but the always-present temptation and promise of the exquisite ecstasy of the white powder had been impossible to resist.

After the night in the diner with Lauren, she had set sail, getting as far away from land and the drugs as she could. This time she would do it the hard way, she vowed — cold turkey. If she made it and lived, it would be for the last time. She would never abuse her body by using again.

She had drifted for days, too sick and too weak to man the boat or raise the sails. She didn't die, but there were times all alone out on the ocean that she wished she could. When the worst had passed, she dragged herself up on deck. She stank and she'd lost weight.

Ten weeks later when she sailed into the private cove of her home in Laguna, she was clean and fit, both mentally and physically. Her body was free from her craving for cocaine. The first thing she did after soaking in the Jacuzzi for the better part of two days was to send Lauren flowers and an invitation to have dinner with her.

Sasha was still thinking about Lauren when the door opened. Hoping it was her, she flashed her eyes to the doorway. When she saw Ingrid and Marty and the looks on their faces, she covered her face with her shaking hands and started to tremble. A low ragged moan came from deep inside her. Ingrid rushed over and took her in her arms. "Sasha, honey, are you hurting?"

Sasha removed her hands from her face; bewildered she looked at her sister. "Ingrid, Ingrid...oh God, Lauren! Please, tell me...where's Lauren?" Sasha wasn't even aware that Sidney and Leah had come into the room. When she became increasingly agitated and confused, Leah gave her something to sedate her.

Sidney saw the fear and terror in Sasha's eyes. It tore at her heart to watch the anguish and torment Sasha was going through. Before the medicine took effect, Sasha moaned Lauren's name over and over. She had truly loved Lauren Serantis, thought Sidney. She felt a brief, surprising moment of jealousy toward the dead woman.

When Sasha finally quieted, Leah told them that she could be under for hours. All they could do was wait and see if Sasha came around sound of mind, or if her mind would defensively shut down rather than face what had happened at the beach house. On edge, Sidney decided to go back to the office instead of waiting at the hospital.

As Sidney ran from the hospital toward her car, splintered thunderbolts sliced through the low-hanging clouds and rain started to fall. Sporadic flashes of white light illuminated the darkened gray skies. The forecast on the news warned of a huge storm cell coming off the Pacific that would bring heavy rains. The coast would soon be socked in.

By the time Sidney reached the turnoff to her office, the rain was threatening to turn into a torrential downpour. The street was wet and mostly deserted as she approached the entrance to the underground parking. Her heart rate quickened when she saw an empty police car and a motorcycle in front of the building in a No Parking zone. She pulled in, got out quickly, and hurried toward the elevator. As she did so, she was struck by something she heard or rather didn't hear. The gate hadn't made its usual clang as it closed against the cement floor.

Looking back as the gate shut, Sidney noted the lights above the barrier were out, making the area too dark to see. Spooked, she started to talk out loud to herself, her voice bouncing off the walls of the mostly empty garage. "You're just tired and imagining things." It didn't help. She couldn't shake the uneasy feeling that gripped her.

Avril met her when she got off the elevator. She had been crying. "I tried to call you on your cell, Sid. You left it in Sasha's room. Leah answered it and told me you'd just left."

"Avril, what is it? Has something happened? What...?"

"Please come into the conference room. Jay Brunelle and two of her officers are here."

Sidney trembled. A portentous shudder ran through her body as she entered the conference room. It was obvious that something terrible had happened. Mark Timmer, one of their long-time investigators, was standing at the window with his fists clenched, staring out at the rain that was falling over the city. Billie and Janine sat at the end of the conference table. Janine was dabbing her eyes with tissue; Billie sat next to her a stricken look on her face.

Two uniformed police officers flanked their chief. Jay Brunelle looked frazzled. She must have been caught in the storm because her clothes were wet. Dressed in jeans, boots, and a T-shirt under a worn brown bomber jacket, Jay was holding a motorcycle helmet in her leather-gloved hand. Sidney looked from Avril to Jay. "Is someone going to tell me what's going on here?"

Jay set the helmet down on the table. If Sidney hadn't been so focused on finding out what was going on, she would have seen the tears in Jay's eyes and heard the trembling in her voice. "Grant Nolte was found dead in his car. Someone blew...he was shot in the head."

It was as if the air had been sucked out of the room. Sidney's brain froze, as she tried frantically to assimilate what Jay had just said.

"Grant...Grant is...is dead?" Sidney was vaguely aware of Leah's arms around her, pulling her close, and the murmur of Leah's comforting voice. She turned, confused. "Leah?"

"Avril told me what happened. I came as soon as I got off the phone."

Sidney shook her head. "Grant can't be dead. There must be a mistake."

Jay was hurting. The sight of Grant's brains splattered all over the inside of his car had driven her to her knees. And seeing Leah now with Sidney... Tearing her eyes away from Leah, Jay focused on what she was there for. "I'm sorry, I know this has been a hell of a shock to all of you, but I need to ask a few questions. What was Grant working on? Was it the Sasha Sheppard case?"

Everyone looked from Jay to Sidney. A moment of confusion crossed Sidney's face, then her eyes widened.

"You think Grant's death is connected to something he was working on?"

There was a hard and impatient edge to Jay's voice as she answered. "Grant was an investigator for this law firm. It's a damn easy guess he was killed because of a case he was working on. And since he was your lead investigator, I would say it's a fair assumption that he was working on the Sheppard case. Am I wrong?"

Sidney was trembling; she knew that she needed to answer Jay and tell her Grant was working on the case, but all she could think of was that Grant might have been killed as a result of something she'd assigned him to do.

Avril answered. "Grant is our lead investigator and is solely on retainer for this law firm. He's been involved with every investigation this firm conducted and yes, he is..." Avril cover her mouth with a trembling hand. "He was involved in the Sheppard case." Avril took a deep breath, then let it out trying to compose herself.

"Had Grant said anything in his reports to indicate that he was on to something?"

Avril and Sidney's eyes met. The entire research team knew that Grant sent a daily report in an e-mail that included where he'd been and who he'd talked to, along with a tentative itinerary for the next day. And Sidney knew that as close as Jay and Grant were, Jay would know that, too. Grant had talked on numerous occasions about the possibility of getting hurt while on a case. That was why he was always careful to keep a daily log of his activities, as a safeguard in case something happened to him.

"We've received several reports from Grant, but nothing that indicated he was onto anything specific." Sidney recalled the last report she'd read. "He mentioned that he was going to Serantis Pharmaceuticals."

Jay was too overwrought to continue. She knew it was futile to ask any more questions tonight and she'd play hell getting any information that was remotely connected to the Sasha Sheppard case. She'd gotten all she was going to get from anyone here. Information that Grant had gathered while working for the defense didn't need to be disclosed until it was presented as discovery. She nodded and motioned to the officers, who turned and left the room.

Before Jay could say anything else, Mark cursed. "You S.O.B.! Grant was more than an employee or a case to us. He was a friend. Out of respect, couldn't your questions have waited until tomorrow?"

Jay's dark eyes flashed him a cold hard look, and her hands gripped the helmet she'd picked up. "Grant didn't have any family...except..." She hesitated. "In case anyone here has forgotten, I am the law in Laguna. Grant's been murdered. I understand you're all in shock, but I'm doing my job. I'm sorry if you feel that's an inconvenience for you."

Leah stepped closer to Jay and gently put her hand on Jay's forearm. "I'm so sorry; Jay, this must be very difficult for you. Grant was like a father to you. This has to be just as hard, or harder, for you than it is for us."

Jay's throat tightened with the emotion she'd held at bay since getting the call after she'd gone home from the precinct and seeing Grant's body with half his head blown off. Leah's touch and the fact that she remembered about Grant crumbled her professional façade. Moisture welled in Jay's eyes. Her voice broke as she looked into Leah's sympathetic eyes. "No matter how long it takes, I'll find the person who did this."

Grant's death had opened an emotional floodgate, and the usual stoic chief was showing her vulnerability. Leah's proximity was dredging up memories and longing. It was more than Jay could handle tonight; she forced herself to turn and walk to the door. She had her hand on the knob, then stopped and turned to look at Sidney. "I will find the person who killed him, and nothing's going to stop me. Not you or your case...nothing."

After Jay left, Mark ran his hand through his thick hair and looked at Leah. "Damn, I'm sorry, Leah. I didn't know. It's just..."

"Mark, it's okay. We're all distraught and emotional here. There's no way you would have known. Grant thought of Jay as the daughter he never had. After Jay's father was killed, Grant watched over the family. When Jay and I were..." Leah felt Sidney stiffen and didn't finish what she was going to say. Instead she put her arm around Sidney's waist and said, "I'm taking Sidney home. I think it would be a good idea if we all went home and got some rest. There isn't anything that can be done right now."

Squeezing Leah's hand, Sidney agreed. "Leah is right. We're all too emotional right now. Decisions concerning Grant will be best made after some rest, and then we can sort through this better. Everyone, please, go home. I'll see you in the morning."

The illuminated face of the bedside clock read 3:30 AM. Unable to sleep, Sidney eased out of bed so as not to wake Leah, who had finally fallen asleep after holding her for hours while she cried. Getting into the shower took all of Sidney's effort. Her arms and legs felt as heavy as her heart. She set the alarm for Leah, left a note, and then headed for the office.

When she arrived at the office, it didn't surprise Sidney that everyone on the team was already there and working. All had red, puffy eyes and looked like they hadn't slept. Tears threatened as Sidney stood in the doorway of the war room. Everyone looked up as Jason approached her and handed her a cup of coffee, then kissed her on the cheek.

"Thank..." Sidney cleared her throat. "Thank you all for being here."

The tightness in her throat made it too difficult to say anymore. She knew the team had stayed and gone back to work scouring through Grant's e-mail reports and listening to the few messages he'd left, looking for anything that might lead them to what he was following up on.

Avril followed Sidney into her office. She found her standing by the window looking out into the darkness. The rain had eased, but the forecast predicted a dismal day. A day that reflected the sadness that everyone was feeling. Avril went to Sidney and put her arms around her. "Honey, I figured you'd be back."

"Did you even leave?"

"No, it was too much of an effort to go home. It's hard to believe, isn't it? When I hear the elevator ding, I expect to see him walk in."

Nodding, Sidney said, "Is Jay right? Was Grant killed because of this case?"

"We both know it's a good possibility that this case and his death are connected."

"His life was taken so violently." They stood quietly looking out at the rain, each trying to deal with her grief. Sidney finally said, "Grant has no family. After the autopsy, Jay most likely will be the one making arrangements for his...I don't even know what arrangements Grant wanted."

"He'd mentioned once to me that he wanted to be cremated. The team talked about having a memorial service. I could call Jay and ask her what she thinks about a service."

"I'd appreciate it. Give her some time, then please call her." Sidney hugged Avril and then picked her keys up off the desk. "I'm going to the hospital. Call me if you need me."

When Sidney looked into Sasha's room, Ingrid was sitting in a recliner beside her bed with her eyes closed, a folder of papers on her lap. Sidney quietly closed the door behind her and went to sit on the other side of the bed by the window. Sasha's eyes were closed, and her dark lashes stood out against her pale cheeks. The room was quiet except for Sasha's even breathing and the soft sibilant sound of the machines. A slender ray of sunlight crept between the blinds and fell across her arm, warming the one place on her skin that wasn't cold.

Before coming in, she'd shared a cup of coffee with Marty, who had told her that Sasha had been in and out of lucidity. Looking at her, Sidney thought of Grant. As often as one heard the words "death is so final", it didn't hit home until it crossed your doorstep, thwarting intentions to someday reach out and to understand, putting an end to second chances to resolve unanswered questions.

She searched Sasha's face. *Do we ever really know anyone? Did I ever really know you, Sasha?*

Chapter Nine

Fourteen Years Earlier

Sidney, Ingrid, and Marty were scheduled to graduate from Pepperdine in a week. The afternoon of Ingrid's party, after Sasha disappeared into the sun on her skim board, Sidney lay out for a few more minutes, not wanting to admit that the brash young woman had been right about her getting sunburned. Then she slipped into the water and swam back to the beach. Before going into the kitchen, she wrapped up in a towel that she grabbed off the chaise lounge. Ingrid and Marty, back from the market, were busy cutting up vegetables and making pitchers of margaritas for the party planned for that evening.

"Hey, we saw you lying on the dock in all your naked white glory. You didn't get burned, did you?"

Chuckling, Sidney answered, "A bit maybe. You're not the first to warn me of getting burned, however, and I wasn't the only one naked out there. A mouthy girl popped up out of nowhere, propositioned me, and told me that I had a cute ass." Sidney grabbed a carrot. "I'm going to shower. I'll be down to help as soon as I clean up."

Ingrid and Marty looked at each other with raised eyebrows as Sidney ran up the stairs to her room, then simultaneously said, "Sasha?"

Ingrid angrily wiped her hands on a dishtowel. "I'd better go up and see if Sasha is here, then warn Sidney that the wayward sibling is home."

Marty shrugged her shoulders. "You know if you go up there and play big sister, Sasha's going to resent it and it'll lead to a big fight. Let it go. Sidney can hold her own, and maybe Sasha will surprise us all and be civil and behave herself."

"If I even suspect that she is using, she's going straight back to rehab. I don't know what she's doing here, anyway. She wasn't supposed to have off-ground privileges for at least another week."

Marty went around the counter and put her arms around Ingrid's waist. "Honey, I told you that Sasha has earned weekend privileges. Maybe she came home because she's lonely and misses her family. Give her a chance — okay?"

Ingrid looked confused, then groaned, closed her eyes, and leaned back against the counter, taking Marty with her. "Damn, I forgot. Some big sister I am." She loved the feel of Marty in her arms. Marty's love grounded her and allowed her the simple pleasure of not being perfect all the time. And Marty wasn't shy about telling her that she wasn't perfect. "Have I told you lately what a great lawyer you're going to be or how much I love you?"

Marty leaned closer into Ingrid and kissed the V-shaped soft spot of her neck before nibbling her way across Ingrid's collarbone.

"Hmm...let me see, I can't recall." Marty sucked Ingrid's earlobe into her mouth. "Darling, you taste like lime. But I love it. What say we leave the rest of this for later and go upstairs and...shower?"

Ingrid chuckled, threw the towel in the sink, and pulled Marty's hips tight against her own. Nuzzling Marty's neck, she teased, "Martina Maria Donahue. And what do you suggest we do about our houseguests? What will they think when they hear you moaning and groaning as I make mad passionate love to your gorgeous body?"

Marty felt her lower abdomen tightening and anticipated pleasure pooling between her legs as Ingrid unbuttoned her blouse and kissed across the soft skin and swell of her breasts. She put her arms around Ingrid's neck and purred. "I'd think they would say I'm one very, very lucky woman."

Later that evening, the sound of music and laughter mingled with the rhythmic sounds of the surf breaking across the stretch of shore along the beachfront of the posh Laguna house. The mood was light. Everyone had eaten too much, not a surprise for financially struggling law students. Most were lounging in groups, involved in conversations about the interesting cases they'd discussed in class that week.

Sidney didn't feel like debating the merits of the latest California appellate court decision so she slipped out to stroll barefoot along the beach. The evening was perfect. Everything in her life was perfect. A balmy breeze gently blew her hair across her face, and a blue moon hung on the edge of the water, casting a shimmering, silvery glow on the waves washing across the sand. She walked all the way around the point and climbed atop the rocks and stood looking out at the endless star-filled night sky and the scattered lights of the boats anchored off in the distance. She didn't notice the figure sitting on a rock in the shadows a few feet away until a voice out of the dark startled her.

"I almost didn't recognize you with your clothes on. Such a shame really, to cover up such a gorgeous body." The young woman that Sidney had encountered that afternoon stood up.

"You again. Isn't it past your bedtime?"

The girl's sensuous laugh raised goose bumps along Sidney's arms and sent shivers down her legs. The young woman hopped onto the rock that Sidney was standing on and leaned in toward her. Sidney could feel her warm breath as the girl whispered in her ear. "You looked so sexy lying naked in the sun, but you're just as sexy standing here in the moonlight. I'm Sasha." Her eyes shone with mischief; she seemed to delight in teasing Sidney.

This is Ingrid's kid sister? Jeez! Sidney stood with her mouth open. *My God, she's so...so... she's...* Sidney moved and started to slip, but before she could fall Sasha's arms went around her waist, and the younger woman pulled her tightly against her. The sounds of the night, the music, and the ocean crashing on the rocks all faded as Sasha looked into her eyes and kissed her.

Sidney was stunned. Before she could react, Sasha kissed her again until she was breathless, then hopped off the rocks, and ran her tongue across her own lips. Smiling, she said, "You taste pretty good, too. We'll meet again one day, Sidney DeRoche."

With that Sasha turned and jogged down the beach. Sidney stood gaping until the darkness closed around Sasha and she could no longer see her.

"What the..." Sidney touched her lips and sat down on the rock. "Now I understand why Ingrid is always so concerned about her sister — and she's gay? That one is going to break many a woman's heart."

She shook her head and laughed at the absurdity of the scene and her statement. "She probably already has."

The next morning the smell of coffee brewing nudged Sidney to open her eyes. She suspected Ingrid was up. Ingrid liked to run on the beach at daybreak just when the sun was coming up. She said it inspired her. It did the same for Sidney. Every morning when they could, the two classmates met up and ran along the jogging path from Pepperdine down to one of the most beautiful stretches of beach in California.

Sidney threw on a pair of shorts and a tank top, grabbed her runners, and headed toward the kitchen.

"I knew it was you that was up. Mind if I tag along?"

"Sure. I was hoping you'd get up. That's why I put the coffee on. I knew you couldn't resist."

Sidney laughed as she glanced at the two cups sitting on the counter. "Sneaky, but very shrewd."

"How about a quick cup before we go?"

Sidney inhaled, breathing in the fresh aroma of the coffee that would jump-start her sluggish body. "You couldn't drag me out of here until I've had my coffee."

They ran beyond the point to the pier, then started back, comfortable with each other's pace. As they ran, Ingrid decided to tell Sidney about Sasha.

"The mouthy girl you met yesterday, who was ogling your body, was my sister Sasha. I'm surprised that Sasha and her friend didn't show up at the clambake last night. On second thought, I'm not surprised."

"Friend?"

"A woman. I'm sure I embarrassed her when I barged into Sasha's room this morning. She was...well, in Sasha's bed, naked. It looked like they'd had quite the party themselves. Sasha was up already and down in the pool, swimming. Even as a little kid she never slept much. Always too hyper. I'm sorry if she came on too strong yesterday."

"Hey, it was kind of nice to have my body appreciated. It's nothing to worry about. Come on, I'll race ya back. Loser makes breakfast."

Marty was sitting on the deck reading the paper and sipping her coffee when she spotted the two women racing each other to the house. She loved to watch Ingrid when she ran. The defined muscles in her legs flexed as her pace ate up the sand, and her toned body, dressed in her running shorts, showed off her physical fitness. She was a head taller than Sidney and most of her six feet seemed to be leg.

Marty shook her head at the good-natured competition always present between Ingrid and Sidney. They complemented each other, and Marty couldn't help but think what a successful law team the three of them would make, each strong in a different area. Sidney reached the deck first and flopped down on her back in the sand.

"You let me win. No fair."

"Never, Sidney, never." Ingrid winked at Marty, hopped over Sidney, and bent over to give Marty a quick kiss. "Good morning, darling, did you sleep well?"

Marty raised an eyebrow as she caught the gleam in Ingrid's eye. She grabbed a handful of Ingrid's sweaty shirt and pulled her down for another kiss. "Hmm. I could ask you the same question, smart aleck. I put on another pot. I'll pour. Who wants a cup?"

Before Marty could get up, Sasha and another woman came through the door of the house. They were holding hands. Sasha kept her eyes on Sidney as she pulled the woman close, put her arm possessively around the woman's waist, and placed a kiss on her neck.

"We're heading out. I need to be back in my cell by eight tonight."

The disapproval was evident on Ingrid's face. "It's hardly a cell, Sasha. More like a very expensive playpen."

Sidney could see the anger simmer in Sasha's brooding dark eyes. Anger that she later learned was a part of who Sasha was. Marty stood up to intervene before Ingrid and Sasha went at it, as they usually did.

"That's hours from now. I was just going to fix breakfast. Why don't you and your guest join us before you leave?"

Sasha stiffened, the anger toward her sister evident, but she held her tongue and didn't respond to Ingrid's comment. "Thanks, Marty, but Sondra has a new place on the beach at Huntington that she wants to show me." Sasha ran her hand over Sondra's buttocks. "Don't you, darling?"

Curious now, Sidney looked the woman over. She was attractive, older than Sasha, maybe in her late twenties, wearing torn jeans and a crop top that showed a gold ring in her navel. Blushing, she seemed uncomfortable with everyone staring at her as she held onto Sasha's arms around her waist, but she did introduce herself. "Hi, I'm Sondra Diodorus...a...a friend of Sasha's."

"I'm sorry, darling, forgive my bad manners." Sasha kissed Sondra on the lips. "Please, wait for me in the car. I'll be right along."

When Sondra went back into the house, Sasha angrily turned toward her sister. "I'm sorry I'm such a colossal disappointment to you and that I'm not as smart or as perfect as you are, but you have no reason to be rude to a guest of mine."

"What? I never said a word."

"You didn't have to. It was written all over your face. If you're going to be the next household word in law and politics, you'd better learn to disguise your expressions and body language better."

Sasha turned to Marty, but her gaze was fixed over Marty's shoulder on Sidney as she bent to kiss Marty on the cheek. "Thanks, Marty. Another time."

After Sasha left, they sat on the deck in silence. Finally Marty got up and said, "Well, that's that. Come on. Let's go in and make breakfast and then clean up."

Over a second cup of coffee, Marty commented, "Do you know who Sondra Diodorus is?"

Both Ingrid and Sidney looked at her, eyebrows raised in question.

"Heiress to billions and reported to be one of the wealthiest young women in the world."

Sidney, Ingrid, and Marty received their degrees from Pepperdine and went on to pass the bar exam with flying colors. Sidney's love and interest remained in criminal law, and she accepted a position as an associate at the Isaac A. Sheppard Law Firm, where all three had interned. Ingrid chose to go to Washington to clerk for a judge on the Court of Appeals, and Marty found a junior position in Washington in corporate law to be close to her. The three talked frequently and got together as often as they could, which wasn't often, due to their busy careers.

One afternoon a few years later while Sidney was buried under a pile of law books, preparing for a case that was on the court docket for the first of the year, a messenger delivered an envelope to her. She recognized the handwriting as Ingrid's. To her delight it was an invitation to the New Year's Eve party at Isaac Sheppard's home. Ingrid had enclosed a note saying that she and Marty were going to be home this year for the holidays. They had stayed in Washington, where Ingrid had gone on to serve as a clerk for a Supreme Court Justice, then as Special Assistant to the U.S. Attorney General. Marty had made senior partner and built a reputation in Washington as a foremost and respected counsel in corporate law. Sidney's diligence and hard work during the same period had earned her a well-deserved position as a senior partner.

The annual New Year's Eve party was a gala event, attended by the very wealthy as well as the politically connected. It justified dusting off the credit card and sparing no expense for a new dress and shoes. By noon on New Year's Eve, Sidney was so excited about seeing Ingrid and Marty she couldn't concentrate. It was the first time in years that she had felt the holiday spirit, and she looked forward to the festive occasion. It had been well over a year since she'd seen her best friends, and Ingrid had said in her note that she had something exciting to tell her, but not to mention anything about it in front of Marty.

After showering, Sidney put on the diamond and silver earrings that matched her necklace and bracelet, then looked at her reflection in the mirror. She'd chosen a black sequined form-fitting dress that came to just above her knees. The V neckline showed a respectable amount of cleavage, and the back scooped low enough to display the toning of the muscles of her back. She sat to put on the black patent leather heels, then stood up and put on the waist-length matching silk jacket. Earlier she had the doorman take her gifts, including the special bottle of Isaac's favorite, Cipriano Syrah, and a Special Reserve Cipriano Merlot that she'd picked up for Isaac's wife, down to the car.

The ride along the coastal highway toward Dana Point allowed Sidney a spectacular view of the extravagant holiday decorations adorning the luxury homes. She seldom put up a tree. Having no one to share it with, there wasn't much point when she was at the office more than she was at home. When she saw the illuminated marker set up to guide the guests, she pulled off onto the road that led to the Sheppard home. Cars lined both sides of the road and the driveway. Valets were shuttling vehicles a few miles down the beach to Ingrid's parents' home. Sidney took a last look in the rearview mirror as she waited for the valet, attributing the butterflies she felt in her stomach to seeing Ingrid and Marty again. A few minutes later she followed the sounds of holiday music into the beach house.

Isaac Sheppard's home was a statement of his success and the success of the Sheppard Law Firm. Festive holiday music, played by a four-piece group of string and woodwind musicians, greeted the guests on the front lawn. To her delight, Ingrid and Marty were standing in the entryway waiting for her. When Sidney entered, Ingrid's grin was as big as the hug she enfolded her in.

"My God, it's so good to see you! We've missed you so much. Why can't I convince you to come to Washington with us? Never mind. Don't answer that. I know where your heart is…criminal law. We just miss that damn superior, argumentative, analytical mind of yours." Ingrid laughed and hugged Sidney again.

It was wonderful to see her friends. They radiated happiness and contentment and were very much in love. Ingrid looked healthy and fit, and Marty was more gorgeous than Sidney had ever seen her. Both seemed to be on cloud nine. Sidney hugged Ingrid back and looked at Marty. "How do you put up with her? Does she ever settle down?"

"Well, truthfully? Never, but I love her anyway." Marty took Sidney's hand. "Come on, let's get you a drink and find a place where we can talk."

Everything about the evening was wonderful — the company, the food, and the music. Marty was dancing with Ingrid's father and Sidney was sipping a Bailey's Irish coffee, admiring a huge

Christmas tree, when Ingrid grabbed her hand and led her into her uncle's study. Ingrid had been excited and nervous all evening. Sidney watched her pace the floor now like the proverbial cat on a hot tin roof.

"What is it? You're acting like a fidgety bride or…"

Ingrid opened the top drawer of the desk and took out a small velvet box. "Marty and I have been together for so long, I don't know why we haven't…well, why I haven't…I've waited too long to do this. I mean if…well, if Marty wants to and she'll accept this ring and my proposal to be my life partner, will you be the best woman at our joining?"

Both of Sidney's hands went to her mouth, then her fingers trembled as she excitedly opened the box. "Oh, it's beautiful. Marty loves you, you big dope, and she'd wear a cigar band if it came from you. Besides, you're right, it's about time." Sidney threw her arms around her and hugged her. "I'm so excited. When are you going to ask her?"

"Tonight, when we go home to my parents' house. I'm going to come up with an excuse to leave early. I have everything arranged. Flowers, candlelight…wine…well, white grape juice. Mom and Dad are staying the night here so we have the house all to ourselves."

"Yes! I'll be at your joining, and I'll be your best woman. Wait — white grape juice…?"

Grinning, Ingrid said, "How do you feel about being a godmother, too? We're pregnant. I mean Marty is pregnant." Ingrid's smile lit the room.

With tears of happiness in her eyes, Sidney crossed the room and hugged her best friend. "It would be my honor."

After dinner Ingrid feigned a headache, and she and Marty said their good-byes. From the tears in Sidney's eyes and the smile on her face when she walked them to the car waiting in the driveway, Marty suspected that Ingrid had told Sidney about the pregnancy. Marty linked her arm through Sidney's. "So, did you agree to be godmother? You know, I wanted to be with her when she told you."

Not surprised that Marty guessed, Ingrid tried to explain. "I'm sorry. I know we agreed to tell her together, before we told the family tomorrow. I just couldn't wait any longer. Sid and I were talking and…"

"Honey, it's okay. If you hadn't beat me to it, I would have told her."

"Thank God that's settled. I've wanted to yell how happy I am for you two since Ingrid told me." Sidney held both of Marty's hands and stepped back. "You looked absolutely radiant. I love you both, and yes, I will be your child's godmother."

Just as the car was going down the driveway, Marty rolled the window down and yelled to Sidney. "Twins. Godmother to our twins."

Feeling happier than she had in a long time, Sidney wandered out onto the veranda and stood listening to the sounds of the music and the waves slapping against the rocks on the beach. It was a beautiful night. The temperature earlier in the day had hit seventy-six degrees, and the night air was crisp and the sky so clear that Sidney could actually see the soft nebulae of Orion. A brilliant shooting star crossed the night sky, and Sidney whispered, "I wish I may, I wish I might, have all my wishes come true tonight."

Sidney heard a voice that seemed to float around her with the gentle breeze from the ocean. "I can't speak for those stars you're looking at, but if you name your most passionate desire I'll make it come true."

Embarrassed, Sidney turned to see a familiar and most stunning woman standing behind her in satin tuxedo pants and a short satin backless tuxedo vest that showed off the skin of her abdomen. "I'm sorry, I didn't know...I was...Sasha?"

Sasha laughed softly and handed Sidney a crystal flute, then filled it from the bottle of champagne she was carrying. "It's me, all grown up, and I still think you're the loveliest woman I've ever had the pleasure to feast my eyes on."

As they sipped on the champagne, they talked and laughed about that day on the beach, when they'd first met. From inside the house the noisy countdown to the New Year had started. Sasha set her glass down, stood in front of Sidney, took the glass out of her hand, and set it down as well. When "Happy New Year" started to echo through the balmy night air, Sasha put her arms around Sidney's waist, then slowly and gently pulled Sidney against her. "Happy New Year, Sidney DeRoche."

She kissed Sidney, and then, just like the last time, she kissed her again until Sidney's lips and body began to respond. Running her tongue lightly along Sidney's lower lip, Sasha said, "I want you, Sidney DeRoche. I've wanted to make love to you from that first day I saw you naked on the dock at my parents' house."

Speechless, Sidney blinked as she took in the audacity of this beautiful, younger woman. She felt her heart beating wildly in her chest. She felt giddy from her attraction to Sasha. A throbbing feeling between her legs stole her breath as Sasha's husky voice promised what had been missing in her life — passion. "If you want to run, do it now. If not, take my hand and let's get out of here."

For the first time in her life, Sidney threw caution to the wind. They became lovers that very night, and it was the beginning of a torrid affair. Sasha was like a drug to Sidney. She could never get enough, and Sasha accommodated and never seemed to tire — or to sleep. At first, on weekends when Sidney was off, they would stay at the house Sasha rented on the beach and make love all night and well into the next day. Many times, on the spur of the moment, Sasha would want to go sailing or use the family's plane to fly off some place to party. At times, Sasha would try to coax her into going with her to the Club Palais du Plaisir, but Sidney always refused. It wasn't a place or a scene she would ever be comfortable with.

After a while, she moved a few of her things into Sasha's beach house and started to stay on nights during the week. Sasha's passion and energy were endless, and before long Sidney's work and her health began to suffer. She started to drag through the days at work, ignoring the dark circles under her eyes and the weight she'd lost.

Seven months later Marty had her babies, identical twins. Sidney and Sasha were going to Washington for the christening. Sidney hadn't told Ingrid and Marty, nor did Sasha's family know they were seeing each other. When Sidney continually made excuses and put it off, Sasha had accused her of avoiding it because she wasn't sure about their relationship. Sidney agreed to tell Ingrid and Marty and the family at the christening.

Sasha, Sidney, Isaac, his wife, and Ingrid's and Marty's parents flew to Washington in Isaac's plane. Ingrid arranged for a limo to meet them and take them to the church. The sight of Ingrid and Marty standing on the church steps waiting, each with a baby in her arms, brought tears to Sidney's eyes. Ingrid's mother started to cry as Ingrid handed her one of the babies. "Mom, you're a grandmother. Meet little Sidney. Marty is holding Belle."

All choked up, tears streaming down her face, Sidney stared at Ingrid, then at little Sidney. "You...you named one of the girls after me?"

Marty handed Belle to her mother and went to Sidney and put her arms around her and hugged her. Everyone was sniffling now. "We wanted to surprise you. That's why we kept saying we hadn't decided yet when you asked a million times about their names. You're our best friend and the girls' godmother."

After the christening, they all went to Ingrid and Marty's townhouse in Georgetown. Marty had prepared brunch for everyone. After the tears and congratulations, Sidney went upstairs with Marty so Marty could breast-feed the babies. Sidney held Belle while Marty fed baby Sidney.

"They're so beautiful, Marty. I know they're identical, but I swear I can tell them apart. Belle has Ingrid's smile, and Sidney has your eyes."

Marty noticed that Sidney looked thinner and more tired than when she'd seen her at the holidays and that she had seemed nervous most of the day. After changing babies so Belle could feed off her other breast, Marty asked, "What's up? You've been distracted. Are you working too hard?"

Sidney was holding baby Sidney against her shoulder, patting her softly on the back. "I...we...Sasha and I have something to tell everyone and we plan to do it while we're here. I asked her to wait until I could tell you and Ingrid first."

Puzzled, Marty was trying to understand what Sidney was trying to tell her when it dawned on her. "You and Sasha?"

"I've been seeing her since New Year's Eve. I'm in love with her, and she says she loves me, too. I'm sorry that I didn't tell you and Ingrid before this...I just...I..."

Marty got up and put Belle and then baby Sidney in their bassinets and then sat down beside a worried-looking Sidney. She took both of her hands in hers. "Honey, we love you both."

Sidney knew that Marty wanted to say something more. "Is there a 'but' in what you're saying, Marty?"

"We love Sasha, you know that, but she has her problems. I don't doubt for a moment that Sasha could love you, Sid. You're a beautiful woman, inside and out. You're loving and kind and one hell of a lawyer with a great future ahead of you. I just hope Sasha knows what she has in you and treats you right."

"She's been wonderful, Marty. I love her so much. I want this to work out for us, and I want you and Ingrid to be happy for us."

"If you're both happy, we will be. Now, I'm going downstairs and send Ingrid up so you can tell her. Shall I send Sasha up with her?"

Sidney really wanted to tell Ingrid alone, but Marty was wise in suggesting to her that it would be best if Sasha were there, too. "Yes, please have Sasha come up, too. We should tell Ingrid together."

Ingrid looked shocked for a few minutes, then went over and hugged Sidney before she went to stand in front of her sister. Sasha didn't blink or lower her eyes as Ingrid stared into them. "I love you, baby sis. I would walk over hot coals for you, but I love Sidney, too. If you screw this up and don't do right by her, you'll answer to me. Clear?"

A small smile crossed Sasha's face as she looked into Ingrid's serious gray eyes. She reached for Sidney's hand. "I got ya, Sis. If I do Sidney wrong, you'll kick my ass. And, you know what, I'll let you. I love her, and I've asked her to move in with me."

Sidney encouraged Sasha to do something with her degree in public relations and image management. Certainly not for the money. Money wasn't a concern to Sasha. Both Sasha and Ingrid had trusts that would allow them the luxury of not ever having to work for a living. Sasha's charm always won out. She told Sidney that she wanted to be free to enjoy life and Sidney and to spend an ungodly amount of money before she was too old to enjoy it.

One night when Sidney's body was too exhausted to make love again, Sasha reached into the drawer of the nightstand and brought out a small amber bottle and a mirror. She sprinkled two lines of white powder from the bottle onto the mirror, rolled a piece of paper, and sniffed up one of the lines. A moment later, her eyes half lidded and glazed over, she lay back against the pillows and stroked Sidney's breast. She smiled and handed the mirror and paper to Sidney. "Try it, darling. It'll make you feel better." She leaned toward Sidney, kissed her shoulder, and put her hand between Sidney's legs. "I want to make love to you again, and I want you to participate."

A chill ran through Sidney's body, and it wasn't the burning desire that she felt whenever Sasha touched her, a desire that she'd never been able to resist.

Sasha's eyes were empty. How could she have missed it? All the signs were right in front of her. She had seen them many times over the years in the eyes of people she'd defended and many of the professional people she associated with. The endless energy and the same vacant eyes. Sasha never ate, and she was never hungry. It was brutally clear now. The unexplainable mood shifts and sudden outbursts that were always followed by flowers and extravagant gifts of apology, then hours of making up and passionate lovemaking.

Sidney felt sick to her stomach. Nauseated, she got out of bed on shaky legs and started to put on her clothes.

Wiping the white powder from her nose, Sasha asked, "Where are you going?"

Tears stung Sidney's eyes. Her hands shook as she put her clothes on. "I don't do cocaine, Sasha. I won't risk losing my license and all I've worked for either."

Sasha coaxed, "Come on, sweetheart, don't be so righteous. There isn't enough here to even worry about. I'm not asking you to make it a habit, just to enjoy the evening with me. Now come back to bed. I'm cold and missing you."

Sasha placed the mirror under her chin and sniffed in the remaining line of coke. Euphoria transformed her face. She closed her eyes and leaned back against the pillows, unaware that Sidney had picked her keys up off the dresser and stumbled out of the bedroom and out of the beach house.

Halfway to the apartment she hadn't yet given up, Sidney pulled over and cried, too shaken to drive any farther. "Stupid. How could I have been so stupid to allow my desire to blind me to everything else? Damn you, Sasha! Ingrid and Marty, your parents, everyone had so much faith in you." Tears still stinging her eyes, Sidney pulled back onto the road and headed home.

Chapter Ten

The Present

The alarm on Sasha's oximeter started to beep. Sidney's entire body tensed as she gripped the arm of the chair, and Ingrid jumped up, knocking to the floor the papers that were on her lap. Both anxiously watched as Sasha's nurse adjusted the sensor on her finger, relaxing when the alarm quieted a few seconds later.

Sidney walked around the bed to stand beside Ingrid. Sasha's body was covered with sweat, and her eyes moved continually beneath her closed lids. The expression on her face was one of fear. Something horrible was going on in Sasha's subconscious.

Wetting a washcloth with cool water, Sidney gently began to bathe Sasha's fevered face and neck. *Where are you, Sasha? What nightmare are you living behind those closed eyes?*

Sasha's dark lashes fluttered as Sidney wiped the sweat from her face. The feel of Sasha's skin stirred memories she had put away long ago. An unwanted emotion washed over her. Was it sympathy or anger? Compassion? Hurt? Or something else? Trying to make sense of the feelings and thoughts she was having, Sidney stepped out of the room into the reception area. She was pouring a cup of tea when Ingrid joined her.

"Everything okay?"

"Yes...I just needed to...to..." Sidney ran her hand through her short blonde hair. Ingrid's knowing eyes searched her friend's face.

"Memories? I'm so sorry. This has to be difficult for you."

"You would know if I lied and said no. It wasn't all bad. Your sister was...Sasha was...gentle and loving and exciting. At times when I look at her, I see the person I loved and wanted more than I thought it possible to ever want or love anyone. When we broke up, I thought I was going to die. It took me so long to trust another woman and to allow my heart to love again. If it hadn't been for Leah..."

Ingrid took Sidney by the hand, led her a few feet to a couch, and sat down beside her. "She looks so vulnerable lying there. One minute I want to thrash her for all the damage and hurt she's done to herself and to everyone who loves her. The next minute I have this overwhelming need to protect her. I can't say that I've ever been able to figure Sasha out or that I've ever known what goes on in that head of hers, but I have no doubt that she loved you, Sid. And, ironically, you and Leah are her lifeline right now."

"I have so many questions to ask her. And I can't help but wonder how receptive she'll be to me representing her."

"Well, we'll have to wait until she wakes up and we ask her. But, I don't think she's going to object. I just hope...I know my sister didn't kill those women. If she saw what happened, witnessed the murders of those women and her lover, how is she going to live with that and remain sane? In her place, I don't know if anyone could."

My dear friend. I pray that you're right and Sasha didn't kill those women. "First thing is to concentrate on Sasha's recovery. Let me worry about her defense. Whatever it takes, we'll help her through this."

Ingrid's conference call with several of her Cabinet members was tense and lengthy. She listened patiently to what everyone had to say. The consensus was that she should leave Laguna immediately and return to Washington. Their concerns were valid. When the call ended, Ingrid sat thinking. Until she knew that Sasha was going to be all right, leaving and going back to Washington would be difficult. She didn't want to do that. She felt a warm hand on her shoulder. She knew without looking that it was Marty.

Looking up into caring green eyes, Ingrid smiled. "Hey, sweetheart, come sit."

Marty eased onto Ingrid's lap and leaned her head on Ingrid's shoulder. "I just called home. The girls are fine. Missing us, but they're fine."

Putting her arms around Marty's waist, Ingrid rested her cheek against her hair. "I miss them, too. I talked to them earlier, and I'll call them in the morning. I always feel better knowing that you're with them when I'm not there. Sweetheart, I want you to think about going home tomorrow. They're at a vulnerable age, and with the situation plastered all over the news they know what's going on. We've tried to answer their questions, but it's too hard to do over the phone. One of us should be there with them."

"I know. When I spoke to Belle, she asked me how Sasha was doing. They saw the news about her being charged. Their birthday is on Saturday. Did Belle mention the party and sleepover she wants?"

Chuckling, Ingrid said, "She sure did. She told me you said you'd talk to me about it. I could hear Sid in the background yelling that she didn't want a sleepover with a bunch of sissy girls. They're as different as two sides of a coin."

Content sitting on Ingrid's lap, Marty tightened her arms around her, wishing they could lock the world out for just a little while longer. With everything that had happened, they hadn't had much time alone. A few minutes later, Ingrid sighed and said, "Honey, I would really feel better if you went home."

"I don't want to leave you, but I know you're right. I told the girls I'd be home on Friday. I worry about Sid. Mrs. Shaw said that she's been moody and stays in her room and blares her music. We do need to sit down and talk to both of them about all this. What do you think you'll decide about going back?"

Ingrid didn't answer right away. She just held onto Marty. Finally she said, "The decision isn't easy. I love Sasha. I'm crazy with worry. The anguish I feel for her and this situation is like nothing I've ever felt before. How ironic. I've disapproved of her and her lifestyle since we were kids, and now she may be paying the price for who I am, not necessarily for who she is. I'll have to make a decision soon. I really don't have a choice. I've never been torn to this extent between my duty and my family. As long as I'm in office, I'll honor my commitment. This country and so many depend on it, but it isn't easy."

They held each other for a few minutes more until Marty said, "I'd best go and let you get some work done. I'll check on Sasha before I turn in. Will you please try to get some rest?"

Ingrid kissed Marty lightly on the lips. "I will, promise."

"Do you need anything?"

"Well..." Ingrid nuzzled Marty's neck. She licked Marty's earlobe before sucking it into her mouth.

Marty groaned and whispered, "I was thinking the same thing."

Ingrid lifted Marty off her lap, then stood and took her hand. "Come on, let's go to bed."

As Sidney walked along the deserted hallway she reflected on what a different feeling the hospital took on at night. The hustle and bustle of day had quieted, and her footsteps echoed down the dimly lit hallway. Whispered voices could be heard off in the distance.

Sidney had gone to the cafeteria to meet Leah. Before they had had a chance to sit down, though, Leah's pager went off and she had to leave. Sidney bought a coffee and went back upstairs. There she was told that Ingrid and Marty had retired early. *Good for them.*

Sidney went to Sasha's room. It was dark except for a dim light above the bed and one on the desk across the room where the nurse sat writing in Sasha's chart. Without thinking, Sidney tucked the blankets around Sasha's shoulders before sitting beside the bed. When Sasha's hand began to twitch, she reached out and held it.

A vase of flowers sat on the windowsill. The blossoms reminded her of the numerous flowers Sasha had sent after Sidney left the first time. Sasha had sent bouquets every day and left messages on her voice mail saying, "I love you and I'm sorry." She pleaded with Sidney to forgive her, saying it was just the one time, that she was clean and would never use again. After six weeks, when Sidney didn't return the calls, they stopped.

Several more weeks went by. Sidney didn't heard a word from her. It was driving her crazy. At times, alone at night in bed, she questioned if she had been too harsh, too judgmental. She couldn't help but worry about Sasha. She loved her and she hated her. Her emotions were all over the place. She missed her and longed to see her, but she couldn't take a chance that Sasha would give up the drugs.

Avoiding calls from Ingrid and Marty had also been difficult. They knew she'd left Sasha, but not why. The last message Ingrid had left pleaded for her to call them. If she didn't, Ingrid threatened to come to California.

One afternoon she interviewed a potential client, a doctor, who had been under the influence of cocaine when he hit and killed a child. On her way home afterwards, too numb to drive any farther, she pulled over. It was too hard to be the objective, unemotional attorney. The doctor had told Sidney that no one knew about his cocaine habit, that he thought he had it under control.

Torn, Sidney couldn't help but think that if he'd gotten help, this tragedy wouldn't have happened. She realized that keeping silent about Sasha's drug use could cost Sasha or someone else their life. She reached for her cell and spoke to Isaac. She told him that she couldn't represent the doctor and asked Isaac to assign the case to another attorney. She then dialed Ingrid's number.

"Hi, I got your messages. I'm sorry I...I haven't returned your calls."

"Damn it, Sid, we've been so worried. Are you ready to tell me now what really went on between you and Sasha?"

"I should have called you and told you weeks ago, but it...I just..."

"It's okay. I think I know. She using again, isn't she?"

"Cocaine, and I think it's been...well, for a while."

"Have you heard from her recently?'

"No, not for weeks now."

Sidney could hear the twins and Marty's voice in the background asking to talk to her. When Marty came on the line, she scolded gently, but was as concerned as Ingrid was about her and Sasha. "Sid, please, honey, don't ever keep anything from us again. We both love you, and we've been worried sick. We're glad you called. Ingrid's on the other line making reservations to fly to California. Hold on a minute."

When Marty came back on, she said, "I'm coming with her. Can you pick us up in the morning at ten at LAX?"

"I'll be there. See you both tomorrow."

The traffic around LAX was as stagnant as the yellow cloud of air that hovered over Los Angeles. Moving at a snail's pace, Sidney circled the terminal several times before she found an opening in one of the parking lots. It was 10:05 when she finally reached the concourse at the gate security checkpoint. Flight 818 from Washington was on time, and the monitor was flashing an "arrived" message. Sidney paced nervously until she finally saw Ingrid's head bobbing above the rest of the crowd. When Ingrid saw her, she handed Marty her carry-on and practically ran the rest of the way. She took Sidney in her arms.

"I'm so glad you called. Please, don't ever scare us like this again. We love you." Ingrid wiped her misty eyes and looked into Sidney's tear-filled ones. "We clear on that?"

Sidney nodded. "I love you both, too. I'm sorry. Where are the girls?"

Handing the carry-on back to Ingrid, Marty hugged Sidney and kissed her on the lips. "Home with my mother. She and Dad jump at any chance to spend time with them and to spoil them." Marty linked her arm in Sidney's and asked, "Are you all right? We've both been worried about you. Every day that you didn't return our calls, Ingrid's threatened to fly out here and hunt you down."

Sidney had disregarded the feelings of her best friends. It felt so good to have them close. "I'm sorry. I didn't know how to tell you...I..."

Ingrid took Sidney hand. "Let's get out of here and stop and get something to eat."

They talked over breakfast. It wasn't easy, but Sidney didn't hold anything back. Staring into her coffee, Ingrid listened without saying a word. When Sidney was done, Ingrid looked up with anguish in her eyes. "I'm the one who's sorry. Sorry because she hurt you and sorry for her. She's my sister and right now, I've never been more ashamed or more afraid for her. She's been using for years, and she's either gotten a slap on the hand or been sent away to a luxury facility to detox."

Ingrid shook her head. "It has to stop or...or one day we'll get a call telling us she's dead or that she's hurt someone. Will you drop us at my parents' house? I want to pick up a car, then I'm going over to Sasha's."

Sidney dropped Ingrid and Marty off and then drove to the office to try to get some work done. The couple was going to Sasha's place to confront her. Sidney was glad that they had not asked her to go along. If Sasha had another woman with her, she didn't want to know.

The light in Sidney's office was turning the colors of twilight as a coral sun sank slowly into the gray horizon of the Pacific. The phone rang. Ingrid was on the line. "Hey, I figured I'd catch you there. Still working? Can you break to get something to eat?"

Sidney looked at the stack of files that she'd hardly touched. "Sure. Where do you want me to meet you?"

"How about that little place off the coastal highway a few miles south from the office? Loperchios, say in fifteen minutes?"

"Did you speak to Sasha? Is she all right?"

"I hope she is. Marty and I will meet you at the restaurant, and I'll explain."

When Sidney arrived, her friends were already there. As she approached the table, she could hear them arguing. Or, rather, she could hear Marty trying to reason with Ingrid. As she sat down, the waiter delivered the food they'd ordered while they were waiting. Sidney commented, "You never argue unless it's about Sasha. Did you see her today? Is she all right?"

Ingrid looked at Marty with a sheepish expression. "I know you think I'm unreasonable when it comes to my sister, and you're the one that takes the brunt of it. I'm sorry."

Marty leaned closer and kissed Ingrid on the lips. "You're right, but it's all right. Tell Sidney what we found out."

"She wasn't there, but the housekeeper was. She told us that Sasha had been away for weeks, but that she received regular checks for household expenses and her salary. I called and talked to Isaac. He handles our trust funds. He told me that Sasha's mail is being forwarded to him, and he sends it on to her. He wouldn't break a confidence and tell me where she is, but he asked me to hold while he called Sasha. She agreed to talk to me on the phone."

"Where is she? Did she sound okay?"

Sidney could feel the vibes of doubt coming from Ingrid. "I asked her straight out about the drugs and how she was going to deal with her problem. She said that it was up to her to do whatever had to be done. Then she asked me to trust her and not to ask any questions and not to try to find her. All she asked me to do was to tell you that she was sorry and that she loves you. That was it, except that she would keep in touch, then she hung up."

Sidney put her fork down, a lump forming in her throat. "Do you believe her? Do you think she's dealing with her habit or just off somewhere indulging herself?"

Ingrid hesitated, the food on her plate long forgotten. "I don't know. She's never given us one damn reason to trust her."

Marty folded her napkin and laid it on the table. "Ingrid Sheppard, Sasha is your sister. You're as different as night from day, but you share the same genes and that annoying stubborn nature. I know you're angry because you love her, and you're worried about her, but you need to trust her on this, and give her this chance. Don't try to find her just yet. If we don't hear from her, we'll start looking."

"Mom and Dad are getting too old to deal with this, Marty. They've been through it too many times with Sasha. I feel responsible for her. She could be somewhere out there doing drugs and at risk of hurting herself, overdosing, or heaven knows what else."

"Sweetheart, I know. I worry about the same thing. When you talked to her, you said she sounded like she was clean. If you interfere now, you...we'll lose her for sure."

Ingrid sat back in her chair. "I can only pray that she's clean. I told her if she needed our help, all she had to do was call, and we'd be there."

Sidney sat quietly looking down at her hands. Ingrid sensed what was going through her mind. "Sid, look at me, please. You're thinking you should've stayed with her and that you could have helped her. Listen to me. It was because you didn't that she had to face her drug problem and she realized that she had to do something about it. If you'd stayed with her, it would have destroyed you both."

Ingrid was right, but it didn't help ease the pain Sidney felt in her heart. "When are you going back to Washington?"

"In the morning. The twins have a doctor's appointment to get their next immunization shots the day after. I go with Marty, but...I can't go in when they give them the shots. I'm there to help comfort them when they come out."

Marty squeezed Ingrid's hand. "You are an old softy, Sheppard, but I love you. And hey! You haven't told Sidney that you were asked to run for the Senate."

Sidney's eyes widened. "Senate?"

"After Marty, you're the first person I wanted to tell. If you hadn't been avoiding my calls I would have."

Marty shot Ingrid a look. "Enough now, we've been over that. Tell her."

"Sid, I've been asked to run for the Senate, and I've agreed. I'm going to do it."

The time was right for Ingrid to make her bid for a seat in the Senate. Her aspiration and desire had always been to be a political voice for what America and the Constitution stood for. Sidney volunteered to manage her primary campaign, and most everyone from the Sheppard Law Firm pitched in as well. From the very first day, Sidney was overwhelmed by the support for Ingrid from family, friends, and the people of California. The only cloud was Sasha. No one but Isaac had heard from her in over four months. When Ingrid threatened to make good on her promise to track her down, Isaac advised her not to, saying that Sasha was working on her problem and was all right.

Ingrid's campaign was exhausting, but well worth it. She won the California Senate seat by a landslide. One evening thereafter, Sidney arrived home to find Sasha sitting on the floor next to her apartment door. Sasha shyly smiled and stood up when she saw her, and Sidney's heart began to race. It was impossible, but Sasha looked even more beautiful than before. She'd put on some weight and looked fit and healthy.

Speechless, Sidney just stared as Sasha took a piece of paper from her jeans' pocket and held it out toward her. Sidney's hands shook as she took the paper and read it. Then she looked into Sasha's clear eyes. Eyes that she could never resist. Her voice quivering with emotion, Sidney said, "This past six months you've been at a comprehensive rehab program?"

Sasha moved a step closer. Sidney felt her breath on her face when she said, "The coke made me feel alive, but not as alive as you make me feel. I can live without the coke, but I can't live without you. I need you in my life, Sid. When I told you I love you it wasn't because I was high on drugs. I fell in love with you that first day on the beach. I had plenty of women after, but I drove myself crazy thinking about you and wondering how it would feel to have you in my arms and to make love to you."

Taking another step closer, Sasha continued, "We didn't meet by chance that New Year's Eve at my uncle's. I knew you'd be there, so when I saw you alone on the balcony, I was determined to make you see me as all grown up and for you to see how much I adored you. I love you, Sidney DeRoche. I'm crazy about you, but if you want me to go, just say the word and I will."

The desire swirling in Sasha's eyes made Sidney lightheaded. She felt helpless to resist. How ironic. Sidney knew well how strong a craving could be. She felt the burn start, build in the pit of her belly, and flow throughout her body. When Sasha reached out and traced her finger along her cheek and then across her lower lip, Sidney's legs trembled. Sasha's arms went around her. One of them moaned. Maybe it was both of them. They fell against the door to Sidney's apartment, each seeking the other's mouth with a fervent urgency. Sidney's hunger was so compelling that she wondered if Sasha's craving for cocaine could even remotely compare.

As Sidney turned and fumbled with the door, Sasha pressed against her backside, pushing her hands under Sidney's skirt. She caressed along the sides of Sidney's thighs, edging her fingers under her panties into the wetness that testified to Sidney's need. The skirt slid to the floor before Sasha kicked the door shut. As if possessed, Sasha kissed every inch of Sidney's exposed skin as she took off her blouse and bra.

Every fiber of Sidney's body remembered and screamed to be touched. She moaned, her skin burning where Sasha's fingers touched. Wanton, demanding, she pushed Sasha to her knees, unable to think of anything but her throbbing clit and the aching torment between her legs.

Sasha pulled Sidney's panties down and buried her face in her soft pubic hair, her mouth watering as she savored the smell of Sidney's desire. "Oh God, I've missed you, Sid. I missed this. The withdrawal from the drugs was nothing compared to being without you."

Her mouth found Sidney's swollen clit, ripping a hedonistic cry from Sidney's soul. "Oh my God, Sasha. Don't stop, please don't stop."

Sasha gripped her buttocks with both hands, holding her tight against her face and using her tongue to taste and to tease.

Sidney's slick, smooth muscles clenched around Sasha's tongue. Her hands gripped Sasha's hair. Her hips moved erratically, pushing against Sasha's face. When Sasha withdrew her tongue, Sidney moaned, crazy for release. "No, Sasha, please..."

"Tell me. Tell me what you want, what you need. Tell me."

"You. I need you...please, Sasha. I need you."

Sasha buried her fingers deep, took Sidney's clit in her mouth, and sucked. Sidney's entire body stiffened as her orgasm ripped through her. Her legs collapsed, and she slid to the floor. Sasha pulled her into her lap and wrapped her arms around her, saying over and over, "I love you, Sidney. I love you."

A few months later, Sidney moved into the beach house with Sasha. They were over the bad time, she felt, and their relationship was solid. Within six months Sasha had successfully started her own consulting business, converting one of the spare bedrooms into an office. With her connections and talent, it wasn't a surprise that she did well and had several influential clients.

Not long afterward, Sidney had to fly to Phoenix to take a deposition for an upcoming case. Leaving the beach house the morning of her flight, she told Sasha that she wouldn't be back until the following day. Her flight to Phoenix wasn't until mid-morning. That left her time to stop by the office to pick up a file she'd forgotten.

Jason took one look at her when she got off the elevator and said, "You look like hell."

"Thank you, that makes me feel a whole lot better." She had been struggling all week with the flu bug that was circulating in the office.

"Seriously, what are you doing here? I thought you were scheduled to be in Phoenix today."

"I'm on my way to the airport. I left a file I need on my desk."

"Sit before you fall down. I'll get it."

When Jason came back with the file, Sidney was coughing so hard he became worried. "Really, Sid. You do look lousy. You push too damn hard. Susan can go to Phoenix to take the deposition. She's worked with you on this case from the start and is as familiar with it as you are. She won't have any problems. Go home, please. I'll call her and make all the arrangements. She'll get there in plenty of time."

"Thanks, but I can make it. I'll have some time to rest on the plane, and I'm staying overnight so I can rest in the hotel after the deposition."

Sidney took the file from him and put it in her briefcase. When she stood up, though, it took all her effort, and she found herself extremely short of breath. The room started to spin. She quickly sat back down. "I think I'm going to be sick." What little she had for breakfast started to come up. Jason made a face and slid the wastepaper basket in front of her. "On second thought, you'd better call Susan," Sidney groaned.

Jason offered to drive Sidney home. She refused the offer, but agreed to take the next few days off. She headed for the beach house. It was closer than her apartment, and she spent most of her time there anyway. Chilled, even though it was the middle of summer, and dog-tired, she turned onto the coastal highway. By the time she reached the house, she was miserable and glad she'd decided not to go to Phoenix.

She groaned when she pulled up and saw an unfamiliar car parked in the driveway. Sasha was supposed to be in San Diego seeing a client. Sidney had thought that she'd be alone to take a hot bath, down two extra strength cold tablets, then go straight to bed. Every bone in her body ached as she walked the short distance up the driveway to the front door. She managed to get her key into the lock and let herself in. Not hearing voices, she walked into the living room — and stopped dead in her tracks.

Wineglasses were littered around the room. Women's clothes were strewn everywhere. On the glass cocktail table were the remnants of several lines of white powder.

It felt as if someone had kicked her in the stomach and then reached in and pulled out her heart. Sidney couldn't breathe. It had to be a mistake. Sasha wasn't doing drugs again. She'd know...or would she?

She picked up a lacy bra that was lying on the table next to the cocaine, quickly figuring out that it didn't belong to Sasha. She was about to go up to the bedroom when she heard a noise coming from the ocean side of the house. In a daze she walked toward the window overlooking the pool. Through the wall of smoked glass, she could see the sparkling water of the pool and the deeper color of the ocean beyond it. Sasha and two other women were in the pool naked. One woman was pressed against Sasha from behind, fondling her. Sasha had the other woman pinned against the rocks of the waterfall, fucking her.

Sidney raced to the bathroom, hung her head in the sink, and vomited. "Oh God! Oh God!" She turned on the cold water in the shower and stuck her head under it until she stopped gagging. After a few minutes, when she thought she could make it to her car, she opened the bathroom door. She found Sasha standing there in her robe, looking as pale as a ghost.

"Sid...baby, I'm sorry...it was...it was just this one time. They don't mean anything to me."

The water dripping from Sidney's hair mingled with the tears that ran down her face. When Sidney tried to push past, Sasha caught her wrist.

"Please don't leave me, Sid. I promise. I'll never touch the stuff again." Sasha saw the look of loathing in Sidney's eyes, let go of her wrist as if she'd been burned, and then stepped back so Sidney could pass.

Sidney knew if she didn't get out quickly her legs weren't going to hold her up much longer. Her rage at Sasha's betrayal radiated off her. She looked into Sasha's dilated eyes. "That is the last time you will ever touch me. Don't call me, ever." She wouldn't see or hear from her again until the day she walked into the exam room at SCMC.

A short time after the split Sidney quit the Sheppard Law Firm and started her own firm, asking Avril and Jason to join her. She got together with Ingrid and Marty occasionally, but when she did they seldom talked about Sasha. Ingrid was well on her way to a promising political career, Marty was extremely busy with her own practice, and both were ecstatic about raising their daughters. Sidney knew that they had repeatedly tried to help Sasha, but that Sasha was caught up in her self-destruction.

It took a few years more, but eventually Sidney met Leah and, with a guarded heart, gave love another chance.

PART TWO
Chapter Eleven

The Present

Sasha's condition continued to improve, and soon Leah felt that Sidney would be able to talk to her. The media was running rampant, roasting Sasha. Rumors and innuendo spread like wildfire. The paparazzi were lurking everywhere — at Sasha's beach house, the hospital, and Sidney's office — waiting to capture anything with their telephoto lenses. Reporters camped out on the street in front of the law firm, hoping to get an exclusive statement. Others were digging into Sasha's past, adding more frenzy and fuel to the already damaging headlines and news reports.

The team worked around the clock to be prepared and to counter any adverse publicity. Nothing was found connecting the murdered women to the lifestyle of the patrons of the Club Palais du Plaisir. A review of their credit card history showed nothing more than the busy lives of three successful, hard-working women.

Frustrated, Sidney sat down and held her head between her hands. A beep indicted that a fax was coming in. Raising her head, she looked at Avril, who went to retrieve the transmission. After reading the message, she uncharacteristically swore.

"Fuck, you're not going to believe this! It's a message from Anderson Cooper saying that he's going to profile Sasha and the murdered women on *Anderson Cooper 360*."

Sidney's head shot up. "You've got to be kidding."

Avril handed Sidney the fax. "Nope, I wish I were. Take a look."

"When?"

"Tomorrow night live from the Time Warner Center and the CNN Studios in New York City. Brace yourself. Marcus Ramey is going to be on the show, and Anderson invited you to be there as well. Ramey must have lost his mind. Bob Redfern is going to crucify him."

Groaning, Sidney read what Anderson sent. "How in the hell can this get any worse?"

Refusing Anderson's invitation to appear on the show was not an option. Not only was Ramey out for Sasha's head, but he was also anxious to smear Ingrid.

Avril went to alert the team. Sidney phoned Leah and left a message asking her to call back. The team went to work sorting through the information and facts to prepare Sidney for anything that might come up. She had little time to get ready to counter or refute anything that Ramey might throw out. She'd have to depend on her skills to do the rest.

By late afternoon Sidney was as ready as she was going to be. She'd decided to fly to New York to be in the studio instead of doing the show by remote. She went into the war room and stood looking at the team, which was still hard at work. She saw empty coffee cups, unshaven faces, women with no makeup on, and many reddened eyes. When she'd gotten everyone's attention, she simply said, "You've all worked very hard. Thank you."

Turning this interview around on Ramey could work in their favor, Sidney knew. It wouldn't be hard to trip him up. He was inept and easily angered. Provoked at the right time, he'd fly off the handle and come off looking like a bully and the rancorous man that he was. Her plan was to expose Sasha's past before Ramey or anyone else could and then present a sympathetic view of a woman who had turned her life around and was now being persecuted by the district attorney. She also planned to subtly insinuate that his reasons for going after Sasha were politically motivated and designed to influence the upcoming Presidential election.

Sasha's sexual relationship with Lauren Serantis would have to be handled with skill, as would her own past relationship with Sasha. Lauren Serantis' exemplary reputation and the fact that she'd founded Serantis Pharmaceuticals when she was in her early thirties and managed it into a Fortune 500 company would be in Sasha's favor. Exposing too much could be detrimental.

Back in her office, Sidney sat at her desk framed by the light from the windows behind her. She felt haggard and dead on her feet. It was going to be a tough day.

Avril groaned and stood up to stretch. "Well, that does it. You've been on Anderson's show before, and I know if anyone can pull this off, you can." She managed a wry smile. "I stink. I'm going to shower. You look as if you could use a few hours of sleep. Jason scheduled you on a red-eye into New York and into a hotel close to the studio. You'll be in New York early enough tomorrow to get a few hours' rest and go over your notes before the broadcast."

Avril went to Sidney and kissed her on the cheek. "Go lie down and get some rest." She started toward the door, then stopped. "Cooper is a good guy. He's fair. I'm glad he's the one doing this.

The other bastards will try, convict, and have her hanging from the highest morality mast before it ever goes to trial."

Pressing her index fingers against her lips, Sidney stared at the door long after Avril left. She was right on all counts. Especially about Sasha being tried by the media. She hit the speed dial to a private number and waited for Blyth Connolly to answer. Blyth was a PR specialist and an image consultant guru. She knew Sasha. They were colleagues. Blyth could create, and she could break. She worked magic. If anyone could, Blyth could manipulate the press in Sasha's favor.

Blyth picked up after the first ring. Sidney was barely able to get a hello in before she said, "Sidney, I've been taking bets on how long it would take you to call. I've been working up a few things. Send me what you can immediately, the good, the bad, and the ugly. As usual, use a secure courier service and no e-mails. I've prepared a statement for the press concerning your appearance on 360. Before you ask how I know, it's been on CNN. I'll start feeding the press the information we want them to have, today. I'm going to enjoy taking a few bites out of Ramey and that tight-assed bunch of homophobic bastards he's associated with."

Blyth finally took a breath. "You there?"

"Yes, just waiting until you finished."

"Good, I'm done. Get that stuff to me. I'll call you." Then Blyth hung up.

"God, what a whirlwind. Her energy and ability to anticipate is uncanny. I'm glad she's in our corner." Stretching her tired muscles, Sidney heard her vertebrae popping. "Avril is also right about getting some rest."

She left Leah another message telling her about the appearance on 360 and that she'd be taking a red-eye that night to New York. The thought of driving home and Leah not being there depressed her. She decided she could pack what she needed for the trip from the clothes and personal things she kept in the suite next to her office.

An hour later, Sidney was lying awake on the bed looking through some papers. Her cell rang. It was Leah. "Hey, I got your message. We're looking good here. I can get away for a few hours. I can be at your office in ten minutes. I miss you."

The huskiness of Leah's voice made Sidney shiver. "Honey, hold that thought. I'm in the suite. Oh, and Dr. Stanhope, I miss you, too."

Leah made good time. When she entered the bedroom of the suite, the bathroom door was open and the shower was running.

The hassles of the day and the fatigue she felt were forgotten when she saw Sidney's shapely form behind the foggy glass shower doors. Walking toward the steam-filled room, she pulled the scrub top over her head and dropped it on the floor. Her fingers went next to the ties of her pants. Naked, she pushed open the shower doors and stood, allowing her eyes to lovingly caress every inch of Sidney's body.

Feeling the cold air on her backside, Sidney turned. A smile brightened her tired eyes as she reached for Leah and pulled her into the stream of warm water and her arms. Sidney buried her face in Leah's neck. She could feel Leah's hardened nipples against her own. Closing her eyes, she groaned and cupped Leah's buttocks. "Just how good a doctor are you?"

The next morning Senator Mack Kincaide paced the floor of the Krause Suite of SCMC, waiting for President Sheppard. He opened the drawn curtains and stood looking out at the Pacific Ocean. He'd arrived unexpectedly at the hospital after deviating from his itinerary at the last minute. He'd been in Los Angles, scheduled to fly to Salt Lake and then on to Washington, when his brother, former President Wade Kincaide, called him and asked if he would go talk with Ingrid. Ingrid had consulted with Wade after the attempt on her life.

The last minute change in the Senator's schedule and his arrival at SCMC had the Secret Service in a state of high alert. Securing SCMC and the area around the hospital to protect the President was a nightmare for them. Having Kincaide at the same location with no preparation or advance notice had everyone on edge and scrambling to adjust.

Kincaide turned so that his back was to the window as the door to the suite opened and Ingrid walked in. She smiled and extended her hand. "Mack, this is a surprise. I knew you were in California, but I thought you'd be back in Washington by now. What's on your mind? You just didn't happen to be in the neighborhood."

Mack appreciated Ingrid Sheppard's candor. That, along with her unpretentious patriotic views of what makes a country great, was why he and Wade admired and supported her. Ingrid didn't mince words and came right to the point. He would do the same.

"First, your safety, and then your political future. I'm here not only as your friend, but as your advisor as well. You've always trusted Wade, and I hope me, to give it to you straight. That's what I'm going to do now. Wade has told me someone tried to kill you. You're driving the Secret Service crazy trying to protect you here at the hospital. Your party is having a meltdown, and the people who care about you are frantic with worry."

Mack searched Ingrid's face. "There's no way to sugarcoat this. If you want to have a snowball's chance in hell of serving a second term and continuing the programs and reforms you've started, you have to leave California and go back to Washington."

Mack ran his large hand through his thick, slightly graying hair, the pain of the past a shadow in his eyes. "You know that I was in a similar position. Heaven only knows what I would have done to protect my brother. If he were in the situation your sister is in, I'd probably do the same thing you have. But your life and your political career are at stake, my dear friend, so I have to try to get you to listen. Your leadership is of paramount importance to this country."

The frustrated look on Ingrid's face told Mack that she had heard it all before from many others.

"Damn it, Ingrid, I'm not saying abandon Sasha. I'm saying let her lawyer and Starr handle it. Staying here is not just political suicide. You're putting your life, as well as the lives of everyone in this hospital, in danger, including your sister's."

Ingrid looked stunned. She'd been so preoccupied that she hadn't thought about the havoc and worry she was creating for others.

"I'm sorry to be so blunt, but you're a sitting duck as long as you stay here, and because you are, anyone around you is, too. Hasn't Starr advised you of this? She knows better than anyone how vulnerable you are here."

Ingrid wasn't surprised when Mack mentioned Liberty. Mack had been the attorney general when President-Elect Brady Lawrence was killed and she assumed the office of the President. It was Mack's brother, Wade who had gathered together Liberty and the Talons, a covert group of antiterrorists, after an act of unspeakable terrorism that had killed many and devastated the country.

"Mack, I would never knowingly put anyone in danger. It's just...this situation with my sister has been... Do you know how difficult it is for me? Sasha needs me to be here with her."

"I do know. You're between a rock and a hard place. It's tough, but I'm not beneath playing on your patriotism. Your country needs you, and burying you would break this country's back."

Ingrid went to the window, staring out at the ocean. She knew he was right. "Marty is flying back today. Sasha's over the worst of it, and I'll leave in a day or so."

Mack relaxed. "It's for the best. To be honest, I don't know if I could do it. I do know what a personal sacrifice it will be for you to leave here, but you know that Sasha will be protected and in good hands. Whatever Wade has told you about Starr comes nowhere close to her capabilities. All the agents surrounding this hospital, your personal detail and mine, could not protect your sister better than this woman can. And Sasha has Sidney DeRoche."

"I hope you're right about Liberty. And Sidney is a very dear friend. I thank God we have her." Ingrid looked at her watch. "I talked to her just before I was told you were here. She's in New York preparing to talk about this mess on CNN with Anderson Cooper."

A knock on the door interrupted them. Ingrid's secretary rolled in the coffee tray. "Is there anything else you need, Madam President?"

"No, thanks, Sylvia." Ingrid poured Mack a cup of coffee.

From her position on the roof of SCMC, Liberty had a clear view of the Pacific for miles. The hospital butted up against a hill that was covered with dense shrubbery. The Secret Service had placed sensors covering the entire area, and agents were stationed around the perimeter of the hospital and on top of the hill behind the hospital.

Shifting her weight off her right leg, Liberty stood with her feet slightly apart, looking out toward the horizon where the gray water coalesced with the blue of the sky. A breeze coming off the water blew against her face and ruffled her hair. She was certain if an attempt on President Sheppard's life were to come while she was at the hospital, it would come from the direction of the water. It was too open and too perfect.

From the water an assassin could target the upper floor of the hospital with a shoulder-fired missile. He could be as far as three to five miles out and still deliver a lethal blow, one that would destroy most of the hospital. Ingrid Sheppard had put herself in a very vulnerable and dangerous position, one that was almost impossible to defend.

Raising powerful binoculars to her eyes, Liberty scanned beyond the tiled red rooftops across the PCH to the Pacific. Her eyes searched beyond the rocky promontories off the shoreline and the boats that were scattered and anchored offshore. She focused on a small fishing boat that had been in the same spot the day before. The boat was just beyond the five-mile parameter the Coast

Guard had established when securing the area off the shoreline in the direct line of the hospital.

The airspace over Laguna Beach had been restricted also, and F-15 jets were in the air 24/7 enforcing the no-fly zone. Registrations of all boats in the area were being checked, and the Coast Guard had tripled the number of cutters patrolling and enforcing the perimeter restrictions.

Every precaution was being taken to ensure the President's safety, but it didn't ease the feeling Liberty had in her gut. She watched the old man on the boat wave as a Coast Guard cutter slowed and eased alongside. They performed a visual check. Seeing the same fisherman they had seen the day before, they went on toward Aliso Beach.

A fishing pole was secured in a notch in the gunwale, the line dangling over the side into the water. The old man sat leisurely cutting bait, a cup and a battered thermos beside him on the deck. Liberty studied his hands and his aged crooked fingers as he worked, following them as the man shoved his cap back on his head and reached for the thermos. With a look of utter contentment, the old man leaned back in his chair, sipped from his cup, and then turned his face toward the sky. The face was that of a fisherman, tanned, weathered, and deeply lined from years of exposure to the sea and the sun. Liberty recognized on it a look of inner peace, the expression of a soul content with life, and acceptance of the day that had been given.

Finding inner peace was something Liberty had never hoped for after so many years of killing, but beyond all odds she had, in the serene mountains of Montana and in the eyes and smile of Kayla Sinclair. As her gaze left the fisherman and worked its way across the water, she wondered if she'd made the right decision by coming out of seclusion to come to Ingrid Sheppard's aid. She was no longer the Ghost, a Talon assassin. Mercifully, because of Kayla's trust and love, she no longer felt dead inside. Gone was her sterile emotionless detachment from the human race. Kayla's love was a gift, a precious gift of life; her love and acceptance had changed everything.

As she looked out across the water, Liberty wondered if she'd lost her edge, if she still had what it took to compete with an assassin and stay alive. It was a talent she'd cursed and wished many times that she'd never acquired.

Kayla and Lone Mountain were never far from her thoughts. She felt an infinite connection to the woman who loved her in spite of her past. That connection kept her grounded even though they were hundreds of miles apart. She longed to be home on Lone Mountain. With the approach of summer, the hours of daylight in Montana would be growing longer and the warmth of the sun would be replacing the snow on the slopes with an array of wildflowers. Nature had been kind, and spring skiing had lasted well into May, assuring a profitable year for the Sinclairs and the Lone Mountain Lodge. When Kincaide's call came, she and Kayla had been planning a well-deserved whitewater rafting trip through the Lower Salmon Gorge for the following weekend.

Liberty shifted her weight again, remembering the look in Kayla's eyes when she had told her that former President Kincaide had contacted her and what he had requested. The look had been one of denial and fear and something else that Liberty couldn't quite read. Kayla had looked at her for a long moment. Then with trembling fingers she had gently touched Liberty's cheek and said, "I need a little while. I'm going to take a walk. When I get back, we'll sit and talk."

Knowing Kayla, Liberty hadn't asked her if she wanted company. She knew where Kayla would go. Up Lone Mountain to Colman's Ridge, the place where Addie, Kayla's first love and wife, had died in an avalanche. There were no secrets between them. Liberty knew about the love between Kayla and Addie and how Addie had died on the mountain. And Kayla knew of Liberty's past and the role the Talons had played during a time when terrorism had gripped the world.

As she sat on the deck, looking out at the mountain, waiting for Kayla to return, Liberty had unconsciously rubbed her hand along the constant ache from an old wound in her right thigh. The snow hadn't left the higher elevations, and Liberty felt the chill of spring cut deep.

Her impulse had been to go and find Kayla, but she had waited.

I should have told her there's nothing in this world more important to me than her and our life together. One word, Kayla, one word is all you have to say, and we'll never mention it again. If you ever looked at me and your eyes reflected disappointment or the image of a killer, I wouldn't survive.

A speck of blue moving between the pines along the trail down the mountain caught her eye. Liberty got up slowly and went inside. By the time Kayla came through the kitchen door of the pub, Liberty had added a log to the fireplace and had a pot of tea steeping and sandwiches ready to put on a plate.

"I made tea. You hungry?"

Kayla had hung her jacket on the peg behind the door as Liberty poured two steaming cups of tea. Serious discussion happened and decisions were always made over a cup of tea. Her back to Kayla, Liberty had reached into the cupboard for the plates for the sandwiches. She had felt Kayla's arms slide around her waist and Kayla's head rest lightly against her back.

"I love you with all my heart. If anything happened to you, I'd go on, but my life would be empty. When you told me about Kincaide's call, I felt an overwhelming fear that I could lose you as I lost Addie. This will put you in extreme danger. There's no way to play that down or minimize it."

Liberty turned and took Kayla in her arms. "Can we take our tea and sit by the fire and talk?" Kayla nodded. Liberty carried the sandwiches while Kayla carried the teapot and cups. After settling on the sofa, Kayla continued, "Every step I took up the mountain I was dead set against you even considering doing this. By the time I reached Colman's Ridge, I had simmered down a bit. That's when the importance of why Kincaide asked for your help hit me. In the scheme of things, when it comes to the safety of Ingrid Sheppard, my uncertainty seems very unimportant."

Liberty set her mug down and cupped her hands around Kayla's face. "Anything and everything you feel or want is most important to me. My life as a Talon does not exist anymore. My life with you does."

Kayla's eyes studied the anguish in the eyes and on the face of the woman she loved.

"Do you remember telling me why you became an FBI agent and joined the Talons? You, my love, are still that person who had strong enough convictions about your country and duty to sacrifice your identity and risk your life to protect it. Kincaide must be very concerned for the President and her sister's safety to have asked for your help."

Liberty started to speak, but Kayla gently put her fingers against her lips.

"If this assassin is successful in killing Ingrid and you could have stopped this, could you accept it? Could we go on and live with that? It's your decision and whatever that decision is, we'll get through it."

Liberty watched a speedboat until it went behind the rocky point and out of sight. Lowering the binoculars, she checked the monitors connected to the sensors on the hill behind the hospital, then walked around the perimeter of the roof. When her eyes went back to the ocean and the old fisherman on the boat, she discovered the boat had moved. It was inside the bobbing orange boundary markers. The canvas top of the boat had been raised, and the fishing pole wedged in the gunwale was cocked at an odd angle. She grabbed her custom long-range sniper rifle, flipped down the bipod, then steadied the rifle on the cement ledge. Quickly, she focused the powerful Leupold scope on the boat. The canvas top partially obscured the view of the old fisherman, but Liberty could see him. His head was slumped forward, and his hands were hanging lifeless by his sides. A piece of rope had been tied around his chest to keep him upright in the chair.

A movement behind the fisherman in the shadow of the canopy raised the hair on Liberty's arms. A figure in a wetsuit was taking a portable missile launcher out of a tube. A jolt of adrenaline surged through her body, heightening her every sense. The boat was within her range. There was no time to warn anyone, and only seconds to take the shot.

Less than a split second later, Liberty pulled the trigger, firing the entire clip of .50 caliber rounds at the boat. She saw the first few rounds hit the old man, ripping open his chest and knocking his body back onto the deck. When the clip was empty, she quickly reloaded and scanned the boat. The figure in the wetsuit was gone. She grabbed her radio and notified the Coast Guard to secure the area and to check the coastline and every boat in each direction. She advised approaching with caution and detaining anyone coming out of the water.

She then called the Secret Service agent in charge of the security at the hospital. The second the shots had been heard, of course, the agents would have converged on the suite that Ingrid was in and the hospital would have been locked down. The protocol for removing the President to safety had begun.

Below, on the fourth floor, Ingrid and Mack had been discussing the tougher sanctions the United Nations had imposed on North Korea when the door burst open and the Secret Service agents rushed in yelling, "Get down. Get down!" Kincaide reacted instinctively, using his body to knock Ingrid to the floor and cover her. Seconds later a swarm of agents, guns drawn, surrounded Ingrid and Kincaide, and one directed, "Get the President out of here!"

Ingrid and Kincaide were lifted off the floor and rushed into the outer hall. An agent quickly drew the blinds of the suite shut while shouting instructions into a radio. The Secret Service was prepared to rush Ingrid and Kincaide out of the hospital to safety immediately. Not knowing what danger threatened, Ingrid protested. She wouldn't leave without Marty and Sasha. The agent who had been lead on Ingrid's detail during her entire term knew his directive and that was to get the President to safety with or without her consent.

"Madam President, you know I don't have a choice here."

"I know all that, Jacob. The shots we heard — was someone shooting at the hospital?"

"Madam President, we don't know the details. As soon as we do, I'll tell you. We do need to go."

"I won't leave willingly until I know my wife and sister are all right."

Ingrid turned to find Marty coming down the hall flanked by two agents. She had been in with Sasha when she heard the commotion. Through the chaotic noise and yelling, Ingrid could hear the cell phone ringing in her pocket. When Liberty Starr had given the phone to her, she had instructed her to keep it on her at all times and to answer it immediately, no matter where she was or what was happening at the time. She pulled the cell out and opened it. "Yes."

"Madam President, there has just been an attempt to launch a missile at the hospital. It is imperative that you leave the hospital now. You and your wife will be taken to Air Force One and to safety."

"A missile! My God, was anyone hurt?"

"No, because the assassin didn't get the missile off. But if the shooter had, his target would have been the fourth floor. It would have taken out most of the hospital, killing and injuring many."

Ingrid was visibly shaken and trying to maintain control of her emotions. "What about my sister? She's in danger here. I won't leave her. Air Force One is staffed with a doctor and equipped to handle any medical crisis. I want her to go with us."

"I understand your concern, Madam President. Your sister has been charged by the state of California with first degree murder. You taking her out of California on Air Force One would not only be damaging to you, but to her. I agree with you, though: she's in danger here. The less you know, Madam President, the less you can say if asked. I need you to trust me. Arrangements have been made. Your sister will be safe. This I promise you."

"I have your word that Sasha will be safe?"

"Yes."

A few seconds later, a pale and shaken Ingrid closed the cell phone and turned toward Marty, who was now by her side. "Marty, are you and Sasha all right?"

"I'm okay, and Sasha was sleeping. What's wrong? I heard the commotion. What's going on?"

How to tell you, my love, how close we all were to losing our lives because I insisted on staying here with Sasha.

Ingrid tried to hide it, but her voice shook just enough so that Marty knew that something drastic had happened. "Seems...it seems that there's been an attempt to launch a missile at the hospital. We're being taken to Air Force One. We have to leave. Sasha will be taken care of."

The color drained from Marty's face as Ingrid's arms went around her to steady her. "Honey, whoever it was is gone for now. Thank God everyone is all right."

Ingrid was trembling. She directed her attention to Mack and the cut on his arm. "Let me take a look, Mack."

"It's nothing. Just caught my arm on the edge of the table when we went down. It's already stopped bleeding. "

Ingrid looked at the gathering of anxious-looking agents. "Thank you all for your quick response. Your willingness to sacrifice your lives to protect me and my family is very much appreciated."

Jacob Russell stepped forward. "We need to go now, Madam President." He looked at Mack. "Sir, Air Force One's destination is undisclosed. Your security detainment will escort you to the back entrance where you will be taken to safety."

There was no questioning the finality in Jacob's voice. Ingrid shook Mack's hand, then hugged him. "Thanks for coming. I'll see you in Washington." With her arms wrapped around Marty, Ingrid looked at Jacob and said, "We're ready, let's go."

"Yes, Madam President."

While agents led Mack to the south stairway, Jacob and several other agents led the President and Marty toward the stairway that led to the roof, where a helicopter was waiting. Ingrid looked back and saw another detail of agents coming out of Sasha's room. They were pushing the gurney that Sasha was on toward the rear elevator. Leah was with them.

When Ingrid, Marty, and her detail reached the roof, the F-15's and two Apache attack helicopters roared overhead, ready to escort the helicopter to Air Force One. Below Mack was hustled into a car and spirited away, and Sasha and Leah were loaded into an unmarked ambulance that was waiting at a service entrance.

Chapter Twelve

Unaware of what had happened in California, Sidney sat in New York with Anderson Cooper and Marcus Ramey, going over some points that Anderson wanted to cover during the interview. There was a knock on the door, followed by one of the show's directors poking his head into the room and motioning to Anderson. Anderson joined him across the room, his face tightening as he listened to what the man was saying. After the man hurried out of the room, Anderson asked Sidney if he could speak with her. Sidney followed him out into the hall out of earshot of Ramey.

"There was an attempt to launch a missile at South Coast Medical Center in Laguna." Sidney gasped, and Anderson put his hand on her arm to steady her. "No one was hurt. The reports we're getting are that an agent stopped the attempt before the missile was launched."

Sidney's hand went to her mouth, and she shook her head in denial. *This cannot be happening.* She felt as if her legs were going to give out. "Are you sure no one was hurt?"

"Our reporters are there. No missile was launched. They also saw a helicopter lifting off the roof of the hospital. It has been confirmed that Air Force One is in the air. No confirmation, but it's thought that President Sheppard is on it. Another unconfirmed report is that the President's sister is missing from the hospital."

"Missing?"

"That's the report we're getting. My directors want to go live to the scene and do the interview, alternating with a broadcast from California."

Feeling lightheaded, Sidney felt all the color drain from her face. "I have a certain amount of say on last-minute program changes," he continued. "I can reschedule the interview and just go to our crew on scene in Laguna, or we can do the interview alternating with the breaking news as they suggest."

With a knowing look, Anderson added, "I'm sure Marcus Ramey won't mind coming back. It's your decision." Anderson's eyes were caring as he asked, "Sidney, doesn't your partner work at SCMC?"

"Yes, she does." Sidney looked Anderson in the eye. "Thank you. Please reschedule, and let me know when. I'll be here."

"You got it. I'll call the limo to take you to the airport."

By the time Sidney reached the front of the building, the limo was waiting.

An overcast sky that foreshadowed a storm was crowded with police and Coast Guard helicopters as a Coast Guard cutter with Liberty on board sped toward the fishing boat. The bow dug deep into the rough sea, and salt water pelted her as she stood rigid at the bow, gripping the railing, her eyes riveted on the small boat ahead. Her thoughts were of the old fisherman. It was little comfort knowing he was dead before her bullets tore a hole in his chest. Liberty wondered if he had family or someone who would miss him or if only the sea would mourn his passing.

Thunder rumbled overhead, and scattered disjointed lightning, reminiscent of the fisherman's gnarled hands, reached out of the clouds into the choppy sea as if protesting the injustice that had been done. The skies opened, and a hard rain battered the cutter as it pushed through the rising swells.

Harbor Patrol and other Coast Guard cutters were already at the scene. All had been given strict orders to keep their distance and told that no one was to approach or board the fishing boat. Wiping the rain from her eyes, Liberty spotted a police boat heading toward the small boat nevertheless, ignoring the warning to keep its distance. A plaintive cry could be heard over the storm as a sea gull, wings spread wide, circled the fishing boat as if boding ill.

Sensing the impending danger, Liberty yelled to the cutter's captain, standing next to her, and pointed to the vessel. "Captain, stop that boat."

"I'll damn well give it a try." The captain got on the police frequency and repeated the warning not to approach or to board. The rain was coming down hard as Liberty watched the police boat come alongside and throw a line on the small boat. *Stupid...son of a...bitch.*

It took place in a matter of seconds, but Liberty saw the scene as if it were unfolding in slow motion. Two policemen jumped onto the boat. One stooped to check the old man. The other was about to pick up the launcher that lay on the deck when an explosion on the fishing boat knocked Liberty and the captain to the deck and sent flames and debris hurtling into the sky and across the water. Liberty scrambled to her feet, turned toward land, and looked toward the rocky point. She couldn't see anything through the rain, but she felt the presence of evil.

I know you're there and I know who you are.

On shore, under the cover of the heavy rain, a figure in a wetsuit crouched between the rocks, holding a device in one hand. Looking through binoculars, Scalzon spotted Liberty standing on the Coast Guard cutter. "So, it's you, Starr. You've just made this game a little more interesting."

The ambulance carrying Sasha and Leah drove along the 101 until it came to a turn-off just beyond Santa Barbara. They traveled through wine country until they came to a stucco wall and a double security gate of solid wrought iron. Crafted into the gate were the words "La Villa Dell'uva" and "Welcome to Santini Vineyards".

After the driver nodded into a security camera, he pressed his thumb against a sensor and the gates opened. They drove past guards standing at the monitoring station inside the gates, then past rolling hills of grapevines until they came to a stately villa that looked as if it were an embodiment of vintage Italy. An older, distinguished-looking man with thick gray hair stood waiting on the cobblestone driveway. Standing next to him was a young girl dressed in jeans, a T-shirt, and boots.

When the ambulance stopped, Leah hopped out of the back, and the drivers lifted out the gurney with Sasha on it. As she was taken into the villa, the older man approached Leah, offering his hand. He introduced himself. "Doctor Stanhope, welcome. I am Armanno Santini." He smiled at the young girl next to him. "And this is my granddaughter, Tiana."

On the back way to LaGuardia Sidney tried to call Leah. When she didn't answer, Sidney left a message saying that she was on her way to the airport and imploring Leah to call her as soon as possible. Then she placed a call to the hospital and the ER. The ward secretary answered. When she asked to speak with Leah, she was put on hold. A few minutes later, a familiar voice said, "Hello, this is Doctor Bryson. Can I help you?"

"Judy, it's Sidney. I'm in New York on the way to the airport, and I'm calling to talk to Leah. Is she there?"

"Have you heard what happened here at the hospital?"

"Yes. I can't reach Leah. I was told that everyone is all right and that President Sheppard has left the hospital and her family went with her — including Sasha. Is this true?"

"The President and her wife did leave, but Sasha didn't go with them. She was taken out of the hospital and loaded into the back of a van. Leah went with her."

"What? Leah did what? A van...?"

"Mike was out for a smoke when it all happened and he saw the van parked by the delivery entrance. He got a look when Sasha was loaded inside. He said the outside looked like a delivery van but inside there was a well-equipped ambulance. We tried to call Leah's cell. When she didn't answer, I checked her office. Her phone was on her desk. We have no way to get in touch with her."

"Damn it! If you do hear from her, please ask her to call me. Tell her I'm really worried and I'm going to take the first flight I can out of New York. Tell her...just tell her I'll be home soon."

Sidney hung up and groaned. "Oh, Leah, what the hell is going on, and where are you?"

Air Force One was heading toward Wheeler-Sack Airfield at Fort Drum in northern New York. While it traveled east, Ingrid and Marty's twins were taken to a secluded underground facility in the upper Adirondack Mountains, close to the Canadian border. The concrete underground de-commissioned nuclear shelter had been converted into a safe place, a compound to ensure the safety of the President, the President's family, and a select group of advisors in the case of an event like a nuclear or chemical attack. It was one of several such places that the President and key members of the government could go that was equipped and had available all the facilities for the continuity of government. Protocol dictated that the President and her family have that level of protection for the time being.

After making a few calls, Ingrid joined Marty in the plane's Presidential quarters. When she entered, Marty was on the phone reassuring the twins that their mothers were all right and were on the way to join them. "Girls, Mom just came in. She wants to talk to you."

Marty mouthed to Ingrid that they had seen the news about the hospital on television and were scared. She handed Ingrid the phone and stood with her arms around Ingrid's waist and her head on Ingrid's shoulder. "Hey, you guys, your mother and I sure do miss you. We can hardly wait to see you both. ... In about three hours, honey. I'm sorry about the quick trip and that we weren't there to go to the compound with you. Your mother and I will come in to see you when we get there. ... Yes, we're both fine, and so is your Aunt Sasha."

Ingrid talked a while longer, then said, "We love you both, too. See you in a while." She hung up.

Ingrid held Marty tight. They stood in the middle of the cabin not saying anything, just holding each other, silently giving thanks that the other was unharmed and they were together. Marty kept her arms around Ingrid and buried her face against Ingrid's chest. When Ingrid felt the tears against her skin, her heart ached. Marty seldom cried, and it broke Ingrid's heart when she did. Her voice shook with emotion. "Please don't cry, baby. I can't bear to see you cry. We're okay. We're both okay. The girls are okay. We'll be with them soon."

"I know, and I thank God for that. I just wish we were with the girls right now. I just want to hold you and them and never let go."

Marty eventually agreed to lie down, and Ingrid went into the office off the sleeping quarters. She understood why Liberty wouldn't tell her where she was taking Sasha, but the uncertainty of not knowing where she and Leah were and if they were all right and safe had Ingrid tense and on edge. CNN was covering the attempt on the hospital; Sidney's interview with Anderson Cooper had been cancelled. That meant Sidney was either on her way to the airport or in the air on the way back to California.

Ingrid dialed Sidney's cell. Sidney answered on the first ring. "Ingrid, I've been so damn worried."

"We're fine and on the way to...a safe place. Where are you?"

"I'm at LaGuardia waiting for a flight to California. I need to know what happened and where Leah is. I was told she left the hospital with Sasha."

"She did and as far as I know they're both all right. I want to tell you what I know, but I don't want to do that on the phone." *You might be in danger, my friend.* "Can I send someone for you? Will you come?"

"Yes, of course."

"Go to the administrative VIP lounge and wait. I'll have you picked up."

When Ingrid hung up, she called for Jacob. "Sidney DeRoche is at the administrative VIP lounge at LaGuardia. Please, arrange to have her picked up and flown to the compound."

Once Air Force One landed at Fort Drum, it was a short flight for Ingrid and Marty in Marine One to the underground facility. Ingrid hoped that by the time Sidney arrived, she'd be able to tell her that she'd heard from Liberty and assure her that Leah and Sasha were all right.

When they arrived at the secluded spot in the Adirondack Mountains, Ingrid and Marty went directly to see the twins. Both girls were still awake watching the news on television. When Belle saw them, she started to cry. Sidney sat with her arms crossed, not saying anything. Marty sat on the bed and took Belle in her arms, then wiped the tears from her eyes and kissed her nose. "We're here, sweetheart, don't cry."

Belle's young voice was muffled, but Ingrid and Marty heard what her fears were. "When we saw the news, I thought you and Mom weren't coming back."

"No one was hurt. We're here. Everything's fine."

Noticing Sidney's defensive posture, Ingrid sat on the bed next to her. The girl's voice quivered as she said, "I told Belle that you both were okay. She gets so emotional. Typical girl."

Ingrid could see that her daughter was trying hard not to cry and touched Sidney's chin with her finger. "Honey, your mom needs a hug. Think you could scrounge one up for me?"

Sidney flew into her mother's arms. "I love you, Mom."

The lump in Ingrid's throat made it hard for her to speak. She held her daughter tightly until she was able to say, "I love you, too." She looked over Sidney's shoulder at Belle. "I love you, Belle. Get on over here and give me a hug."

Holding her daughters, Ingrid told them, "Your mother and I are with you now. We love you both, and we'll never leave you."

Marty's eyes were moist as she nodded, too. She put her arms around the girls and kissed Ingrid lightly on the lips. "I love you all so very much. Did you both eat?"

Belle nodded and Sidney said, "We helped Hanna clean up. There are leftovers in the fridge."

"Okay then, why don't I put on some popcorn and cocoa while you two get ready for bed, then we can talk a while?"

After the girls were asleep, Marty went to soak in the tub and Ingrid headed into her office. On her desk were numerous memos, documents, and papers that needed her attention. The explosion on the fishing boat had killed four police officers. Any evidence left on the boat by the assassin had been blown to smithereens or was on the bottom of the Pacific.

Ingrid took a file from her briefcase, opened it, and took out a picture of Liberty Starr. She was a handsome woman, sure of herself in spite of the limp. When Ingrid had consulted with Wade Kincaide, he said that Liberty might be the only one who could help her. She and one other were the last of the Talons, he said. Liberty had gone into seclusion in the Rocky Mountains of Montana. He offered to contact Liberty, but he told Ingrid that he was unsure if she would help. He feared that her patriotism had died along with the betrayal she'd suffered and with those she'd killed.

Now, looking into the cold eyes of Liberty Starr, Ingrid found it easy to imagine how deadly she could be. Wade had trusted Starr with his life, but could Ingrid trust her the same way? She had very little choice, it seemed.

A light knock on the door interrupted Ingrid's thoughts. "Come in."

Lettie, the girls' nanny, entered the room and said, "Madam President, Sidney DeRoche just arrived. She's in the kitchen."

"Thank you. Did you ask Hanna to rustle up something?"

"Your wife is in the kitchen heating up leftovers. She asked me not to wake the cook."

"Lettie...wait."

"Yes, Madam President?"

Ingrid took off her glasses. Her eyes revealed the fatigue she felt. She smiled at Lettie, who had been with them since the girls were born, long before she became President. She was not only their valued employee and supervised the care of the children when she and Marty were gone, she was a dear friend. Lettie loved Belle and Sidney and doted on them as if they were her own grandchildren. "Do you think you might consider calling me Ingrid?"

A hint of a smile touched the corner of Lettie's equally tired eyes. "Yes, Madam President, I'll consider it. Is there anything else you'll be needing tonight?"

Smiling, Ingrid replied, "No, please go on to bed. I'll see you in the morning. And thank you for all you do for us. I can't tell you enough how much we appreciate you."

Lettie's eyes welled with pride before she turned to leave. "Thank you, Madam President."

When Ingrid walked into the kitchen, Marty and Sidney were sitting at the counter drinking tea. Sidney looked awful, like she was on her last legs. Ingrid went to her and hugged her. "I'm glad I caught you before you got on the plane to California."

"I've been frantic with worry. Anderson told me about the attempt on the hospital. It's all over the news about the explosion. What in God's name happened?"

Sidney's voice shook, knowing they wouldn't be standing there if the assassin had succeeded.

"Honey, I know...I know. Everyone's all right. Let's take our tea and go into the living quarters. It's more comfortable, and I'll tell you everything I know."

They settled down on a couch, and Ingrid explained what had happened, why Liberty hadn't told her where Sasha was being taken, and that Liberty had promised to contact her. They talked for a long time. Marty, refusing to leave Ingrid's side, fell asleep on Ingrid's lap.

When the phone rang, Ingrid reached for it, waking Marty. It was Jacob. "Liberty Starr is at the entrance to the property."

A surprised look crossed Ingrid's face. "Liberty is here? Yes, have her brought to our quarters."

Marty sat up as Sidney asked, "Liberty Starr is here?"

When Liberty entered the room, Ingrid looked into the same cold eyes she had pondered earlier. "Are my sister and Leah all right?"

"Yes, Madam President. Both are safe and in a place where they will remain so. Your sister is doing well and every medical convenience is available to Doctor Stanhope for her care."

Ingrid visibly relaxed, though her mind was racing. A direct non-stop flight out of L.A. took a little over five hours. Why was Liberty there and how did she know where the compound was? Then it dawned on her. She took the cell phone that Liberty had given her out of her pocket. She looked at it, then set it on the table. *That's how.* "I was told you saved our lives and the lives of many in the hospital. Words cannot express my gratitude. I'll never be able to thank you enough. I know you warned me. I wasn't ready to listen."

Liberty looked directly into Ingrid's eyes. "Sometimes having no choice is what it takes. Your love for your sister left you no choice but to stay. Then you had no choice but to leave the hospital and go to a place of safety for the sake of protecting her and others. Your sister is safe and so are you and your family."

"Why are you here?"

"I believe the person who tried to launch a missile at the hospital boarded a plane for New York a short time after the attempt."

"I was told you saw this person on the boat."

Liberty's eyes changed to the color of ice. "I saw a figure on the boat, but there wasn't time to focus on anything but getting the shots off." *That's not true, I could see the old man and how his chest tore apart when the bullets hit him, and I could see the hands of the shooter.* Liberty inwardly flinched as she mentally traced the scars that had been inflicted on her body.

Ingrid picked up on the vibes coming from Liberty. She wanted to know what Liberty wasn't telling them. "Do you know this assassin?"

Liberty looked at Ingrid, but she wasn't seeing her. She was remembering how she'd walked right into a trap and never saw the face of her torturer. She could still taste her own blood and vomit as she lay half-naked and blindfolded, facedown with her hands tied behind her back. Scalzon had tortured her for hours to get information about the Talons, especially the Talon called the Ghost. Liberty remembered the pain she had felt as she lay on the floor of the warehouse near dead, waiting for Scalzon to finish her.

Her voice revealed little emotion as she answered. "You'll know the name. I believe the assassin is a terrorist that is known by the name Scalzon. We've gotten close to this person many times, but Scalzon always manages to slip away, leaving many dead behind.

"Stopping this terrorist became the entire focus of the Talons at one point. We suspected that Scalzon was hiding in Afghanistan with the Taliban. Three of us went into Kabul. A source that had given us reliable information several times before told us that Scalzon was planning to attack Begram Airfield. We went to meet with the informant and were ambushed. I was left for dead, the other Talons didn't make it."

Absently, Liberty's hand went to the side of her neck. Her fingers traced along the scar from the wire Scalzon had wrapped around her neck to immobilize her.

"Scalzon is a master of disguise and can change appearances as quickly as a chameleon. We assumed that Scalzon was a man, but I've always had a gut feeling that Scalzon is a woman."

Ingrid knew well the inhumanity of mankind and about the methods torturers used. It sickened her to think of the many lives that had been taken by wars and by terrorists like Scalzon.

"My concern is that my family is safe and that my sister and my friends remain safe until this assassin is found. I don't want anyone else in harm's way."

With intense gray eyes, Liberty looked directly at Ingrid. "We don't know if it was you or your sister the assassin was after. If Scalzon killed those women, your sister probably knows why. The attempt on the hospital, if successful, would have gotten you both. Unfortunately, Doctor Stanhope knows where Sasha is, so her returning to Laguna is not possible until I find this assassin. Her life would be at risk."

Liberty glanced at Sidney. "Ms. DeRoche's life is in danger, too. The assassin will think she knows where Sasha and her partner are and will do anything to get that information out of her.

Even with security twenty-four hours a day, DeRoche cannot be protected in Laguna. She'd be safer staying here."

Sidney's ire flared. "I'm sitting two feet away from you. You can direct your concerns to me."

Without looking at Sidney, Liberty stood. "I'm not needed here. I'll not see you again until this is over." *One way or another.* "You can reach me by using the cell phone I gave you."

When Liberty started toward the door, Sidney stepped in her path, determination evident in her eyes.

"I can't tell you how grateful I am to you for preventing the attack on the hospital. And I've listened to everything you've had to say, but I'm going with you. Staying here is not an option. My partner is with Sasha and Sasha is my client. I cannot defend her from here, so don't even try to tell me I can't go."

Liberty's eyes narrowed. She knew she'd be looking over her shoulder every step and didn't need the distraction, but Sidney DeRoche was Sasha's attorney, and from the look of defiance in her eyes it would be futile to argue with her. She gave her a long hard look and nodded. "Are you ready to leave?"

Chapter Thirteen

Sasha woke lying on her side facing the open screen door to a veranda. She could feel a gentle breeze and smell the subtle aroma of blossoming grapevines. Her head throbbed, but her thoughts were clearer than they had been in days. Clear enough to be thankful that the voices and the images of madness she'd been lost in had quieted.

Rolling onto her back, she thought about the unexplained commotion at the hospital and the ride to this place. Even in her daze, she had known that her Uncle Isaac, her sister, and Marty were at the hospital. She wondered where they were now. Sidney's face and voice also hovered in the back of her mind. Had Sidney been at the hospital? And if she had been, why?

Why isn't Lauren with me? Were we in an accident? Is Lauren hurt?

Every time Sasha tried to push her memory past the point of being in the restaurant with Lauren, Constance, and Kim, she felt herself being pulled into a terrifying black hole where voices and images stole away her very breath. As she pushed the covers back to sit up, pain radiated up both arms. She felt a cold fist in the pit of her stomach, then nausea, as she gripped the bedpost and managed to get her legs over the side of the bed. She'd been through withdrawal enough times to know agony, but she had never felt so close to going over the edge and never finding her way back.

Lightheaded, her nightgown drenched with sweat, she eased up from the bed and stood gripping the bedpost. She needed to pee. She looked across the room through an archway to where she hoped was a bathroom. Just as the room began to spin, an arm went around her waist and she heard, "You're still too weak to be up by yourself. Let me help you. You're probably feeling pretty shitty right now."

"I...I was trying to...the bathroom."

"Lean against me."

"The catheter...didn't I have a catheter?"

"You did. I removed it yesterday. Less chance of getting an infection."

Frustrated because she didn't remember, Sasha looked down at the floor. Leah guided her slowly toward the bathroom saying,

"In time the blackouts you're experiencing should become less frequent."

Halfway to the bathroom Sasha became short of breath and had to stop. Leah tightened her grip around Sasha's waist. "I've got you. I won't let you fall. Just try to take a deep breath and look straight ahead. The first time up is always the hardest."

Nodding, Sasha took in a breath. "You were at the hospital. I don't...know your name. Who are you?"

After a few more steps Leah answered, "Leah Stanhope. I'm the doctor who's been taking care of you."

She'll know what happened. Before Sasha could ask, Hattie, the older woman who had put her to bed when she arrived, came in the room with two younger women in tow. One was carrying a tray, the other a pot of coffee and cups. The woman carrying a tray placed it on the table and said, "Doctor, let us help you." The younger women assisted Sasha the rest of the way into the bathroom.

"Thank you, Mrs. Russo." Leah looked at the tray of food. "It's early. I hope you didn't get up and go to a lot a bother because we're here."

"Please, call me Hattie, Doctor. No one's called me Mrs. Russo in a very long time. It wasn't any bother at all. I'm up before dawn every morning. The work in the vineyards starts before sunup, and the workers need to be fed." Hattie started fussing with the tray. "What you both ate last night wouldn't fill a bird. You must be hungry and your patient needs to eat to get her strength back."

"Yes, she does. Thank you, Hattie."

"Page put a tray in your room, but if you'd like, you can come down to the kitchen and eat. There's always a fresh pot of coffee and tea brewing." Hattie motioned at the food on the table. "I fixed a light breakfast for your patient. If she needs anything more, just let me know."

Leah could see the kindness in the older woman's faded brown eyes. Hattie had not asked why they were there, but she was extending every kindness in welcoming them to Santini Villa. "Please call me Leah. My patient's name is Sasha. Thank you for the food."

"I know. I recognized the young woman from her pictures on the news. Mr. Santini said you both will be staying a while at the villa. You're most welcome, and you both are safe here. Anything you need for Sasha's care is available."

One of the women came out of the bathroom. "Doctor, Sasha would like to bathe and have her hair washed. Gwen and I would be glad to help her. With us both helping, we could get it done in no time. She wouldn't have to be up long."

Leah thought a moment before answering. "Her dressings do need changing. I could take them off, then replace them. I think she'll be too weak to stand in the shower. The tub would be better as long as she doesn't use her hands or submerge them."

Hattie smiled at Leah. "It'll be okay. Page and Gwen are also doctors."

Leah looked at Page. "Doctors?"

"Yes. We moved here from Chicago to be close to Nonna. We have practices in Santa Barbara. I'm in family practice, and Gwen is a psychiatrist. You look tired, Doctor Stanhope. I heard you up several times last night checking on Sasha. Why don't you go get something to eat, then rest? We'll take care of her."

Leah looked at Hattie. "Ah, I can see the resemblance now. Both are your granddaughters?"

"Page is my granddaughter, and Gwen is her partner. And both, along with Tiana, who you met yesterday, are my pride and my joy." Hattie beamed as Page put her arm around her shoulder and gave her a kiss on the cheek.

When Page went back into the bathroom, Hattie started to change the linens on Sasha's bed. "You can trust them. They'll take good care of her. Please, go, eat, and rest."

Anxious, Sidney looked at her watch again. They would be landing in L.A. soon. She glanced over at Liberty, who had her head back against the seat with her eyes closed. They'd hardly spoken two words during the five-hour flight from New York. Liberty mostly stared out the window as if in deep thought. Sidney was having trouble concentrating on anything except Leah and whether Leah and Sasha were safe.

Liberty was right. They didn't know who committed the murders. But if Sasha was a victim, too, and could remember, Sidney hoped she could tell them what happened at the beach house. Three women and Grant were dead, as well as the fisherman and the officers that were killed in the explosion. It was a good bet that the deaths of the two officers who responded to the 911 call were connected also.

First class was full. Many of the passengers were working on laptops or had files and papers spread out in front of them. Sidney shivered. An uncomfortable feeling washed over her. Turning slightly, she looked over her shoulder to see a slender man standing in the aisle a few feet behind her seat. The man bent over to pick something up off the floor. His head lowered, he turned as he stood and pulled the bill of the baseball cap he was wearing down farther over his eyes. Before Sidney could get a good look at him, he walked toward the back of the first-class section.

Something about him didn't sit well, but Sidney attributed it to being on edge and imagining things that weren't there. Before she could say anything about it to Liberty, the captain announced that they would be descending to a lower altitude in preparation for landing at LAX. Before the "Fasten Your Seat Belt" light went on, Sidney started to gather her things. She soon forgot about the man in the aisle.

They were among the first to get off the plane. Shortly after they cleared the boarding area and walked through the concourse toward the baggage area, Liberty took Sidney's arm and pulled her close. One look at Liberty's eyes and her set jaw warned Sidney not to ask why and to just keep moving. Halfway to the security checkpoint, Liberty stopped in front of the ladies' room and whispered, "Go in, wait a few minutes, then come out and put a smile on your face."

Sidney knew right then that she should have said something about the man on the plane. She forced a smile and said, "I'll only be a minute."

Liberty nodded and leaned back against the wall next to the door and casually looked back the way they had come. The concourse was crowded with people, making it hard to see and easy not to be seen. When Sidney came out of the ladies' room, Liberty guided her down the concourse toward the security checkpoint. Sidney glanced at her. "What's wrong?"

"Maybe nothing, but I had a feeling. I thought someone might be following us."

"There was a man on the plane."

Liberty dragged Sidney toward a newsstand. "What man?"

"A man wearing a baseball cap. He was standing looking at us. When I turned and saw him, he bent to pick something up off the floor. But there was something about the way he pulled his cap down and he lowered his head that struck me as strange."

"Could you see his face?"

"No, not really. The cap hid it. Odd...when he bent over I could see his hands. They were smooth and slender, like a...dear God, a woman's."

Liberty tensed, and every muscle in her body tightened. Her eyes grew dark as she positioned Sidney so she was behind her, away from the foot traffic. She threw a bill on the counter and grabbed a newspaper. "We need to get out of here — now."

On the move again toward the end of the concourse, Sidney's heart pounded. "Are we in danger? No one can get a weapon past security...can they?"

"If it's Scalzon, she doesn't need a weapon. Her hands are deadly. She could kill you with that pen in your pocket or with one blow."

This was all too real. Sidney's legs were shaking so badly she didn't think she was going to make it past the security checkpoint a few feet away. "My God, how did she know we were going to be on that plane?"

"She's planted a transmitter on you. That's how she knew. That's why she left California, to follow you. Just stay calm. She's not looking to kill either one of us right now. She'll continue to track you hoping you'll lead her to your client. It looks like Sasha Sheppard is the one she's after."

Sidney stopped dead in her tracks. *That puts Leah in extreme danger.* "Can't you do something to stop her here, right now?"

"By now the man you saw could look entirely different. And, before you ask, yes, Scalzon can change identities that quickly. In a place as crowded as this, even if I could identify her, she would kill many to create a diversion to escape." Liberty pulled Sidney's arm. "Come on, this is not the time for explanations. Keep moving. We need to get to the car."

When they reached the parking garage, the car was parked right where Armanno said it would be. Liberty ran her hand behind the front bumper and found the key, then opened the trunk and took out the bag that Armanno had left for her. She opened it and removed the 9-millimeter pistol and tucked it in the waistband of her jeans. She stuck an extra clip in her jacket pocket. She put the case with the sniper rifle and ammo on the floor of the back seat and threw her newspaper over it. When she turned to get in, Sidney was standing numbly watching her. "Get in."

The authority in Liberty's voice jolted Sidney out of her stupor. She stumbled into the car. Tightly gripping the steering wheel, Liberty maneuvered the car out of the airport garage. "Did she get close to anything you still have with you?"

Confused, Sidney looked at Liberty. "I don't think so. My carry-on was in the overhead. I was awake, so no one touched my briefcase or laptop. Those were under the seat in front of me."

"Where was your suit jacket?"

Sidney thought for a few seconds before it dawned on her. "The flight attendant hung it up in the first-class closet."

Liberty took the exit to the Pasadena Freeway going in the opposite direction from Santa Barbara. After a few miles, she pulled off at a restaurant and parked. "Take off your jacket."

Sidney slipped it off and handed it to Liberty. After searching the jacket for a few minutes, Liberty's hands stilled, and she sat back in the seat. Her right hand came up and between her index finger and thumb was a tiny black chip. "Your transmitter. It's probably not the only one. She's no doubt less than a half-hour behind and not worried about losing us in the airport or in the parking garage.

"I know how she thinks, how her mind works. I'll guarantee you that there's another one on you in something you carry with you all the time, something that was planted before you even left for New York. She's probably been tracking you for a while. That's how she was able to follow you to the compound. When she saw you leaving with me, she knew I'd get around to looking for a transmitter, so she planted another as a decoy for me to find hoping I wouldn't look any further."

"But she was able to board the plane. How is that possible? The Secret Service purchased our tickets under assumed names just minutes before we boarded and restricted any ticket sales for the flight after."

Liberty thought about the many different identities she had used as a Talon assassin and ironically how easy it had been to do what was needed. "It would scare you if I told you how many clever ways there are to get on a plane at the last minute that wouldn't be scrutinized. An example would be using Secret Service or Federal Air Marshal identification. Even replacing the pilot."

Liberty got out of the car and opened the door to the back seat. She removed a small scanner from the bag. She ran it over Sidney and her overnight bag and found nothing, then scanned Sidney's cell phone and her laptop case. She found another small tracking device in the laptop and put it in her pocket with the other one. *Check and soon to be checkmate.*

"Get in the car." As they pulled back onto the freeway, Liberty turned Sidney's phone on and set it on the seat between them. "Your IMEI, International Mobil Equipment Identity, probably has been linked to a private tracking satellite that cloaks its presence. When your phone is turned on, the satellite can pinpoint your location and not even the government's sophisticated equipment can detect it."

Her features hard, Liberty stared straight ahead. "It won't be long now before we're at the crossroads." They drove in silence. Sidney couldn't help but look constantly in the side view mirror. *I'm in a damn car running from an assassin with a woman that scares the hell out of me, and this woman is the only one who knows where Leah and Sasha are. Leah, I need to hear your voice, baby, telling me you're all right.*

They reached a point where the highway split in four directions and pulled over. Liberty tossed the transmitters and Sidney's cell phone out the window into a field. "You can relax. No one can follow us now. We're heading back toward the coast."

After Leah left Sasha's room, she lay across the bed with her arm over her eyes. She was tired, but couldn't sleep. She wanted to hear Sidney's voice, but Armanno Santini warned her that any call placed to or from Sidney's cell phone could be traced. The attempted attack on the hospital was the big news on every channel; Sidney had to know and was probably out of her mind with worry. Armanno had assured Leah that Sidney had been told she was safe, but she wanted to know that Sidney was safe, too, and to tell Sidney how much she loved her.

A heinous killing had brought Sasha Sheppard back into their lives, turning things upside down. She thought back to how she met Sidney and the difficulties they both had to overcome when they fell in love. Sidney had been burned badly, and Leah's long-term relationship with Jay was ending as their careers took them in opposite directions. They had tried, but it hadn't been working for a while. When Jay reenlisted for another tour in the Middle East, it was over. By then, Leah had no intention of even becoming involved with another woman, let alone falling in love. Then she met Sidney and fell head over heels — literally.

It was Leah's first weekend off in weeks. She'd decided to go jogging along the ocean path in Heisler Park. The sun was a blazing red and blinding as Leah came around a bend. She didn't see the jogger stooped in her path, tying one of her laces, until she hit Sidney, flew over her, and landed on the asphalt. When she caught her breath and picked herself up, she looked to see what she'd run over. Sidney was sprawled out on the ground holding her wrist in obvious pain.

"I'm sorry. I'm so sorry. Are you hurt?"

"No... Yes... I...I think my wrist is broken."

Leah knelt down beside Sidney. "Please, let me see." Gently supporting Sidney's wrist, Leah ran her finger lightly over the bone. "Without a doubt, it's broken. There's a first aid station up ahead. We can get an immobilizer for your wrist, then I'll drive you to the ER. Do you think you can make it or should I call an ambulance?"

"If you can help me up, I can make it."

Leah took Sidney to the ER, set her wrist, then drove her home. The next day she stopped by Sidney's apartment to see how she was doing, then again the following day. After six weeks Leah found that Sidney was constantly on her mind; she was hopelessly in love.

Chapter Fourteen

Leah woke, surprised that she'd actually dozed off. After showering, she dressed in the clean clothes that Hattie had brought, then went to check on Sasha. Page was sitting in an easy chair reading while Sasha slept. When Leah entered the room, Page lowered the book to her lap and spoke softly, "She was tuckered out. She did well getting cleaned up this morning, and she ate a little breakfast and some soup for lunch. Before she went back to bed, she walked a little around the room."

"Good. That'll help her get her strength back. How did her wounds look?"

"Good. I went ahead and cleaned the suture lines, then redressed."

"Thank you for doing that. I appreciate it." Leah looked at the clothes she had on. "And for the clean clothes your grandmother so kindly provided."

"An amazing woman, my Nonna. She's always prepared for everything." Page could see the fatigue and deep lines of worry on Leah's face. "Were you able to get some sleep?"

"Surprisingly enough, I did. It's been...hectic at the hospital."

Page looked over at the sleeping Sasha, not wanting to say anything that she might overhear. "Understandable. A lot has happened."

"That it has. And I'm worried about my partner. She was in New York when...we left the hospital and I haven't spoken to her since. It all happened so fast and now... I'm sure she's—"

"Just as worried about you as you are about her. I would feel the same way if it were Gwen. Speaking of which, Gwen and I are going to take turns staying with Sasha tonight. The villa has a beautiful solarium with a waterfall. You could take a swim in the resistance pool. It's a wonderful place to relax. Or, you could take a walk through the vineyards to the bluff overlooking the ocean."

"You and Gwen need your sleep. You both have practices. Don't you have patients to see tomorrow?"

"Gwen doesn't have office hours tomorrow, and I have partners who can cover for a few days."

Leah went and stood next to the bed. She was pleased to see that Sasha's color was better. Her washed dark hair framed her face. She was truly a beautiful woman.

As hard as Leah tried to rationalize and tell herself that Sasha was in Sidney's past, her gut still churned every time she thought of them together. She turned and walked toward the door. Getting some fresh air sounded good; she needed to put her thoughts in perspective. "I think I'll take you up on your offer and take that walk."

The rental car slowed, then took the exit. The driver pulled around to the side of a convenience store and gas station just off the freeway ramp. Dusk was approaching and the neon lights that wrapped around the building buzzed and turned on, illuminating the lone occupant's face. Scalzon contemplated the dot on the grid displayed on the LCD screen of the hand-held receiver. It had shown no movement or change of position in over an hour. Scalzon had doubled back twice to search the area where the GPS indicated they should be and had found nothing.

Her eyes narrowed suspiciously as she slowly sat back in the seat. "Well, it appears you've found all the transmitters, and of course you know about the phone. Unfortunate, but you would have disappointed me if you hadn't." Amused, she looked again at the GPS receiver. "Nice move. You think you have me in check, but don't be so sure. The next move is mine."

Scalzon sat remembering Liberty's athletic, fit, and very lethal body. It aroused and excited her, thinking about Liberty's resistance when she'd tortured her. With sadistic pleasure, she'd taken her time, but Liberty didn't break and that had pleased her all the more.

"You were a challenge, though you made the mistake just like the rest of not seeing what was right in front of you. I was just a go-between. The go-between that the Talons thought would lead you to Scalzon. You, dear Liberty, were the one chosen to gain my confidence. Your seduction was flawless. Unknowing you willingly walked right into my web. Even when I left you for dead, you never knew that you had been so close to the very quarry you were after. How ironic that I didn't know you were the Ghost, the one that made it possible for the Talon to get so close so many times."

A twisted need to finish what she'd started with Liberty burned in Scalzon's mind. "Having another go at you is a stimulating thought. I wonder, are you still a loner and as cunning, Liberty, or do you have a weakness?"

Traffic was light, enabling Liberty to keep a better eye on the rearview mirror. Glancing over at Sidney, she could see that she'd finally relaxed a bit and had given up sitting on the edge of the seat. They would be at the vineyards soon, and Armanno would have two more guests. The retired Talon commander was loyal and a patriot, and when she asked a second time for his help, he offered his resources and his home without hesitation. Villa Dell'uva was Armanno's refuge away from his past of espionage and covert actions. After the "accident" that was meant for him killed his son and rendered his daughter a paraplegic, Armanno had turned the villa into a fortress. From that day on, he had devoted his life to protecting his family from the ghosts of his past.

Family. Kayla was never far from Liberty's thoughts. *I know the ache DeRoche feels for her lover. I miss you, Kayla, more than I ever thought possible. I want to hear your voice. But to do so would be too dangerous for you.*

The possibility of her not coming back had not been spoken, but Kayla knew how to contact Armanno, and Armanno had given his word that if anything happened to Liberty he would go to Lone Mountain and tell Kayla himself.

Liberty struggled with the acceptance and unconditional love Kayla gave her. In her heart, she knew she wasn't worthy, that she could never atone for her deeds as a Talon. The faces of those she'd killed tormented her.

My sweet Kayla, your love and faith give me reason to live. It's not fair to put you through this and the uncertainty of not knowing if I will be coming back to you.

Barely perceptibly, Liberty's hands shook as she gripped the steering wheel. She struggled to overcome the emotion and ache she felt in her heart. *I gave you my word. I promised you that I would never leave you again or walk the path of the Talon.* Liberty kept her eyes on the rearview mirror. She'd taken enough detours to make sure they hadn't been followed. Glancing over at Sidney, she said, "It won't be long. We're almost there."

Leah ran into Page in the hallway in front of Sasha's room. "How was your walk? When it started to get dark, I sent Tiana to find you."

"Tiana did find me. It's beautiful here. I took your advice and walked to the bluff. What a view. Tiana showed me through the tasting room on the way back. For someone so young, she knows a lot about making wine."

"Yes, she does. Tiana knows more than many who have been in the business a long time. One day she'll take over and run both the Santini and Cipriano vineyards as well as many other business holdings of both her grandfathers. And you're right, it's beautiful here. Gwen and I love it. At times I'm tempted to give up medicine and become a vintner." Page smiled and Leah could see the truth in her eyes. "Sasha was up and walked to the bathroom, but she's still pretty weak."

"It'll take a while. She lost a lot of blood. If I draw a CBC, can we send it to a lab?"

"I can have it picked up and have it run, stat."

"Thanks, Page. I'm sure the last unit of blood she received was helpful, but I'd like to make sure."

"Several times today Sasha asked questions about how she was injured and where her partner is. I don't think you'll be able to put off telling her much longer. She's anxious to talk to you."

Leah ran her fingers over the bridge of her nose. She didn't want to be the one to tell Sasha. She was a stranger. It would be too impersonal.

"Leah, Armanno would like you to join us downstairs for dinner." Page looked at her watch. "In about fifteen minutes."

"I'd like that. That gives me enough time to wash up."

Looking in on Sasha, Leah was relieved to see her sleeping quietly without the tremors and the restlessness. Having worked up a sweat walking, she showered then went downstairs. She hadn't realized how hungry she was until she tasted Hattie's fresh halibut broiled in lemon sauce with roasted bell pepper risotto. Armanno had chosen a Sauvignon Blanc to go with the meal, and Leah found herself enjoying the meal and the company. Armanno was a gracious host and an interesting man. Leah suspected there was much more to the unpretentious, humble winemaker than initially met the eye.

Mist gathered on the front window of the car and an evening fog swallowed the beams from the headlights as Liberty drove along the private road toward Villa Dell'uva. Barely able to see the light from the lanterns that lit the entrance and the gates of the villa, she came to an abrupt stop, jostling Sidney. "What is it...is something...?"

"We're here. This fog is so thick I didn't see the gates until I practically drove into them."

Sidney shivered as she looked out the window, seeing nothing but dense fog. When she heard a tap on the window, she jumped. "Jesus! Scare the hell out of me..."

As Liberty rolled her window down, a bright light flooded the inside of the car, blinding them. Shielding her eyes, Liberty asked, "Do you think you can douse the light?"

When the light went out, they heard a sound of metal moving, indicating that the gates were opening. A head poked through the open window. "I'll turn on the fog lights along the road. You can follow them to the villa. Go on ahead. I'll call Armanno and tell him you're here."

After dinner Leah returned to her room, went out on the veranda, and sat looking out into the fog. Her thoughts were filled with Sidney and the hospital and the danger they all had been put in. During dinner Armanno had said he was expecting to hear from Liberty soon. He also assured Leah that he would locate Sidney and arrange for her to receive a secured cell phone so they could talk.

The sound of the ocean off in the distance evoked a feeling of such emptiness. Leah remembered the many nights she and Sidney had sat on their own veranda, or stopped for dinner at a little pub called Hennesy's, known for its special ambience, and experienced the fog that rolled over the streets of coastal Dana Point. She needed Sidney, to hear her voice and to know she was safe.

When she went inside, Leah undressed and got under the covers. The bed felt strange and much too empty. Lying in the dark, Leah wondered how long they would have to stay at the villa. She was needed at the hospital, where, not surprisingly, the attempt on the President's life had caused chaos.

Rolling over, she punched the pillow, trying to get comfortable. She finally began to doze off, when she felt the covers lifting and someone getting in the bed. The familiar scent started her heart pounding. A split second later an arm slid around her waist and a cheek pressed against her back. When Leah started to turn, a very welcome but shaky voice said, "Please, don't move. Just let me hold you for a minute."

Giddy, Leah leaned back into Sidney's embrace, thinking nothing in the world had ever felt so good. When she felt the moisture from Sidney's tears on her back, she turned and took Sidney into her arms. "Honey, please don't cry. Don't cry."

Burying her face against Leah's neck, Sidney sobbed, "I was out of my mind with worry. If anything had happened to you, I...I couldn't have..."

"Sid, I'm fine. No one was hurt."

Sidney started to say something, but Leah put her finger gently on her lips, then kissed her. Returning the kiss, Sidney groaned, then said, "You have no idea how frantic I was. We need to—"

"Honey, I do know, and we will talk, but not right now." Leah unbuttoned Sidney's blouse, kissed her throat, then kissed across her collarbone, working her way to the swell of Sidney's breast. In short order, the bra joined the blouse on the floor, followed by Sidney's slacks and panties. They were lying facing each other. Kissing, tongues exploring, fingers touching and caressing. Leah ran her hand over Sidney's bare back and buttocks, then sat up and leaned over to place a kiss behind Sidney's knee, eliciting a moan. Shifting, she put Sidney beneath her, straddled her, and splayed her fingers over Sidney's abdomen, slowly moving them up over her ribs to cup her breasts. She caressed Sidney's nipples with her thumbs until they were rock hard.

Sidney watched through half-lidded eyes and dilated pupils, her breath catching as Leah lowered her face and whispered how much she wanted to make love to her. She traced the sensitive skin along the ridge of her ear with the tip of her tongue, and Sidney groaned. Her swollen clit seeking firmer contact, Sidney moved her hips. She tried to capture Leah's nipple in her mouth. When Leah reached between them and ran her fingers through Sidney's wetness, all thoughts of talking vanished from Sidney's head. Their lovemaking was filled with passionate emotion, body, heart, and soul.

Spent, they slept, the danger they were in forgotten for the moment. Sidney woke with a start but relaxed when she felt Leah curled up around her. She lay in the dark listening to the rhythmic breathing of her lover, savoring the taste of Leah on her lips and the feel of her breath against her skin. How often had she done the same thing. Nothing had ever tasted, or ever felt, as good as tonight, though.

Leah stirred in her sleep, and Sidney lovingly brushed her fingers through her hair. With a ragged breath, she remembered the terror she'd felt when she was told that someone had attempted to launch a missile at the hospital. She never wanted to feel that fear again. She couldn't fathom what her life would be like without Leah.

Sidney dreaded the light of day when she would have to come face to face with Sasha. She knew that given the drugs that were in Sasha's system, it was possible that she'd never remember what happened. Tough questions needed to be asked. *How am I going to tell Sasha that her lover and the others are dead and that she's being charged with their murders? Then tell her that an attempt was made to kill her or Ingrid or both?*

It was a lot to hit her with. Sidney was afraid Sasha wouldn't be able to handle it.

Dozing off again, Sidney woke to a tap on the door. When she reached for Leah, she was gone, but Sidney could hear the water running in the bathroom. Pulling the covers over her naked body, she cleared her throat and croaked, "Come in."

Page entered, carrying a tray of fruit. She was followed by Gwen, who was carrying a pot of coffee and cups. "Whoever you are, you come bearing the right gifts. That coffee smells heavenly."

Page laughed and introduced herself. "I'm Page and this is my partner Gwen. Nonna said that you'd gone straight upstairs, when you arrived, without having anything to eat. We heard the water running and knew someone was up and thought you both might be hungry — by now."

Sidney blushed as the women placed the tray and coffee on the table in front of the fireplace. "Thank..." Sidney cleared her throat. "Thank you, Leah is...," looking at the door to the bathroom, "showering, I think. I'm Sidney, Leah's partner and Sasha's lawyer."

"Welcome to Villa Dell'uva. Your lady has been plenty worried about you. We're not staying. We'll have time to get acquainted a bit later. Tell the doctor that her patient is doing fine. I changed her dressings this morning. She's been up and walked and is going to try some breakfast."

Page looked at Gwen, who added, "She's asking questions. The television in the room was removed so she hasn't seen anything on the news. It might be best if she was told what happened. I'm a psychiatrist. If I can help or if there's anything I can do, I'm here."

"Thank you. I plan to tell her today. I don't know how she'll respond. It's good to know you're here."

Gwen saw Sidney eyeing the coffee and poured her a cup. "How do you take it?"

"Black, thank you. I so need a cup."

Handing Sidney her coffee, Gwen said, "We do have an understanding of the situation. It's all over the news. I have to say even with the little time I've spent with Sasha, it's difficult to believe she could be capable of murder. You'll be treading on fragile ground. It could very well push her over the edge."

"I know and I..."

They heard the water shutting off in the bathroom, and Gwen said, "We can talk more about this later."

A few minutes after Page and Gwen left the room, the bathroom door opened. Leah stood in the doorway, toweling dry. "Hey, I was hoping you would sleep a while longer. Did I hear voices?" Leah spied the coffee and recognized the contented look on Sidney's face while she sipped from a cup. "Page and Gwen or Hattie?"

Through the years, the sight of Leah's wholesome beauty and naked body had always unfailingly evoked desire in Sidney. Leah had never looked more beautiful to Sidney than today, however.

"Page and Gwen and they brought..." Sidney took a drink of her coffee and pointed to the tray. "Sustenance. You know I can't begin to function without my morning coffee. Page said to tell you that she changed the dressings and that Sasha was up and walked."

Taking another sip of her coffee, Sidney groaned her pleasure as she looked at Leah standing naked before her. "Hmm, delicious. They said for you to enjoy your breakfast."

God, I love it when she does that. Leah threw the towel in the bathroom and walked over to the bed and took the cup out of Sidney's hand. "They did, did they?"

Chapter Fifteen

Sasha poked at the food Hattie brought her. They'd talked for a few minutes, and the older woman had encouraged her to try to eat in order to regain her strength. Hattie meant well and she was right, but every bite made her stomach feel queasier.

Pushing the breakfast tray away, Sasha wondered again where she was. Everyone referred to it as the villa, but who owned it? Her mind had been fairly clear when they left Laguna, and even though there were no windows in the back of the ambulance, she was certain they had headed west on the coastal highway and traveled for about three or four hours. When they arrived, she could hear sea gulls in the distance and smell the light fragrance of spring grape blossoms. She owned a home in Montecito, and it was an easy guess that the villa was on a vineyard somewhere near there. Lauren loved the house and its incredible view. She called it "la finestra al mare", the window to the sea.

She looked around the room. Everything appeared so normal, but for her nothing was. She felt like she'd fallen down the rabbit hole. Her world had turned upside down, and she couldn't remember why. She had a lover she adored and a life that no one was talking about.

She wasn't stupid. The wounds on her wrists looked like self-inflicted cuts. On her worst day, even coming off the cocaine, when she'd wished she were dead, she never contemplated suicide. So where had the wounds come from?

The pale stuccoed walls reminded her of the walls in the home she shared with Lauren. She felt a sharp pain in her head and closed her eyes. She started to shake as a picture flashed in her mind of white splashed with red. When she opened her eyes, she raised both hands to her face and cried, "I'm going to go crazy if someone doesn't tell me what's happened and where Lauren is. Something is wrong, terribly wrong. Lauren, baby where are you? God, please, where is she?"

Sasha laid her head back on the pillow, fighting the panic and the darkness that threatened. She could see Ingrid's face. Her sister had never looked so afraid. What had happened that had put the fear in Ingrid's eyes?

Pushing her covers back, Sasha unsteadily got to her feet. She couldn't breathe. The room was too hot. Her shaking legs took her to the doors and out onto the veranda to the railing. Lightheaded, she leaned against it and tried to fill her lungs. The smell of the ocean jolted her. It reminded her of when Lauren had applied the sunscreen to her back — before they'd gone out to meet Constance and Kim for dinner.

Tears ran down her cheeks. In her mind she could see a lone sandpiper mocking her from a shadow that fell across Lauren, who was lying so still on the deck. Trembling, her hands went to her face. A guttural sound tore from her throat. "She's dead! Dear God, Lauren is dead!"

Tiana was riding home after visiting with her grandfather and Hattie. She sat on her horse a few yards away from the house, talking to a few of the workers. When she heard Sasha cry, she looked up. She saw that Sasha was in trouble and holding onto the railing. She pulled back on the reins, turned the horse toward the house, and dug her heels in.

Page was just coming out of the tasting room when she heard Tiana yelling. When she turned her way, Tiana pointed to the veranda. Page looked, then took off running.

Leah and Sidney had taken the dishes back to the kitchen and were talking with Hattie when Tiana burst in. "Nonna! Nonna! The lady upstairs, she's out on the balcony, and she's in trouble. Page is already on her way up."

By the time Leah reached the stairs, Page was at the top of the landing. When Leah reached the room, Page was standing still on the veranda and Sasha was holding onto to the railing. When Leah started toward her, Sasha cried, "Don't touch me. None of you touch me! Someone is going to tell me what's going on and where Lauren is!"

Leah went to move a step closer. Sasha swayed, looked down over the railing, then warned, "Don't come any closer."

"We just want to help you inside, Sasha. You're still weak. You could fall."

"Please, don't touch me. Just tell me where Lauren is and why I'm here. That's all I'm asking."

Sidney and Tiana helped a slower Hattie up the stairs. When they reached the room, Sidney's heart was pounding. Leah saw Sidney entering the bedroom and motioned for her to stay back.

Hattie shook her head. "The poor woman is frightened to death. Can you blame her? Not knowing what has happened to her or her partner. She does not escape her nightmares even when she's awake."

The truth of what Hattie said stunned Sidney. Had she rationalized and allowed her failed relationship with Sasha and Sasha's past to harden her heart? Had she been insensitive to Sasha as a person whose life had been thrown into chaos and a maelstrom of murder? Being honest with herself, she admitted that her focus had been on serving as Sasha's attorney and containing the backdraft for Ingrid and her reelection, not on Sasha's loss or what Sasha might have witnessed if she'd been in the house during the murders. *My God, how callous of me. Sasha most likely watched her lover and those other women being butchered!*

Someone had to reach Sasha. Sidney prayed she could do that. She stepped out onto the veranda behind Leah and Page. Moving slowly, she stepped to the side so Sasha could see her and stood still. Confused, Sasha blinked when she saw Sidney. As Sidney slowly walked toward Sasha, she spoke softly, "Sasha, it's Sidney."

Sasha's eyes never left Sidney. "Sidney, I thought I was...you were in the room at the hospital?"

Sidney took a step closer. "We were all there. Ingrid and Marty and your Uncle Isaac."

Sasha squeezed her eyes shut and swayed backward against the railing. "I've tried to...Sid...something...I just can't...remember."

When Sasha opened her eyes, they were pleading and filled with tears. Sasha's sorrow tore at Sidney's heart and her conscience. For the first time since she'd opened the file that Ingrid sent and looked at those pictures, she truly saw the woman she had once loved and cared for. Emotion blurred her eyes as she took a step closer and held out her hand. "Please, Sasha, come inside with me. I'd never hurt you. Please, I'll tell you what you want to know."

Trembling, Sasha braced herself against the railing with both hands. She nodded and reached a hand out toward Sidney. Grasping it, Sidney drew Sasha away from the railing and into her arms. Sasha's body sagged against hers in trust. Sidney held her as Sasha sobbed.

"It's okay. You're safe. I've got you." Sidney looked over Sasha's shoulder at Leah. Her face held an unreadable expression as she turned and went inside.

"Page is going to help me take you inside. Is that okay?"

Sasha held onto Sidney and raised her eyes searchingly. "Please, promise that you'll tell me what has happened to Lauren."

"I promise."

Once inside, Sidney and Page put Sasha to bed. Hattie told them that Leah had gone to get a sedative. Concerned that too many people in the room would frighten Sasha, Hattie took Tiana and went downstairs.

When Leah came back into the room, she avoided eye contact with Sidney, who was sitting on the bed holding Sasha's hand. She spoke, her voice gentle and compassionate. "You've had some tough days, Sasha, but you're getting better, and you'll continue to get better. You're having blackouts and flashbacks due to an emotional trauma and the combination of drugs you had in you when you came into the ER."

Sasha's eyes widened, and her fingers tightened around Sidney's hand. "Drugs?" She stared at Leah, confused. "I haven't used any kind of drug in a long time. I've been clean since the day I met Lauren."

After a few moments of awkward silence, Leah said, "Sidney has some things to tell you. Then when you're ready we can talk about your condition. I can give you something mild to help to calm you."

Struggling to control her emotions, Sasha took in a shaky breath and said, "Thank you, doctor, I appreciate it, but I'd rather not take anything."

Leah saw the fear that clouded Sasha's eyes and wondered if she was going to be able to handle what Sidney was about to tell her. "It's your call, but if at any time you feel you...need something, I want you to tell Sidney."

An erratic heartbeat was visible against the side of Sasha's neck as she looked at Sidney. "Can we talk now, Sid?"

Leah got up to leave. Sidney squeezed Sasha's hand encouragingly, then said, "Yes. Would it be all right if Page stays with you while I speak with Leah for just a moment?"

Nodding, Sasha watched as Sidney followed Leah out the door, closing it behind her. They walked down the hall to a sitting area.

"What is it, Leah? Tell me what you're thinking."

Leah started to say something, then turned and stared out the expanse of windows that overlooked the vineyards. "It's nothing."

"It's something. You're tense and uptight. That's not like you. Please, talk to me." When Leah didn't respond Sidney asked, "Is it because Sasha was once my lover? Or do you feel she's guilty? Is that it?"

Angry, Leah swung around. "Your *ex-lover* is my patient. Since when do you feel you have to ask me if I am discriminating against a patient for any reason?"

Sidney closed her eyes, hung her head in frustration, then looked back at Leah. "I'm sorry, that's not what I meant. I know that you would never—"

"I hate that this is coming between us. I know we talked about it, and I know why we both chose to be involved. I don't know if she's innocent or guilty. What I do know is that people are dead, and someone tried to take out an entire hospital. There's an assassin out there. If that person murdered those women, it's not a far stretch to assume that the attempt on the hospital was to get Sasha because she survived. That puts you in danger and that frightens the hell out of me."

"Don't you think I feel the same way about your safety? For God's sake, you disappeared from the hospital with Sasha. And that scared the hell out of *me*."

"I'm her doctor. That's different."

"Different how? It puts you in just as much danger. I also have a job to do and the responsibility to defend her life."

When Leah didn't say anything, Sidney turned to go back to Sasha's room.

"Sid, please wait."

Sidney kept walking. "I need to get back. We're not getting anywhere with this. We can talk about it later."

Leah fell in beside Sidney. When they reached Sasha's room, Sidney caught Leah's eye. "Do you think you should be in the room with me when I talk to Sasha?"

"It probably would be better if you talked to her alone. Gwen and I have discussed this, and if it looks like she's not handling it then we can intervene. Right now she's fragile and still recovering from the effects of the drugs and her wounds. Physically, she's still weak, but she's healing. Psychologically, what happened in that beach house has severely traumatized her. Gwen feels it's possible, and I agree, that Sasha's mind might not be able to cope and it'll take her under. On the other hand, we just saw what happened because she needs to know. She's not coping with that either, and who can blame her? How can we decide for her what's worse? Anyway the decision's been made." Leah wanted to reach out and touch Sidney, but instead she simply said, "I'll be downstairs."

Sasha stared down at her shaking hands, trying to hold on as Sidney sat beside her on the bed. "I'm afraid, Sid. I'm so terrified to hear what you're going to say. But, I need to know why we're here and what's happened to Lauren."

Sidney leaned forward and held one of Sasha's hands, then brushed a stray piece of hair from her face. "Are you sure you want to do this now? We can wait until you're stronger."

Unwavering, Sasha looked directly into Sidney's eyes. With a forlorn sense of loss and a profound emptiness in her soul, Sasha whispered, "Please, tell me."

Not knowing what was going to happen, Hattie drove Tiana home to the neighboring Cipriano vineyards. Gwen had returned from a trip to the market in Santa Barbara. She and Page sat with Leah at the counter in the kitchen. No one made an attempt at conversation as they waited. When the intercom rang, they all jumped. Leah hopped up to answer it. "Sid?

"She knows everything. God, if someone told me what I just told her I'd...I don't know what I'd do. She just lay there and listened, not saying anything. I...I'm afraid...that this..."

"She's probably in shock. Gwen is here, we're on the way up."

When Sidney hung up, she went back to sit beside Sasha on the bed. Sasha's eyes were closed, and she was deathly pale. Sidney wrapped her hand around Sasha's. Her skin was cold as ice. When Sasha opened her eyes, Sidney looked into the fires of hell and saw incredible pain and suffering.

Sasha's voice was raw, her words ragged. "You never asked if I killed Lauren or if I killed the others."

Holding Sasha's cold hand to her cheek, Sidney tried to hold back the tears that welled in her eyes as she swallowed the lump in her throat. "I don't need to ask."

"Thank...thank you for...being here." The gate opened, and Sasha's body shook as she sobbed. "How could anyone do that, hurt her like that? I loved her. Dear God, I loved her so much."

From the doorway Leah and Gwen watched, both thinking it best to wait and let Sasha express her grief. Gwen motioned for Leah to follow her back out into the hallway. "It looks like Sidney has it under control, for now." Aware of the concerned look on Leah's face, Gwen asked, "Do you want to talk?"

Leah shoved her hands in the pockets of her jeans, then leaned against the wall and put her head back. "No, but thanks."

"This has to be a difficult situation for you all. Sidney seems like a compassionate person. A trait rare in an attorney of her reputation."

"Yes, she is. Sasha is lucky to have her."

"She's fortunate to have you too. During CNN's coverage of the attempt on the hospital, it was mentioned that President Sheppard and Sidney went to college together at Pepperdine."

"Yes, they're very good friends. Ingrid and her partner, Marty, and Sidney, all went to Pepperdine. Marty is an attorney also."

"I see. Then Sidney and Sasha knew each other."

As Gwen suspected, her words hit a sore spot. Leah pushed herself away from the wall. "Yes, they did." Leah looked tired as she looked toward the door of Sasha's room. "Do you mind? I think it best if I wait awhile before going in."

"Sure. In a bit I'll go in and see if I can be of some help. Armanno was sorry that he and Liberty were not here when Sasha went out on the veranda. He's arranged for Sasha to have someone with her around the clock."

Nodding, Leah said, "It's a good decision. It's so difficult to know what may be going through her mind now."

"The person who'll be with Sasha is Beth. She has a high security clearance and she's a top-notch bodyguard with a medical background. No need for you or Sidney to sit up with Sasha all night. If anything comes up, Beth will alert you. Page and I are here also."

Leah had seen the woman downstairs talking to Liberty Starr. When the woman saw her watching, she smiled politely, but Leah could see the same edgy and dangerous look that Liberty had. "Thanks, Gwen. Armanno gave me a cell phone. I need to call the hospital. I'll talk to you later."

Chapter Sixteen

Several children ran beside the woman, begging for pesos, as she hurriedly walked along the broken sidewalk in the small Mexican town. As she crossed the street toward the cantina on the corner, a man standing in front waved his arms threateningly at the impoverished children, yelling for them to move on. Leering, he said in broken English, "Come, señora, we have cold drinks. Anything you wish." He held open the peeling rickety door of the cantina and gave her a toothless grin. "Come, señora."

Scalzon walked into the musty smoke-filled bar, removed her sun glasses, put them in her shirt pocket, then stood for a moment, allowing her eyes to adjust to the dimly lit room. Briefly, she took note of a man who was watching her as he leaned against an old jukebox in the corner. Her eyes scanned the room, noting every person and the locations of the exits. The man she came to see sat at a table toward the back of the room.

As she approached, the man stopped shoveling food into his mouth and pushed his chair back, then looked at her with a cunning eye. "Ah, señora, it's been a long time since you have honored me with your presence. I was beginning to think you did not like my company. Was the special order to the liking of our mutual acquaintance?"

As did many others, Ramón thought Scalzon a go-between. Either that or he played the game out of fear. A peon, he would provide anything for a price. He was a flunky, a front man for the Mexican cartel that controlled a big piece of the drug traffic into the States. In return, the cartel allowed him to operate various illegal businesses, taking a hefty percentage off the top, including selling off bits of an arsenal of weapons that had been stolen from U.S. military reserve units in the States. Scalzon had paid a high price for the plastics and the small shoulder-fired SAM that she'd left behind on the fishing boat.

Her eyes roamed over the belly that hung over Ramón's belt. He reeked of body odor, and his shirt was stained with sweat and food. He was a despicable man, and Scalzon knew he'd doubled the price the cartel asked for the SAM, pocketing the difference.

Pulling a chair out, she moved it to a position to Ramón's right so she was facing the room before she sat down and placed the canvas bag she was carrying down on the floor. Fixing Ramón with a threatening glare, she leaned back in the chair. "You forget the rules. Asking too many questions can be hazardous to your health."

The woman's penetrating cold eyes always unnerved him. He reached into his pocket for a handkerchief to wipe away the sweat that was running down the side of his face. His gaze darted briefly toward his men, who were watching intently from the bar. He'd never liked dealing with this woman in person. She walked in the shadow of El Diablo and had the look of *muerte* in her eyes.

"Señora, forgive my bad manners." He motioned to the bartender, and an unopened bottle of mescal and two glasses appeared on the table. His hands shook as he poured, praying to the dead maguey worm lying at the bottom of the bottle to devour the evil spirit that had entered the room. "Drink up, my friend."

Scalzon reached across the table and switched glasses, then held her glass up in a salute. She waited until Ramón nervously picked his glass up and downed its contents. He wiped his mouth with the back of his hand and asked, "What is it I can do for you, my friend?"

Without drinking, Scalzon set the glass down. She reached into the bag, retrieved a stack of bills, and placed it on the table in front of her. "Information."

Ramón's puffy eyes widened, and his tongue snaked out and licked at the mescal still on his lips as he looked at the money on the table. A murmur ran through the room, and Ramón's greed almost made him forget his wariness and fear of this woman. "What do you want to know?"

"A little over three years ago you had a package delivered to an address in the States. It was ordered by a contact by the name of Kestral who did business with you often. I want to know where that package was delivered."

Shrugging his shoulders, Ramón scratched his scraggy beard. "Three years is a long time, señora. I am growing old. My memory is not all that good."

Reaching again into the bag, Scalzon took out two more stacks of money, piling them one on top of the other, then glared at Ramón. "Is your memory coming back to you?"

He picked up one of the bundles of cash and thumbed through it. The black of his pupils dominated his eyes. "Si, señora, I do recall delivering a package to a place called Lone Mountain."

"Lone Mountain?" Scalzon's eyes narrowed. "Where?"

"A place with much snow on the mountains. Much too cold for me — Montana."

Picking up the glass of mescal, Scalzon downed it, enjoying the cheap burn as it hit her stomach. Getting to her feet, she started for the door only to have her path blocked by one of Ramón's men. In broken English, he slurred, "Why don't you stay and have a drink with me…" He gestured toward the bar, "…and my friend?"

When he put his hands on her hips, Scalzon brought her knee up hard into his crotch. As he doubled over, she clasped her hands together and brought them down on the back of his neck. He hit the ground hard and never moved. The other man who was standing at the bar started toward her but stopped dead in his tracks when he saw the cold, dangerous look in her eyes that said she derived a sadistic pleasure from inflicting pain.

"No? You've changed your mind? Little man, you don't want to fuck me now? Wise decision." As she exited the bar, she could hear Ramón's amused laughter and his words, "*Estúpido hijo de una puta*, you let the woman scare you because her balls are bigger than yours."

Outside, Scalzon put her sunglasses on and walked down the street to the end of the block. She could hear the tinny music emanating from the cantina. The smell of fried food and the cries of shopkeepers hawking their goods filled the stifling air. When she crossed to the other side of the street, she looked back at the cantina. She smiled as she took a small black detonator out of her pocket and got into the car.

"You're too easy, Ramón and too busy counting your money to notice the little gift I left for you under the table." As the car turned the corner, she pressed the button. The explosion sent a ball of fire hurling upward into the sky. "Enjoy your profit in hell, Ramón."

Kayla and her sister, Cassie, finished packing their supplies and equipment for a hiking trip to the Swan Mountain Range. Three or four times a year they hiked and explored the forty-seven miles of trails near Swan Crest east of Kalispell. The range's 6000-foot altitude and complexity of terrain made for a perfect workout in the off-training season, enabling Cassie to maintain her strength and providing endurance conditioning of her lungs and legs. Snow remained on the high-altitude trails well into July, and Kayla shoved an extra sweatshirt in her backpack along with one other change of clothes.

"Well, I guess that's it." Picking the checklist off the kitchen table, she reviewed it: Food, water, first aid kit, a change of clothes, flashlight, sunscreen, sun glasses… "My sunglasses. Where are my sunglasses? I had them a minute ago."

Cassie closed her own pack, fastened it shut, then strapped her sleeping bag to it. She wondered how long it would take before her sister found the sunglasses right where she'd left them — where she always carried them — in her right shirt chest pocket. "Thanks for coming with me, Sis. I'm looking forward to hiking the upper Pintler Creek. It'll give my legs a good workout. If I'd just worked harder, maybe—"

"Quit beating yourself up, Cassie. You overcame a lot after the accident. Have you forgotten that your feet were frostbitten when you were buried in that avalanche? We weren't sure you wouldn't lose one or both of them."

"I remember, but—"

"No buts. You were more than ready. Remember, I helped train you and I know what I'm talking about. You've never slacked and you did work hard. If your run had been earlier in the day, before the course conditions changed so drastically because of the warmer temperatures, you'd have had a good chance at taking the Silver. Turin is behind you. Your goal and focus now is 2010 and Vancouver."

Laughing, Cassie pulled the baseball cap down over Kayla's dusky blue eyes and reached for the sunglasses in her sister's shirt pocket. "I love you, big sis. You never give a centimeter, do ya? Come on. Let's get going." Cassie handed Kayla her "lost" glasses. "The sun will be up long before we get there if we don't get a move on."

"Would you throw my pack in the truck? I want to call the lodge and tell Nathan we're leaving and that I'll have my cell phone with me just in case..."

Cassie knew the "just in case" was if Liberty tried to contact her. As was Kayla's way, she kept her emotions and feelings bottled up inside. She hadn't talked with anyone about why Liberty left Lone Mountain or where she'd gone. She'd simply said that Liberty had been asked to do a favor.

"Have you heard anything from her?"

"No, and I don't expect to. She'll come home when the job's done. And if she does and I'm not here, I want Nathan to tell her where we've gone."

Yesterday, after listening to the news about the attempt on the hospital, Kayla had paced the floors for hours, then grabbed her jacket and gone for a walk. Both Cassie and their brother, Nathan, were worried. Kayla was a rock and the strongest woman Cassie had ever known, but she was a recovering alcoholic. After Addie,

Kayla's first love, died in an avalanche on the mountain, Kayla had turned to the bottle, then disappeared for a few years.

"You were pretty upset yesterday. I know you can't talk about where or what Liberty is doing, Sis, but I'm here if you need to talk."

Tears welled in Kayla's eyes, and her heart filled with pride as she hugged her younger sister. "I love you, too. Sometimes it's hard for me to realize that you're all grown up and have gotten so wise. Now, go on. Put our stuff in the truck while I call Nathan. Then we'll go and hike those trails and we'll see if you can keep up with me."

"Put your money where you're mouth is, Sinclair. If I can't keep up with an old woman like you, I'll buy dinner when we come down off the mountain."

"Deal. Bring your wallet. And it'll be a place of my choice."

Cassie grabbed the two backpacks and retorted, "Dream on, and don't cry poor when you have to pay up."

Chapter Seventeen

Armanno took a Cuban cigar out of the humidor on his desk and appreciatively passed it slowly under his nose. "Ah, Cuban *Totalmente a mano*, a weakness I willingly admit to. I would offer you one, Liberty, but I know you do not indulge." Armanno stood. "Please, join me."

Leading the way, he opened the door of his office, then followed Liberty into an area that extended the entire length of the backside of the villa. The solarium was completely enclosed with bulletproof glass, and sections were artfully decorated with stained designs. The retractable roof allowed in the rich smell of the soil and the ocean along with the fragrance of grape blossoms. A waterfall flowed into a therapy pool, and an aviary of birds and an array of plants and greenery thrived.

Gesturing to one of the comfortable chairs, Armanno said, "Please, sit and join me in a glass of wine." In the center of the table sat a bottle of Cipriano Petite Syrah and two glasses. Armanno picked up the bottle and removed the cork. "It is a gift from Sebastian Cipriano, Tiana's other grandfather, a rare bottle from his private cellar."

"Yes, I remember him."

After pouring the wine, Armanno handed Liberty a glass. He picked up his own and leaned back in his chair. Eyeing Liberty with respect, he said, "It must have been a difficult decision for you to make when Wade Kincaide asked you to help Ingrid Sheppard." He raised his hand when the color of Liberty's eyes deepened. "You don't need to explain. You and I are the last of the Talons. Unfortunately, the world will never know of the sacrifices of so many to protect this country."

"No, nor will it know of the innocents who were killed."

"As commander of the Talon, there is not a day that goes by that I don't blame myself for those deaths."

"You're not responsible, Armanno. You were betrayed and a victim, just the same as the rest of us. You lost your son and Maggie lost..."

Recognizing the depth of pain that appeared in Armanno's eyes, Liberty fell silent, her inadequate words left unspoken. Sipping their wine, they sat in silence, each reflecting upon their chosen paths and the anguish their choices had brought.

Armanno finished his wine and fastened his gaze on Liberty. He said in a sober voice, "We all lost. Long before the Talons were stalked and murdered, they'd lost their souls, condemned to their fate, isolated from their families and those they'd loved."

Armanno spoke harsh words soured by unfulfilled revenge. "Brady Lawrence's death was much too easy. He didn't suffer enough to appease the agony of the souls he betrayed. The Talons were a collective of the very best and most patriotic agents this country had to offer. Good men and women went to their graves thinking that their country had turned its back on them. How many thought that President Kincaide had ordered their elimination? We both have used force and done what was necessary to complete a mission. We did what we had to do. I've never liked to kill, but I would have enjoyed watching Brady and his assassin die a very slow and painful death."

The very fiber of Liberty's being also harbored a profound hatred for the betrayal and murder of the Talons. During a year of self-imposed isolation with her adopted people, the Navajo of New Mexico, her broken body and bones had healed. Not even the healing powers of the sacred earth of El Santuario de Chimayó could cleanse her tormented soul.

As Armanno talked, Liberty grew increasingly uneasy. Thoughts of Kayla, an acute awareness of her, raised goose bumps on the back of her neck. After years of killing, Liberty had existed in the shadows, allowing nothing or no one in. At first it was necessary for survival, but with each successful kill she'd lost what little was left of Liberty Starr and became the Ghost, the Talons' deadly assassin. Weary, on the run, and wounded, she'd stopped to rest in a pub in northwestern Montana and met the most extraordinary woman. Kayla stole Liberty's heart and changed her life.

"You survived and found someone to share your life who loves you. You served your country. Was it fair of Kincaide to ask you to put what happiness you've found and your life at risk again?"

Liberty had selfishly thought the same thing at first, but Kayla's understanding and reasoning had allowed her to make the decision she did.

"You've done no less by allowing us to stay here at the villa, Armanno. Sasha Sheppard has been charged with multiple counts of murder and Orange County's DA is out for her hide. If they find her here, you'll be charged with harboring a criminal and with aiding her escape."

"Just as you chose to answer Kincaide's plea for help, I could do no less. We are the last, but we will always be the President's Talons."

Armanno filled their glasses once again before continuing. "I've been thinking about what you told me. You are sure the person who made the attempt on the hospital and blew the boat was Scalzon?"

"The way it was planned and executed screamed Scalzon. There are not that many suppliers of C-4. I made some inquiries, and I'm certain it was her."

Armanno lowered his glass as his eyes narrowed. "You said her. You think Scalzon is a woman?"

"I have for a long time. Remember, it was Scalzon's contact who led me into a trap. I believe that woman was Scalzon. I should have seen it. If I had, we wouldn't have lost..."

Reverting to Italian, Armanno reinforced, "*Non eravate responsabile delle loro morti.*"

A suspicion brewed in Armanno's mind as he took a drink of his wine. "If Scalzon was the one behind the murders, she got careless and thought the Sheppard woman would be dead before the authorities arrived at the murder scene. Leaving her alive would have been too risky, and Scalzon never took risks. Assassinating President Sheppard outright would have made her a martyr and turned the people's sympathy to her party. But with Sasha dead and all the evidence pointing to her as the murderer? That's all it would've taken to bury the President's chance of being reelected in the same grave with her sister." His insight had him following the same thread as Liberty. His dark eyes narrowed, and Liberty could see the seed of mistrust forming in his mind the same as it had in hers.

"Scalzon is a psychopath, devious and cunning. Capable of weaving a web that made us think one thing, but there was always another agenda."

"You're thinking that we're being led by the nose to believe one thing, but it's a smoke screen to cover something else." Liberty nodded slowly.

"You know it's never as it seems with Scalzon. We need to explore the possibility that the murders were not a politically motivated scheme to keep Ingrid Sheppard out of the White House, but a diversion. If you're right, and the attempt on the hospital was to get Sasha Sheppard and not her sister, it makes sense that Scalzon is afraid that Sasha will remember what happened and why. Now that you've destroyed the tracking devices, Scalzon will look for another way to get to her."

"Which makes her dangerous to anyone who might get in her way, including Jay Brunelle, the Chief of Police of Laguna. Jay's a good cop and was close to the DeRoche investigator that was killed. He might have left something, or Scalzon might think he did, that could get Jay killed. She's smart and tough, but she's no match for Scalzon."

Armanno sat back in his chair and steepled his fingers against his lower lip. "Jay Brunelle...the name is familiar." His eyes showed that he did remember. "The pilot you met in the Middle East when we were so close to finding the last of Nusair's terrorist cell. Does she remember you? Will it be a problem?"

"The one time we met was a few days ago. It was dark, and she couldn't see my face. Even with my hair its natural color and not wearing dark contacts, it's possible that she'd recognize me if she got close enough. I used Jay as a cover when we were tracking Nusair's cell. We spent a month together in an intimate relationship. If she did recognize me, though, there's no reason to think she'd connect me to the terrorist's assassinations. As far as Jay was concerned, I was just another lonely Australian too far away from home." *No, Armanno there was more to it than that, but it's not relevant and not something you need to know.*

A sound deep in Armanno's throat expressed his amusement. "Australian, huh? You were always good with accents. Must come from the many languages you speak." Armanno's demeanor turned serious as he sat forward in his chair. "Do you remember the mission in Bosnia? Agent Erramuzpe was able to extract the information buried deep in the subconscious mind of one of the rescued Bosnian officers by using a neurotransmitter. It might work on Sasha Sheppard, if she would agree to try it."

A sixth sense gripped Liberty. Kayla was in danger She tried to concentrate on what Armanno was saying. "Yes, I remember. It's worth a try. If the drugs are administered properly, it possibly could work."

"Tonight is not a good time to approach this. In the morning, we can talk to the doctors and her lawyer to get their opinions. If they think it's safe, it could be discussed with Sasha. If she agrees, we could have some answers soon."

Distracted, her thoughts elsewhere, and feeling on edge, Liberty asked, "Armanno, can you handle this tomorrow?" *Am I just spooked? Should I contact Kayla?* "There's something I need to do." *Jay needs to know about Scalzon.*

Intuitively Armanno knew what was on Liberty's mind and said, "You're going to talk to Jay Brunelle."

Liberty's face revealed little as she mentally traced the scars Scalzon left on her body. "If we hold back pertinent information about our suspicions about Scalzon from her, it could get her killed...or worse."

"If she suspects you were involved in Sasha's disappearance from the hospital, she will arrest you."

As Liberty stood, her face held a hardness that Armanno was familiar with. "That's not going to happen. Contact me on the number I gave you if Sasha remembers anything." For a long moment Liberty gazed out at the rolling hills that stretched to the Santa Ynez Mountains, thinking about the mountains of Montana and Kayla. A few minutes later she was on the highway heading back toward Laguna.

Since telling Sasha about the murders and their aftermath, Sidney hadn't moved too far away from the chair beside her bed. Emotionally exhausted, Sasha finally drifted into a restless sleep. Leah came in and stood behind Sidney. "Hey, why don't you go and lie down awhile? I'll wake you if there's a problem."

Not taking her eyes off Sasha, Sidney put a hand over the one that Leah was resting on her shoulder. "Thanks, but I couldn't sleep. You go get some rest. Beth is here with me."

Feeling an unreasonable sense of rejection, Leah removed her hand from Sidney's shoulder. Sidney was shutting her out, and at the moment there was nothing to be done about it. She looked across the room at Beth who had discreetly occupied herself by reading Sasha's chart. She had taken off her jacket, exposing the weapon and holster clipped on her belt at the back of her faded jeans. A steady diet of gunshot wounds in the ER had made Leah leery of guns. "You never touched your dinner, Sid. Can I get you something from downstairs?"

"Thanks, I'm not hungry."

What's going on in your mind, Sidney? You're not responsible for any of this so why do I see the look of guilt in your eyes? Leah bent and brushed her lips against Sidney's hair. "I told Judy I'd follow up with her tonight. She's been covering both the ER and Intensive Care." Not wanting to burden Sidney and add more to what she was already dealing with, Leah kept her thoughts to herself. *With the number of admissions down to nothing and all the sudden discharges since the attempt on the hospital, the hospital will be damn lucky to keep its doors open.*

Leah went downstairs and ran into Armanno going into his study. "Leah, can we talk for a moment? I have something I'd like to run past you."

Armanno discussed the possibility of retrieving Sasha's memory by using the drug therapy. Leah had read several research papers on the subject. She thought it was feasible, but felt it was also risky. The procedure could push Sasha permanently into her nightmares and a world of darkness. "We'd have to research the results of the procedure and get an expert opinion before we approach Sasha with it. I can make a few inquiries and we can ask Gwen's opinion. She may know someone in the field."

After speaking with Armanno, Leah went back to Sasha's room, hoping to get a few minutes alone with Sidney so they could talk. The distance between them was making her crazy. Sidney stood with her in the hallway for a few moments. "Sid, you're dead on your feet. Go lie down for an hour. I'll stay with Sasha." Leah ached to hold her, but Sidney's body language, with her arms wrapped around herself, warned her off.

"I wouldn't sleep."

Frustrated, Leah returned to her room and called the hospital to talk with Judy. The situation at the hospital was critical. Admissions had continued to drop drastically. The administrator was frantic, and a meeting of the board of directors was scheduled in the morning to discuss closing the hospital for a few weeks. Leah knew if that happened many employees would seek jobs elsewhere. The hospital would suffer the ramifications of that decision and would never reopen.

Rain, propelled by strong winds, began to pound at the villa, adding to the forlorn feeling in Leah's heart. She sat in front of the fire, listening to the sound of the storm outside. Even though Sidney was a few feet down the hall, the distance felt immeasurable. The king-sized bed, that just a few hours ago held them in passion, seemed empty now.

"What in the hell do you mean, no one knows where she is! Son of a bitch, it's illegal for the Secret Service to interfere and just waltz her out of the hospital. I'll have that bitch Sheppard impeached for this." Marcus Ramey was livid as he ranted and raved at Jay Brunelle over the phone.

Gritting her teeth, Jay impatiently listened, wanting to reach through the phone and grab Ramey by the neck and dangle him out of the window of her truck. She didn't have time for his bullshit indignation. "When you say the Secret Service, you mean Ingrid

Sheppard, don't you? The President had nothing to do with Sasha Sheppard leaving the hospital. And if the Secret Service did, they're denying it. President Sheppard has gone on record saying she had no knowledge of the plans to remove her sister from the hospital, where she is, and that she has not been in contact with her."

"On the record? You know this, how? I'm the fucking district attorney and I don't know this."

You stupid... You don't know your ass from a hole in the ground. You'll do anything to discredit Ingrid Sheppard so the likes of you can put another self-centered neoconservative slug in the White House. Another brain dead obstinate who will again serve up the American people and all the other duped innocents of the world on a platter so his cup and that of his wealthy cronies runneth over with oil.

"Bob Redfern sent me a copy of the statement President Sheppard's attorneys prepared and her press secretary read at a White House press conference this morning. It's been on all the stations for hours. Doesn't anyone in your office listen to or watch the news?"

Sputtering, Ramey sounded like he was choking. "Redfern sent the statement to *your* office?" Jay muted the phone and chuckled. She could just imagine Ramey's ugly mug turning red with rage.

"When you find Sasha Sheppard, and you'd fucking better do it fast if you want to keep your job, I want her handcuffed and her ass dragged back here and thrown in jail. She'll get no special treatment. Do you hear me, Brunelle?"

Slamming the phone shut without answering, Jay threw it on the seat beside her. "You damn jerk, the entire country can hear you."

As much as she would like to, Jay couldn't put off making the trip to Grant's house. He had a cat that had showed up on his doorstep one day and never left. She'd have to find him a home and handle the arrangements for Grant's cremation, then settle his affairs. She knew her investigators had gone through the house and found nothing out of place. Now, she had to close the house. Grant had no one else except her and a housekeeper who had called her sobbing when she'd heard the news of his murder. Mrs. Dudly had been cleaning and preparing meals for Grant for twenty years and was at a loss as to what she should do.

As she drove toward the bluff, Jay thought about everything that had happened. About the women who had died, Grant's death, the officers who had lost their lives. Then the attempt on the hospital, the death of the fisherman, and the explosion that took more lives. Jay had been on a police patrol boat heading toward the scene when she heard the directive from the Coast Guard. She took a good guess as to why the urgency was necessary and was reaching for the mic to reinforce the warning when she spotted the police boat from Dana Point and the officers boarding. No one would ever know if the officers who were killed had heard the Coast Guard commander repeating the warning not to board the fishing boat.

The force of the blast rocked everything on the water for miles, knocking Jay off her feet and breaking windows on shore. The assassin had planned to blow the boat and used enough C-4 to vaporize it and anything else, making sure there wouldn't be any evidence or bodies to recover. Why? Jay thought about that. Maybe to create more chaos to keep everyone running around chasing their tails...?

After the blast, Jay remembered seeing a Coast Guard cutter heading back to shore in a hurry. The rough sea and heavy rain made it difficult to see, but Jay was certain that the person standing at the bow was the woman who had identified herself as Liberty Starr at the crash site along Big Sur. The feeling that she knew this woman from somewhere gnawed at her gut. When she'd contacted the Coast Guard and the commanding officer of the sector, all she was told was that there had been an agent on board the cutter. No name, just an agent who had top secret clearance.

Ingrid Sheppard and the Secret Service were gone, and Sasha Sheppard had vanished. No one knew or was admitting that they knew where Leah was, either, and that had Jay worried. All she got when she called Leah's cell was her voice message. Calling Sidney's office wasn't any more informative. She was told that Sidney was in New York and they didn't know when she planned to return. Her assistant, Jason, politely said he would make sure that Ms. DeRoche got the message that Jay wanted to speak with her. She was getting nowhere with this case.

Pulling up in Grant's driveway, Jay rolled down the window. She sat trying to get her emotions under control. She couldn't recall ever being in Grant's home when he wasn't there. When he had mustered out of the Army after Vietnam, he'd come home and gotten a job as a patrol cop on the Los Angeles Police Force. He used his savings to put a down payment on fifteen acres on the bluff overlooking the Pacific in Laguna. Now the property was worth a fortune.

Off in the distance the deep throaty blast of a ship's horn sounded. She thought about the many times she and Grant had walked to the top of the bluff and stood sipping on beers as they watched the ships making their way along the corridor coming in and going out to sea. Her eyes stung as she swallowed the lump forming in her throat. Tonight, the mournful sound of the horn was a eulogy to Grant and reflected the sorrow in Jay's heart.

Grant's cat sat on the railing of the porch as if waiting. His eyes seemed to be searching for Grant. Jay opened the truck door and stepped outside. "Well, there's no point in putting this off." Jay scooped the cat up and scratched behind his ear. "He's not coming home, boy. You hungry? What say we go see what we can scrounge up?"

Removing the yellow tape from the door, she inserted her key into the lock and pushed the door open. Looking around the room, Jay appreciated the care and respect her investigators had taken when they went through the house. Everything was the same, but the house felt hollow and empty. The realization of Grant's death hit her like a fist, knocking the wind out of her. It took all she had to walk across the hardwood floors toward the kitchen. The sound of her footsteps echoed deafeningly throughout the room.

Jay put the cat down and opened cabinet doors until she found his food. She filled both the food and water bowls before walking down the hall to Grant's study. Standing outside, she took a deep breath before opening the door. She wanted so much for it all to be a mistake, wanted to find Grant sitting at his desk, laughing and telling her stories about the "good old days". The tears came then, but Jay didn't care. She walked into the room, picked up the sweater from the back of the chair, and brought it to her face. It smelled like Old Spice and pipe tobacco, and her heart ached. She sat in Grant's chair and looked at the top of his desk. Grant was organized and kept everything neat. Jay reached down to turn on the computer. Her finger was on the button when she froze and swore.

"Son-of-a bitch!" The back cover of the computer was slightly askew. Pulling the unit out, she could see that the cover was missing half the screws. After removing the remaining screws and inspecting the CPU, she took her cell out of her shirt pocket and pushed the speed button to the station. "This is Chief Brunelle. Patch me through to Dobbs."

A few minutes later Dobbs answered, "Dobbs here."

"Hey, Gene. When you were at the Nolte house, did you remove the hard drive of the computer in Grant's office?"

"No, Chief, I left you two messages asking about it while we were still in the house."

"Messages?"

"Yeah, I left a message on your cell to call me. When you didn't return my call, we left everything as it was. I included the information about the missing hard drive in the report that I put on your desk this morning. No point in bring the computer in unless you..."

Damn. "Your report is still on my desk. Did you see anything unusual? Was the house secure when you arrived?"

"We used the key you gave us and checked all the windows and the doors. Nothing except the computer looked disturbed. And we only knew that when we checked it."

"Were there screws missing?"

"No, I removed them. When I saw the hard drive was gone, I reattached the cover with two and put the others in the ashtray on the desk."

"Dispatch an investigating team back to Grant Nolte's house. I want the computer brought in and everything dusted for prints. I'll be here."

After hanging up, Jay looked around. A barely visible scratch on the back door lock indicated it had been picked. No easy feat considering the locks Grant had installed. Just as Jay suspected, it didn't look like anything else had been taken. She picked the cat up and went to sit on the front porch to wait for her investigators to arrive.

Jay thought about what Grant would have had on his computer. He always sent a back up copy of any investigation he was on to himself, to the DeRoche office, and to his computer at home. If Grant was killed because of something he found during an investigation, she was determined to find out what it was. She made a mental note to check for any messages from him. Grant sometimes e-mailed her if he found evidence of criminal activity on the part of non-clients.

Harry Sweeney paced the sidewalk in front of Mallory's Bar and Grill waiting for Jay to arrive. His stomach growled in response to the smell of deep-fried fish and chips and Mallory's spicy chowder. Grumbling, he stopped and looked at his watch as he saw Jay's truck coming down the street. "It's about time."

Harry had read Hank's autopsy report of the murdered women and was about to call Jay when the phone rang. It was Jay asking if he could meet her at Mallory's. She'd read the report, too, and wanted to talk to him about something — and not in her office. Hearing the edge in Jay's voice, Harry knew it was something important. He suspected it was more than the autopsy reports that Jay had on her mind.

Jay hurried around the corner, carrying her briefcase. "Sorry to keep you waiting. I had to sneak the hell out of the building or I'd have had a string of damn reporters on my tail. You done for the day?"

Harry nodded. "I'm never done, but I'm off duty."

"Good, we can talk over dinner."

"My stomach's been growling since I arrived." Harry followed Jay into the bar, convinced that he should have stood at attention and saluted. He admired Jay's no nonsense approach and shared her disdain for the blood sucking newsmongers. His mind flashed to an image of a younger smiling captain in an Apache A-H 64 giving him thumbs up after the rescue chopper plucked him out of the desert. Tonight, he felt that same intensity vibrating off her that he'd witnessed during her tour of duty in the Middle East.

As they entered the pub, Jay glanced at Mallory, held up two fingers, then headed toward a booth at the back of the bar. A few minutes later Mallory delivered two steaming bowls of clam chowder, along with two mugs of beer to the table. As she set the tray down, she nodded to Jay, then looked at Harry. "Haven't seen you in a while. L.A. keeping you busy?"

"L.A. is an old-fashioned kind of town. Murder never goes out of style."

Mallory went back to the bar. Harry devoured his chowder, then picked up his beer. "I'd forgotten just how good Mallory can cook." Preoccupied, Jay didn't hear him until he asked whether she wanted another beer.

Both her hands were wrapped around a mug that was still more than half-full. Jay tilted it toward Harry. "This will do." Jay had her mother's warm tawny-colored eyes, which at the moment were darkened with anger. "Have you read Hank's autopsy reports?"

Here it comes. Harry knew it wouldn't take long for Jay to build up a head of steam when she read the reports. "Yep, finished up just before you called." Jay pulled a folded copy of the autopsy reports and her notes from the department's investigation out of her briefcase, along with the report on Sasha's lab results. She summarized the information they held.

"Hank was right, Lauren Serantis died last. He put her death sometime between two and two-thirty AM. Kim Lang and Constance Williams died about midnight."

Turning a page, Jay continued, "Here's what we know from our investigation. Four people arrived at Loperchios for dinner at about nine PM. Lauren Serantis' credit card was charged at ten-fifteen for four meals and one bottle of red wine. They went into the lounge for a nightcap. At ten twenty-five, Sasha Sheppard used her credit card to pay for a round of drinks.

"The bartender and the cocktail waitress both remember a fifth person joining them — a woman who'd been sitting at the bar. The waitress remembers feeling that something odd was going on at the table and that Sasha Sheppard appeared to be sick all of a sudden. She offered to call an ambulance, but the woman said that Sasha had had a little too much to drink. The waitress thought that strange because Sheppard only had a glass of wine with dinner and an ice tea she didn't finish in the bar. When they left, the woman had her arm around Sasha's waist and was practically carrying her out. And the other three women seemed nervous."

Jay gripped the mug so tightly Harry thought it would break in her hands. "Credit card receipts and witnesses put them leaving the bar at eleven-fifteen. Constance Williams' car was left at the restaurant. It's a fifteen-minute drive to the Serantis beach house. The two women died about midnight and Lauren two hours later. Sasha Sheppard's credit card was used at the club at three AM."

After a moment of silence, with a sarcastic tone, Jay said, "Marcus Ramey expects to convince a jury that Sasha Sheppard started the killings about a half-hour after they left the bar, then two hours or so later killed her lover. Then somehow covered in blood, doped up on Ketamine and Rohypnol, was able to drive across town to the Club Palais du Plaisir. Where she supposedly was seen snorting cocaine that never showed up on the toxicology report and still managed to drive back to the beach house to cut her wrists."

Harry added, "It was a woman's voice who called in the nine-one-one at four-fifteen AM."

"You know what I think — Sasha Sheppard is being set up. She was drugged. Our killer is this fifth woman. This woman, or someone associated with her, used Sasha's credit card at the club to establish the drug binge. After Sasha's wrists were slashed, the caller waited until she thought Sasha had bled out enough to die, then called in the nine-one-one."

Harry leaned back in his chair. "Neat, cold, and calculating. You thinking what I'm thinking that these murders were a professional hit? Maybe to assure that Ingrid Sheppard doesn't make the White House home for the next four years."

"I think our killer is very clever and is leading us around by the fucking nose."

"I agree, Jay. And, Ramey, the bigot, was so damn eager to charge Sasha Sheppard with the murders that he jumped the gun without waiting for the autopsy reports or until we could investigate more thoroughly. The stupid S.O.B. went for three counts of first degree murder. Unbelievable. I'd hate to be in his shoes."

"Truer words. You're right. I wouldn't want to be in Ramey's shoes when Sidney DeRoche gets through with him. The bastard didn't have a case. Bob Redfern called me right after he'd read the reports and Hank's findings. He was livid and out for blood. He went after Ramey. The charges against Sheppard have been dropped."

"Holy shit." Harry fished in his pockets to pull out a stub of a cigar. "Have Sidney and Sheppard been told the charges have been dropped?"

"Bob was going to contact Ingrid. I have no doubt that the President will know how to get in touch with DeRoche. The press has crucified Sasha Sheppard. No doubt DeRoche will have plenty to say about that. Bob plans to hold a press conference to announce that the charges against Sasha Sheppard have been dropped. Ramey will grovel and give an official apology, but it won't do him any good. Redfern wants his hide and his job, and DeRoche will publicly castrate the bastard."

A rare smile crossed Harry's face. "I'd like to see that." He took a sip of his beer, then in a somber voice said, "That leaves us with a killer that's going to be hard to catch. Anything on the two officers that were killed?"

"The autopsy showed their necks were broken long before their car went off that cliff. Bad cops aren't too hard to find. My guess is that they were involved and then became a loose end and were silenced."

"I'm sure sorry about Grant, Jay. He was one of the good guys."

Jay gazed into her beer and nodded. "He sure was."

"There's a whole lot more to these murders than we know, Jay. I never thought for a moment that Sasha Sheppard committed them. I've seen a few murders in my day, and from the time I set foot in the Serantis beach house I had a feeling it had the makings of a professional hit that was made to look like Sheppard did it all drugged up. The only person that might be able to help nail this killer or know what was behind these murders would be Sasha

Sheppard. And it's my guess that can't be setting too well. This person will attempt to silence her."

Chapter Eighteen

Kayla slipped the backpack off her shoulders and put both arms over her head, locked her hands together, and stretched. "I'm glad we made it this far today. It's a perfect spot to make camp." She looked up at the clouds that had kept temperatures comfortable all day for hiking, then pointed to a grassy knoll. "Let's pitch the tent over there. It's high enough so we won't get wet if the melt-off swells the river."

Cassie removed her pack and walked a few feet to a pebbly beach. Squatting, she looked at the water with an expression of pure bliss on her face. "God, I just love it up here." She worked for the Forest Service when she wasn't training for the 2010 Winter Olympics. "There's a position posted in this district. When I start back to work next week, I think I'll apply."

Surprised, Kayla started to say something, but decided not to. It was a selfish thought. She liked being able to see Cassie every day when she was home. A transfer would mean Cassie would only be able to be home on her days off. "I'd miss you, but it is beautiful here. I can understand why you'd want to transfer."

"It's not that far a drive. Besides, when Liberty comes home, I'll be lucky to see you for the rest of the summer." Cassie looked at Kayla and winked. "If you know what I mean, big sis."

Kayla blushed. She missed Liberty and longed for her touch and to have her home. Liberty had stormed into her life, and brought desire and passion and love. "Cocky, aren't we? Why don't you use all that energy to help me set up camp?"

Waggling her eyebrows, Cassie hopped up and unstrapped the compact tent from her pack. By the time the sun sank behind the mountain, they had camp set up, kindling gathered, and a fire started. Within a short time they had finished eating, secured the campsite, and their packs were hung in a tree a safe distance away. Sitting around the fire drinking coffee, they rested in comfortable silence, each enjoying the peacefulness as they listened to the sounds of nature around them. After a bit, Cassie yawned, stood up, and walked to the river to rinse her cup. "I'm going to hit the hay. You coming?"

"You go ahead. I'll be along in a bit. If we get an early start tomorrow, we can make Granite Butte. Are you up for a bit of rock climbing? We could take the upper trail."

"Climb the face? You bet. But only if you think you can handle it. Wouldn't want you to strain yourself."

"In your dreams. Good night, Cassie."

"'Night, Kayla."

Kayla's mind filled with thoughts of her lover as she sat listening to the rhythmic sound of water flowing. Had she been wrong in not asking Liberty to stay? Would it get Liberty killed? Though it was a gradual change, she could see that Liberty was beginning to forgive herself for what she'd done as a Talon. She no longer kept a loaded gun under her side of the bed, and she didn't tighten up as often whenever a stranger entered the pub or approached her. Looking up at a gibbous moon, Kayla placed her fingers lightly over her heart and closed her eyes. *Come home, sweetheart. Please, just come home to me.*

Ingrid had been on a conference call well into the early hours of morning with Hu Jintao, the leader of the People's Republic of China. Within moments of hanging up, Marty appeared in the room and handed her the message from the Attorney General of California. "Bob said it's urgent and to call him back as soon as you can." Ingrid took in Marty's robe and slippered feet. "Did you get some sleep?"

"The bed isn't as comfortable as the one in Washington, but it'll do. Bob sounded anxious to talk to you. It must be important."

Ingrid was tired and her mind was on overload. Her first thought was that something had happened to her sister or that they had found her. She knew, though, if that were the case, Sidney or Liberty would have contacted her and Bob would have told Marty. "What do you think this is about?"

Handing Ingrid the phone, Marty said, "Honey, we won't know until you call him back."

The conversation with Bob was short. After Ingrid hung up, she went to sit next to Marty on the sofa. She sat for a moment without saying anything, then covered her face with her hands and started to cry. Marty, tears in her own eyes, gathered Ingrid into her arms. This woman she loved with all her heart was the President of the United States and the voice of a powerful country. She made decisions on a daily basis that affected millions of people and intervened in world crises with calm control. This gentle, unassuming, and powerful woman was crying like a baby in her arms. "I love you, Ingrid Sheppard."

Hoarse with emotion, Ingrid tried to tell Marty what Bob had told her. "They...Bob...the charges..."

"Honey, I heard. You were on speaker, and you repeated it twice after Bob told you." Marty tightened her arms around Ingrid, and they sat holding on to each other. A short while later, Ingrid placed a call to Liberty to tell her that the charges against her sister were being dropped. She asked where Sasha was and for a phone number. She wanted to be the one to tell her sister and Sidney.

Liberty gave Ingrid the information and told her to use the secured phone. When Ingrid said she was flying to California to get Sasha, Liberty reminded her that Scalzon was still out there and was hunting Sasha to kill her. "Please give me a few days before going to California. Your sister may be able to identify Scalzon and that makes her a target. She's better off where she is right now until I can find Scalzon and end this."

Lowering her head, Ingrid closed her eyes for a moment. When she opened them, she said, "You're right. Sasha's safety is more important than my selfish needs. I'll wait. When you first spoke the name Scalzon it wasn't unfamiliar to me. This terrorist-turned-mercenary has been on the top of terrorist lists of many countries. After the attempt on the hospital, I put all my resources into gathering information. Intelligence fingered Scalzon for the series of resort and hotel bombings in Morocco and Egypt as well as other countries around the world. This person is more than willing to work for any terrorist or extremist group, including Osama bin Laden. Anyone, who'll pay the price. Our intelligence tagged Scalzon for a recent bombing in Mexico that killed a known arms dealer."

"That's where she got the C-4. Scalzon is extremely intelligent and dangerous. My suspicion is she's a woman and can effortlessly morph from one identity to another, passing as a man or a woman. She leaves no predictable pattern. Most likely she hides in plain site in an unassuming identity."

"A woman? I'll be damned. What can I do to help you find her?"

"You and your family stay safe. I'll find her. To do this, I'll need to be under your sanction with a top clearance that will allow me to travel freely and by any means available."

"I can arrange that. You'll have that authorization in the time it takes me to make a call."

Liberty gave Ingrid the information where Sasha was, then said, "I'll be in touch."

It was early on the West Coast when the call from Ingrid came. Sasha broke down and sobbed after she talked to Ingrid. A pall of sorrow hung over the room as she wept for Lauren, Connie, and Kim. Sidney held her in her arms as grief poured from Sasha's heart.

"Dear God, Sid, why? Why would someone want to do this? If the evidence hadn't proven that I didn't do this monstrous thing, how could I have gone on? How could I have ever been sure that in some demented frame of mind it wasn't me? "

Beth stepped outside the room to allow Sasha the privacy to grieve. Leah, Page, and Gwen followed, each feeling the same compassion and helplessness, unable to imagine how one could survive losing the person you loved through such violence. No words spoken could ease Sasha's agony. Through the open door, Leah saw the tears that were running down Sidney's face as she held Sasha. Sidney was Sasha's lifeline, and Leah didn't fault Sidney's compassion or her kindness.

Gwen stepped closer to Leah and in a low voice said, "At least she can have the peace of knowing she wasn't responsible, but her ordeal isn't over. She may never get over this tragedy. She's going to need therapy and a lot of support. Until whoever did this is caught, she'll also need protection."

Now that the charges had been dropped, Leah didn't feel there was any immediate need to discuss or risk retrieving Sasha's memory. When Sasha was stronger, if she chose to pursue the treatment, it would be her decision. As Leah's eyes drifted back to Sasha's room, she shifted uncomfortably, feeling very much an outsider and that she was intruding on something very intimate as she watched Sidney with Sasha. The familiarity between them spoke of their past.

"Sasha's medical condition is stable. And you're right. She'll need help and therapy. You're more qualified to help her with that than I am. The hospital needs me right now." Unable to hide the emotion she was feeling, Leah knew she needed to get away from there.

Gwen and Page were waiting in the sitting area outside Sasha's room when Sidney came out a few hours later, looking exhausted. "She's emotionally drained and has cried herself out." Sidney's tired eyes searched the room. "Where's Leah?"

Gwen exchanged looks with Page. "She left to go back to Laguna. They needed her at the hospital."

Shocked, Sidney stared at Gwen. "She just left...without telling me?" Her face paled. "Did she leave me a message?"

"Sidney, with the state Sasha was in, you had your hands full. I don't think Leah wanted to disturb you. She did say she would call you when she got to the hospital."

"But...I thought no one was to leave the villa because of the danger it would put them in. Nothing has happened to change that."

"No, and Armanno did try to talk to Leah. He reinforced what danger she could be putting herself in, but Leah was adamant about leaving and Armanno was not going to physically stop her. He did send two of his people with her. The board of directors at SCMC is considering closing the hospital. Leah is afraid if they do, even if they say it's only temporary, the hospital will not reopen."

Confused and shaken, Sidney turned and walked down the hall toward her room to call Leah.

Up early, Kayla and Cassie broke camp and were on the trail before the sun chased the chill of morning away. When they came to the trailhead of Granite Butte, they veered to the right, to the trail marked Experienced Level, which would take them to the rocky face of the butte. Halfway along the trail, Kayla stopped and stood perfectly still. Raising her fingers to her lips, she looked at Cassie who understood and stood quietly.

Kayla listened for a long minute, then motioned for Cassie to continue up the trail. "I thought I heard something. Too light-footed to be a bear. Could be a mountain lion stalking us, but I don't think so. Plenty of game this spring, so it's unlikely a cougar would be hungry enough to attack us. Never know, though. Probably just my imagination, but be on the alert."

"Will do. Do you think we'll reach the cliffs with enough light left to make the climb?"

"Barring any unforeseen delays, we should." Kayla had deliberately let Cassie lead. Last night before she turned in, she'd caught the smell of a campfire not too far from their campsite. She couldn't shake the feeling of being watched. It was odd, because the sounds of the forest had quieted and that had bothered her.

Dressed in his pajama bottoms, Bob Redfern stumbled down the stairs of his home in his bare feet to answer the persistent ringing of the doorbell. He'd been up most of the night waiting for a return call from Ingrid and had just gotten back to sleep. He flipped on the porch light and looked through the side window to see Jay Brunelle impatiently pacing in front of his door. As he opened the door he said to his wife, who was standing at the top of the stairs, "Go back to bed, honey, it's Chief Brunelle."

Jay's face was flushed as she hurried inside. "Sorry to wake you, Bob, but I have something very important I want you to see."

Bob knew whatever it was that brought Jay to his home so early had her excited. "It looks like you slept in your clothes. Come on, I'll fix some coffee."

Jay followed Bob into the kitchen and took a seat at the counter while Bob pushed the button overriding the timer on the coffeepot. While the coffee was brewing, Bob took two mugs out of the cupboard and set them on the counter. "Let's see what you have." He sat speechless as Jay laid out the reports and documents she found in Grant's safety deposit box. The last message she received from Grant contained a small note saying that he'd put the deed to her share of the property in his safety deposit box. She'd read over it every time until it hit her that Grant didn't have the deed, she did. She had access to Grant's box. In it she found what Grant had discovered that would blow this case wide open.

When Jay was done showing Bob the documents he was shaking. Infuriated, he slammed his hand down on the kitchen table, making Jay jump.

"Nine people dead because Lauren Serantis was going to stop a drug her company was going to release when she found out the test results had been tampered with. These bastards hired someone to kill three women to frame Sasha Sheppard for it, in the process ruining Ingrid's chance for reelection. Their assassin would have taken out an entire hospital and everyone in it to get to Sasha Sheppard because if she could remember she would blow their little scheme to hell and back. All to put a defective drug on the market that could potentially endanger the lives of thousands so they could pocket billions. Who knows how many people would have died by the time the FDA got off their asses."

Bob stalked across the floor and picked up the phone. After making several calls, he said to Jay, "My dear mother always said that the most dangerous cutthroats of all were the ones that sit in big houses. I have no intentions of waiting on the bureaucracy of the Department of Justice. We're moving on this now before the warrants I've asked for are leaked and those bastards can destroy any evidence."

In no time the search warrants had been served and Bob and Jay stood together supervising the removal of numerous computers and records from the offices of Serantis Pharmaceuticals and the homes of two members of the board.

As the door slammed shut on the last truckload, Bob's cell rang. He answered and listened for a few minutes. "How long will it take you to get those warrants? Make the arrests and read them their rights twice — in front of witnesses. Everything by the book."

When he hung up, he turned to Jay and said, "David McCall wired a total of $5 million to a Swiss bank account before the murders. Out of respect to Serantis, Jillian Bennett proposed that the release of their new wonder drug be delayed. The two of them have been doing a little illegal insider trading during their mourning by buying up shares of the company that had dropped after Lauren Serantis' death. They planned to buy up what they could, then make a killing when the drug was released. It's enough to arrest and hold them both until we can go through their computers. My office is being bombarded with calls. I need to get back."

Bob opened his car door, but before he got in he looked at Jay and said, "Good work, Chief."

Han Kiong's detailed portrait of a killing played in Jay's mind as she stood in the middle of the bedroom where the women had been brutally murdered. The darkened bloodstains throughout the room were testament to what had happened there. Constance Williams had been killed tied to the bed. Kim Lang died on the floor with her hand outstretched, crawling toward her lover. Lauren Serantis died on the deck trying to run for her life. Three women with everything to offer and live for were murdered so a few greedy people could line their pockets.

Jay walked through the house. Everywhere she looked she saw personal little things that told of their lives. A reminder on the refrigerator saying, "Pick up the laundry. I love you." Two toothbrushes in the holder and a lipstick left on the vanity. In the living room were pictures of Sasha and Lauren smiling at each other.

Opening the doors that led to the deck that overlooked the Pacific, she stared at the bloodstains where Lauren had died. Anger raged in Jay's gut. She went to stand by the railing to rid her senses of the stench of their unconscionable deaths. She wanted this killer so bad she was shaking inside. When she heard a noise behind her, Jay stiffened and her hand went to her holster. Before she could draw her weapon, a voice said, "No need to draw your weapon."

With the sun in her eyes, Jay turned to see Liberty standing in the shadows at top of the stairs that spiraled up from the beach.

"This is getting to be a habit. If I'm right, you're the one who broke into Grant's house and took the hard drive from his computer."

"If I had the hard drive, no one else would have access to it. It was possible he put something in his notes, something that only you would know and the killer would want, that could get you killed. I watched the stuff being hauled out of Serantis Pharmaceuticals and the homes of David McCall and Jillian Bennett. The attorney general's office didn't have too much difficulty finding what I'm sure McCall and Bennett thought were cleverly hidden bank accounts."

"It doesn't surprise me that you already know about Serantis Pharmaceuticals. Something tells me you had something to do with the attorney general's office knowing about McCall's buying up the stock and where to find the information about the bank accounts."

The feeling that Jay knew this woman was so overwhelming she moved so the sun wasn't blinding her. As she did, Liberty stepped out from the shadow.

Jay searched Liberty's face for a moment before her eyes widened with recognition. "Nicole...Nicole Stephens?"

Cassie and Kayla made good time until they came to a tributary that branched off the river where they usually crossed. Cassie took off her pack and stood on the bank. "Spring melt. It looks pretty high. We can't cross here. It wouldn't be safe. Besides, we'd get wet. I'm going upstream a ways to see if I can find another place where we can cross."

Kayla slipped off her pack and dropped it to the ground. "We'll make camp and start the climb at first light."

As Cassie worked her way upstream along the bank, Kayla stooped to unzip her pack to get an energy bar. When a shadow fell in front of her, she turned to see a woman pointing a pistol at her. "If you yell, I'll put a bullet in your sister's head."

Kayla was stunned, but her instincts and the unemotional cold look in the woman's eyes told her that this woman meant what she said. She swallowed the lump in her throat and said, "What do you want?"

"I want you. Pick up your backpack and start back down the trail. If you hesitate and your sister returns before we leave, she's dead."

Kayla lifted her pack and stood. "Good choice. Now get moving." Scalzon picked up Cassie's pack and threw it in the fast-moving water.

Angry, Kayla started toward Scalzon, then stopped when Scalzon raised the pistol. "What the hell did you do that for?"

With a look of amusement Scalzon said, "You're wasting valuable time. Do you prefer we wait for her to return? It just might be easier to kill her now."

Be cool, Kayla. Just get far enough away so Cassie isn't in danger then think what to do. Kayla slung her pack over her shoulders and started back along the trail at a fast pace, knowing that Cassie would follow. Somehow she had to let Cassie know the danger they were in, to not approach, and to stay out of sight.

Meanwhile, upstream, Cassie found a place where they could cross. She worked her way back to where she'd left Kayla. Not seeing her, she called out her name. When she didn't get an answer, she looked around and saw that both packs were missing. First confusion, then panic started to set in. She turned around in a circle calling Kayla's name.

After a few moments she stopped and tried to control her breathing and calm down. Her mind was frantically trying to think of what to do when she spotted two sets of footprints on the damp ground leading back the way they had come. One set of tracks had the same tread as hers and had to be Kayla's. She knew that Kayla would never leave her willingly. Something or someone forced her to do it. Taking in deeps breaths to quell the nausea she felt, she knew that Kayla was in trouble and needed her help.

Whoever had Kayla had to know that she'd follow. Instead of taking the trail, Cassie started to run along the tributary toward the river. If the water wasn't too high, she could follow a trail that paralleled the river in the same direction the footprints were heading. She pulled out her cell phone and turned it on. The signal was weak, but she was able to get a scratchy connection to Nathan. She darn near went to her knees with relief when her brother answered on the second ring. Cassie yelled into the receiver as she ran, "Nathan, the signal is low. Someone has Kayla. I'm following them back toward the trailhead of Granite Butte. Find Liberty."

Chapter Nineteen

Jay's eyes swept over Liberty. After the breakup with Leah she had been lost. Lonely and hurting. She'd let an attractive Australian pick her up in the base cantina, a woman who said her name was Nicole Stephens. They'd had a brief affair during her last tour of duty in the Middle East. The hair and eyes were a different color, but the woman standing in front of her was, without a doubt, Nicole.

Jay's confused brown eyes never left Liberty's. "Everything seemed good between us. You just disappeared one day. No note, no goodbye, nothing." Finally breaking eye contact, Jay turned to stare out at the Pacific. "You've lost your Aussie accent. That night at Big Sur you told me you had been asked to look into the murders by Ingrid Sheppard. Who do you work for? The CIA, Special Ops?"

When Liberty had spotted Jay in the base cantina, she knew the look. The attractive captain was trying to drown her sorrow and would be vulnerable. It was easy to strike up a conversation and, with the base under construction, plausible to explain that she was one of the civilian builders being housed on base. A week later when she told Jay her bunk in the barracks was being allocated to a higher-up, Jay invited her to stay at her quarters on base, a small one-bedroom apartment in a fourplex until another bunk became available. She'd used Jay, but she also developed feelings for her.

Understanding Jay's distrust, Liberty quietly answered, "I don't work for any government agency. Not any more." After a moment's hesitation, she continued, "I needed a place to stay that wouldn't draw suspicion. I left the way I did because it was the only way. I was involved in something that I couldn't explain to you, and it could have brought a lot of trouble down on you. We weren't in love with each other. We were casualties of our own wars and needed each other."

As angry as she was, Jay knew Nicole, or Liberty, was telling it as it was. "It was bad timing — for both of us." *But the sex was unforgettable.*

They looked at each other for a long moment, then Jay cleared her throat and said, "I should arrest your ass and throw you in jail. You broke into Grant's house and stole his hard drive, and I'll bet my badge that you're the one who took Sasha Sheppard out of the hospital and hid her out."

"If I did those things, it was best for everyone. Sasha's life is still in danger and if Nolte's hard drive fell into the wrong hands, dangerous for you."

"When did you become my guardian angel? I'm capable of watching out for myself, and if given the chance, protecting Sasha Sheppard."

You wouldn't say that if you knew who you'd be going against. "I understand they dropped the charges against Sasha Sheppard even before you found the evidence that would have cleared her. The best of capitalism, alive and well."

"You have to admire Lauren Serantis. Even though she'd invested everything in the development of this drug, she was going to blow the whistle on the lot of 'em. If they'd been successful and this scheme went unexposed it would have endangered many. Money is a strong motivation for murder. These people conspired, and paid a bundle, to kill Serantis and prevent her from stopping the release of Novastol."

"The person they hired is the very best. A very clever assassin, who created an intricate web, leading everyone to believe that Sasha Sheppard did the killing in a drug-induced rage."

"You know who this killer is, don't you? And you're going to tell me."

Just as Liberty started to say something her cell rang. A worried look crossed her face as she took the cell from her pocket and saw that it was Armanno. Flipping open the phone, she said, "What is it?" The color drained from her face as she listened. "How long ago... You've sent your plane? I'll be at the airport in ten minutes."

Shaken, Liberty turned to leave.

"Hey, hold on. You have a habit of disappearing. You're not leaving until I get an answer to my question. Do you know who this killer is?"

The warning in Liberty's eyes and in the tone of her voice was deadly. "I don't have time for this."

Jay unhooked the handcuffs from the back of her belt. "Make time or I'm placing you under arrest."

Liberty shifted her weight and threw two blows and a kick that caught Jay off guard and swept her off her feet. Stunned, Jay landed hard on her back. Liberty was halfway through the living room when she was tackled from behind, knocking both her and Jay to the floor. Jay was a match for Liberty in strength, and after landing a few good blows of her own, she was able to straddle Liberty and pin one of Liberty's arms behind her back. Breathing hard, Jay used her weight to keep Liberty face down on the floor. "Don't you fucking move or I'll break it. I want this killer just as much or more than you do. You can lead me to her. So where you go, I go, or you're not going anywhere but to jail."

Tightening her hold, Jay applied more pressure to Liberty's arm. When Liberty nodded, Jay eased her hold. Liberty quickly brought her head back, hitting Jay on the bridge of her nose with enough force that Jay lost her hold. A second later, her face filled with rage, Liberty was straddling Jay, holding a knife against her throat.

Holding her breath, Jay froze. The knife was cutting into her skin. A long moment passed as Liberty stared wild-eyed down at Jay. Finally, Liberty said, "You heard my conversation and know I'm going to the airport. A jet is waiting for me. A life is at stake. I can't have you doing anything to interfere with that plane taking off."

The knife cut deeper as Jay carefully chose her words. She had to take the chance that Liberty wouldn't kill her. "You can kill me, but I don't think you will. Or you can stop wasting time and take me with you, and we can sort this out on the way to wherever you're heading."

Liberty lowered her face until it was less than an inch away from Jay's. "When I let you up, if you make a move to stop me, I'm warning you, I will kill you. Now get the hell up and don't say a fucking word."

Cassie's lungs burned as she ran along the river, cursing when she had to make her way through water up to her waist and around obstacles that slowed her down. If she could reach the trailhead first, she might be able to surprise whoever had Kayla and do something to help her. Something bobbing in the water caught her eye, and her heart froze. Her limbs trembled as she stumbled along the bank to get a better look. Going to her knees in relief, she covered her face with her hands and cried, "It isn't Kayla. It's my pack."

Getting to her feet, she broke a branch from a nearby tree and waded out as far as she could. Using the branch, she was able to snag the backpack out of the water. Hauling it along would slow her down, but it could mean her survival if whoever had Kayla went deeper into the wilderness instead of staying on the trail. "Thank you, God, for water proofing."

The energy Cassie had expended was telling. She needed to hydrate. She retrieved a power bar and a bottle of water from her pack, then slung the pack onto her back and started to run again, stopping only to answer her cell when it vibrated in her chest pocket. She fumbled, nearly dropping the phone in the water. "Nathan?"

"Cassie, tell me what happened." When Cassie heard Liberty's voice, she started to cry. "Cassie, you need to listen to me carefully, okay?"

Trying to compose herself Cassie said, "Yes, I'm listening."

"Tell me what happened."

Cassie told what little she knew, then Liberty said, "I believe Kayla has been taken by a woman who is very dangerous. No matter what happens, or what you see, you are not to approach Kayla or let this woman see you. She'll not hesitate to kill you and Kayla. The reason you aren't dead already is because you were needed to contact me. If you become a threat, she'll hurt Kayla until you show yourself, and then she'll kill you." *Scalzon, you bitch! This isn't about getting Sasha anymore. By now you know that the people who paid your price have been arrested and it's over. It's me you want.*

"Cassie, I don't question your skills or your ability, but don't be fooled. This woman is as comfortable in the forest as you are. You said they're heading back down the trial toward where the truck is parked. You know the area well, make your way back, but stay out of sight and don't get near the truck. It could be rigged to explode. Keep your cell on vibrate and call me if you see them. Do you understand me? You need to do exactly what I'm telling you."

"Yes...yes, I understand."

"I'm on my way."

"Please hurry."

They had been in the air for an hour. At a speed of 440 knots, Armanno's small jet would land in Kalispell in a little over an hour. Liberty opened a closet and took out a pair of fatigues, boots, and two camouflage jackets, not surprised that Armanno kept the plane as well-equipped as it was when the Talons used it for missions. *You're only going with me so far, Jay, but you'll freeze your ass off without a jacket.* Throwing one of the jackets at Jay, she said, "It can get cold where we're going." Her eyes went to Jay's boots. "Those will do." She turned her back and started to strip out of her clothes.

When Liberty removed her shirt, Jay sucked in a breath. She'd explored every inch of this woman's body. The burns and scars on Liberty's back hadn't been there when they'd made love. She'd seen wounds of torture; someone had painfully worked Liberty over. "Jesus, what the hell happened to you?"

Liberty turned and shot Jay a look that sent a shock wave through the cabin, stopping Jay cold. Liberty was preparing for the most important battle of her life and didn't need Jay breaking her concentration. "Cut the chatter. I'd just as soon send you head first out that door."

Silently Jay watched as Liberty changed, then reached in the closet to retrieve a case. In it was her custom-made sniper rifle. Next she took out a Sig P226 9MM and several clips. After placing a clip in the weapon, she shoved the pistol in a holster, then threw Jay a clip. She carried the same weapon. Last was a knife that Liberty placed in the sheath of her boot. *Jesus, she looks like she's going to war. She could have killed me easily back in Laguna, but she didn't. Who in the hell are we going after?*

Liberty took out her cell and placed a call. "Nathan, we'll be landing in..." she looked at her watch, "thirty-two minutes. Is the helicopter there?" *Kayla, please hang on. Know I'm coming.* Without another word she hung up and sat rigidly, looking straight ahead. She was going to a place in her mind she'd locked away. A place where the Ghost, the Talon assassin, still existed.

Observing the deadly look in Liberty's eyes sent a chill down Jay's spine. She'd seen the same look in the eyes and on the faces of the spooks and operatives of Delta's Special Forces during her time in the Middle East.

Kayla kept up a good pace, wanting to put as much distance as possible between her and the woman behind her. Her adrenaline was pumping so fast that it was making it hard to think. One minute she and Cassie were enjoying the hike, the next she had a gun stuck in her face and this woman was threatening to kill them both. Nervously, Kayla glanced over her shoulder, hoping for a chance to slip her hand into her jacket pocket and get her cell, but the woman's eyes never left her. With every step, Kayla was frantic with worry that Cassie would catch up with them.

She could hear the sound of the river through the trees on her left and knew they were coming to a stretch where the river met the trail and switchbacked up a steep, rocky terrain. Those familiar with the trail knew to wait until one hiker made it to the top before following to avoid being caught in a rockslide and ending up in the river below. *If I can get ahead and loosen the rocks to create a slide, she could lose her footing. The water is swift enough to carry her downstream. I can double back and find Cassie.*

Just a few more yards to go. Kayla's heart was pounding as she climbed. The woman stayed close behind. All Kayla needed was a couple of feet between them. Halfway up Kayla decided to take a chance and pretended to fall forward. Bracing herself on her hands, she dug her boots in and kicked at the loose rocks. When the rocks under her started to slide, she took a deep breath and scrambled on all fours toward the top. Without looking back, she started to sprint across a clearing toward the trees. She thought she was going to make it when she heard the shots and felt dirt and rocks spitting up against her boots and legs. Kayla stood dead still, waiting for the bullet that would take her life. "If you so much as twitch, the next shot will take your head off."

Cassie had reached the spot where the river path and the trail intersected and zigzagged up and over the shale-ridden side of the hill. She'd have to climb it and work her way down on the other side to pick up the path along the river. She froze when she looked up and saw a woman standing at the crest. Backing away, she heard shots and a woman's voice threatening. Fear for Kayla propelled Cassie up the hill. When she got to the top, she saw Kayla standing with her back to a woman who was walking toward her. When the woman was a foot away, she said, "Turn around."

When Kayla turned and saw Cassie, she managed to raise her hand to signal Cassie to stay put before Scalzon hit her across the face with the gun, knocking her to the ground. To Scalzon it must have looked like a defensive move, because she didn't turn around. When she pressed the gun against Kayla's skull, Cassie yelled, "Noooo."

Scalzon swung around and fired twice, hitting Cassie and knocking her backwards. She plunged down the hill. Blood streaming down her face, Kayla struggled to get up off the ground as Scalzon moved toward where Cassie had gone over. Cassie's body was bobbing up and down in the turbulent water. Before Scalzon could get another shot off, Kayla was able to get close enough to launch herself at the woman, knocking them both to the ground. She held on as Scalzon hit her about the head and face. Then everything went black.

Kayla was jerked from unconsciousness when she felt the wetness on her face. Sputtering, she opened her eyes to see Scalzon standing over her holding an empty water bottle. Her hands were tied behind her, and when she tried to get up she fell back. Excruciating pain tore through her head, and she spit blood from her mouth.

"I should put a bullet right between your eyes. If you say a word, I'll cut your tongue out. Get up."

Closing her eyes, Kayla felt the cold ground under her. She hurt all over and didn't know if she could get up. *I don't care if she kills me. Dear God, is Cassie dead? Did she kill her?*

"I said get up. Do you want your lover to find you gutted in this very spot? She will if you don't get up and start moving."

Liberty! Oh God, she's after Liberty. Kayla forced herself to focus. In her mind she pictured herself on the top of a mountain preparing to make that one run. All her work came down to one run. For years she'd trained her body and her mind to displace distraction — cold, pain, or anything that would cost her a split second in the race for the Gold. In her chest beat the heart of a champion. Her love for Liberty was stronger than her defeat.

Kayla rolled to her side, got on her knees, then struggled to stand. Taking a moment to steady herself, she turned her head to wipe the blood that was running down her face on her sleeve. Then, with an unsteady gait, she started to walk toward the trees and the trail. With every painful step she vowed that this woman was not going to use her to kill Liberty.

Chapter Twenty

"South Coast Medical Center. This is Diane."

"Diane, this is Sidney DeRoche. Is Doctor Stanhope there?"

"She was, but she's in a meeting, Sidney. I'm not sure if I'll see her before I leave, but I can transfer you to her service so you can leave a message."

"Thanks, Diane, I've already left several messages. If you do see her, please tell her I called."

"Will do, Sidney."

Sidney hung up, angry and annoyed that Leah hadn't called. "You just walk out of here without saying a word to me and you've not returned my calls?" Throwing the cell on the bed, she left the room and walked down the hall to stand in front of the door to Sasha's room. Her anger had settled into an ache inside. She knocked lightly and waited.

"Come in."

When Sidney stepped inside, Sasha was dressed and standing by the window. "You feel like company?"

"No, but you, yes. Please come in, Sid."

"I checked on you a while ago. You were lying down. Did you sleep?"

Sasha shook her head. "Every time I close my eyes I see horrible images and I hear the screams. I hear Lauren calling my name. I want to wake up and for this all to be a bad nightmare. But I'm awake and Lauren is still gone." Tears filled Sasha's eyes as she turned back toward the window. "I still can't remember what happened. Just bits and pieces. Where do I go from here? How can I go on?"

Closing the distance between them, Sidney stood next to Sasha, put her arms around her, and gently hugged her.

"You'll go on because you have family and friends who need and love you, and who'll be there for you. Ingrid and Marty want you to come and stay with them. They want the girls to get to know their aunt." Sidney tightened her arms around Sasha. They stood that way for a few moments until Sasha voiced her fears.

"What if they never find the person who killed them? I can't hide or stay here forever. I need to take care of things. Arrangements need to be made for Lauren's...for her...services."

"Honey, did Lauren have any family?"

"No, no family. Just me. Lauren's attorney handled both our wills and directives." Sasha shook as she buried her face in her hands. "Dear God, Connie and Kim are dead, too."

She looks so pale and so thin. She's living a nightmare. How much more sorrow and pain can she endure? What would I ever do if I lost...Leah? Sidney took Sasha's hand and led her over to the sofa. "Come sit with me, please." Still holding Sasha's hand, Sidney said, "I'll call Connie's office. Everything will be on file. You don't have to do this alone."

Trying to express the gratitude she felt, Sasha raised her eyes and looked at Sidney. "You being here and your kindness have kept me going." *I loved Lauren, but I never stopped loving you.* Sasha struggled to find the words she needed to say to Sidney. Her voice shook as she spoke.

"We never saw each other or talked after that day you came home and found me with those women. No one forced me to start on the cocaine again. That was me kidding myself that I could handle it and telling myself what you didn't know...I knew that I'd betrayed the love we had for each other." Sasha raised her eyes that were filled with pain. "I...I'm so sorry, Sid."

A hand reached in and squeezed Sidney's heart. It still hurt. "Thank you for telling me now. That's all in the past. Let's leave it there, okay?"

Squeezing Sidney's hand, Sasha said, "You've been a dear friend, Sid. Just saying thank you will never be enough."

Pushing a strand of dark hair from Sasha's forehead, Sidney kissed her softly on the cheek. "You would have done the same for me."

"Yes, I would have. Gwen was here just before you came in. When I asked her where Doctor Stanhope was, she said she'd gone back to Laguna. I remember Uncle Isaac telling me you fell in love with a doctor that worked at SCMC. Is Doctor Stanhope your partner?"

"Yes, she is. I'm sorry. With everything, there hasn't been a time to tell you that. Hey, are you up for a surprise? Well, I guess if I tell you it won't be a surprise."

"What is it?"

"Ingrid is on her way here. She should be here any time now."

"God, she doesn't need to do that. She shouldn't do that. She has a reelection campaign to worry about, and all this couldn't have helped any. Please, call her and ask her not to come."

"Even if I tried I couldn't keep her away. The reason Ingrid hasn't been here with you is because of her concern for your safety.

She would jeopardize everything she's worked for, and her career, to protect you. Up until a few hours ago, she didn't know where you were. If she had, she would have refused to say because you would have been taken back to Laguna and put in jail. You would be too vulnerable and too easy to get to there. When the charges against you were dropped and the people behind the scheme were exposed, nothing was going to keep her away. Sasha, never doubt that Ingrid loves you very much."

They both looked toward the door when they heard, "Sidney's right. I do love you very much and I wasn't about to stay away."

Ingrid stood in the doorway wearing sneakers, an old pair of jeans, and a hooded sweatshirt. Sasha's hand went to her trembling lips. "I can't believe Marty let you out of the house wearing those clothes. Aren't you supposed to be the Prez?"

Moisture filled Ingrid's eyes as her long legs crossed the room. She lifted Sasha off the couch and took her in her arms. "Always the smart mouth."

Sasha sobbed as her arms went around her sister. "There's so much I want to say...to tell you."

Both sisters were crying when Sidney slipped out of the room and went downstairs to the kitchen. Hattie was adding vegetables to soup that was simmering on the stove. "Handsome woman. She's much taller and younger-looking in person. If you're all hungry, I made soup."

Hattie rinsed her hands and dried them on her apron, then put the tea kettle on. "You look like you could use a cup of tea."

"It shows, huh? A cup of tea would be great, Hattie. Mind if I take a walk first?"

"It's a good evening for a walk. The breeze off the ocean keeps the air in the valley clean and the sky clear. Take the path behind the villa. When you see the sign that says Cipriano turn left. It will lead you to the bluff overlooking the ocean. It's just a short distance. There's a sweater hanging next to the door."

The path took Sidney along a stretch of grapevines. She returned the waves of a few workers as she walked by. When she reached the sign she turned left, and a few minutes later she was on the bluff. A gazebo sat on the highest point, allowing a spectacular view for miles. She'd never felt so lonely in her life. Taking a deep breath, she tried to sort things out in her mind. She didn't know how long she'd been sitting there when she heard Ingrid's voice. "Beautiful, isn't it?"

"Hey, you. What's that you have in your hand?"

Holding up two long neck bottles, Ingrid chuckled. "Well, it ain't tea, and Hattie was the one who suggested I bring them along."

Ingrid twisted the cap off of one and handed it to Sidney, then sat beside her, opened the other, and took a sip. "A view like this makes me homesick. Sometimes I wonder why I want to serve another four years in the White House. It's been hard on Marty and the girls. And it's been hard on my sister." Ingrid looked at Sidney. "Your eyes are puffy. You've been crying. Sasha told me that Leah left."

"And I thought I was good at cross-examining." Sidney looked out at the water. She loved everything about the ocean. The smell, its serenity, and its power. Nothing was as mesmerizing as a stormy sea or as soothing when it had appeased its anger and lay calm and peaceful. She'd prepared her best presentations and worked through many a problem while pondering the mystery of the sea. "Yes, she did. Page and Gwen are here, and the hospital needed her."

"I'll ask you what you asked me in the hospital. Why do I get the feeling that's not the entire story? This case, Sasha being back in your life, has taken its toll on your relationship with Leah. I know you, Sid. Think about it. You wanted to protect me by representing Sasha. You were in conflict and emotionally sealed yourself off from Leah."

Did I? Have I taken an emotional step away from Leah?

Ingrid slid over and put her arm around Sidney's shoulders and pulled her close. "Remember all the nights the three of us studied until dawn, then sat together like this and watched the sun come up? We were so arrogant. Hot shit, so impatient to show the world what we had."

Remembering, Sidney laid her head on Ingrid's shoulder and smiled. "We *were* hot shit, but it's hard to believe we were ever that young and idealistic. God, it seems so long ago. You and I were so arrogant, weren't we? But not Marty. She was our rock. You lucked out when she caught you."

Ingrid smiled and took a sip of her beer, then said, "True, that I did. She's the love of my life and she's given me two beautiful daughters."

They sat quietly until Sidney sighed and said, "You may be right about me emotionally shutting Leah out. Any advice on how I should fix this?"

"You've a good start by understanding how Leah might feel. Leah knows you love her, but no woman is above jealousy, and

192 ❖ J.P. Mercer

funny things can go on in the head when it comes to an ex-lover. Get down on your knees and tell her you're sorry. Make love to your woman."

Sidney turned and looked at Ingrid. "Why, Madam President, Miss know-it-all. Is that how you solve all your problems? Does Marty fall for that one every time?"

Ingrid's face broke a big grin. "No, but I do keep trying."

Putting her head back down on Ingrid's shoulder, Sidney said, "I miss her so much. All I want to do is go home, but I promised Sasha I'd be here for her. She's lost, and she's going to need professional help to get through this and for those who love her to be close."

"And she will. I'm taking her home with me. We'll be leaving when you and I get back. Before you say anything, I need to tell you that the person they hired to murder those women has taken a hostage, and Liberty Starr and Jay Brunelle have gone to Montana. Trust me. I'll keep Sasha safe. No one will get to her. I promise you that. And she'll get all the love she can handle."

"A hostage! My God, why?"

"We'll have to wait to know the motivation and pray that Starr and Brunelle can get this sick bitch."

"Bitch?" Sidney couldn't believe what she was hearing. "My, God. It's the woman on the plane! This just keeps getting worse."

"A very dangerous woman by the name of Scalzon. She's a mercenary and one of the world's most wanted terrorists. McCall and Bennett paid a high price to make sure that Lauren Serantis didn't pull that drug. I was thinking about the cost to bring a drug to market, about $200 million. If Serantis had pulled the plug, the stocks wouldn't have been worth the paper they were written on. Serantis Pharmaceuticals would have folded. Creates a lot of pressure and encourages exactly what happened. I want to put my support behind the recommendation made to Congress that a separate agency be created to continuously monitor drug safety. We need to eliminate loopholes like a drug's fast-track status, which can be bought, and we need to enact tougher watchdog regulations. Too many proven and potentially dangerous side effects are being ignored, and harmful drugs are being marketed. Novastol was one of them. The FDA should not be politically susceptible to pressure and should be above graft and corruption."

In front of Sidney sat her friend dressed in jeans drinking a beer, but every inch of Ingrid Sheppard shouted that she was the President of the United States. Sidney delighted in the conviction on Ingrid's face as she talked. "You just answered your own question why another term. This country needs you and that's why you'll win this election."

"Maybe so."

"And organizing this agency will take time and hard work. You'll have to appoint someone that can wade through all the legal bullshit they'll throw at you."

After taking her last sip of beer, Ingrid stood and held out her hand. "Yep. You think you know someone who might be interested? It doesn't pay much."

Taking Ingrid's hand, Sidney stood. "I might."

"You ready to talk to that woman of yours?"

Sidney nodded. "I am. I just hope she'll forgive me."

Ingrid grinned. "I hear tell that you're a most convincing mouthpiece. And..." Ingrid kissed Sidney on the cheek. "You'll get your chance soon enough. I believe that's your lovely lady coming along the path now."

Sidney turned. "How...?"

"Air Force One is a bit conspicuous. Uncle Isaac sent his plane for me, and I sent it to pick Leah up. It's less than a half-hour flight. Stay, talk with her, then take her and just go. Turn off your cell. Find a place with no television and don't buy a newspaper. I'll call you next week."

Sidney's eyes were on Leah, who had stopped a few feet away. Ingrid walked toward Leah and gave her a hug, then waved to Sidney and went on down the path toward the villa. Simultaneously, Sidney and Leah blurted out, "I'm sorry." Leah opened her arms. Sidney ran into them and buried her face in Leah's neck. Ingrid looked back and smiled, feeling pretty damn good.

Nathan's eyes scanned the sky over the snow-capped peaks as he paced alongside the helicopter. His stomach was fisted into a ball of nerves and he was fighting the urge to vomit. After Cassie had called and told him Kayla had been taken, he'd called Armanno, who told him to do nothing until Liberty contacted him. He warned Nathan not to contact the authorities or it could cost Kayla her life.

Nathan was torn. Liberty had come into their lives out of nowhere at a time when she was needed. Kayla fell in love with her, and he had no doubt that Liberty loved her in return. Cassie adored Liberty, and Nathan liked and respected her. But Nathan had always been afraid that Liberty's past would one day haunt them all. That day had come.

A glint of silver appeared over the mountain. Nathan stopped pacing and stood watching as the plane descended and landed at Glacier Park International Airport. When the door opened, Liberty and another woman climbed out and scrambled down the stairs. Liberty walked straight to the helicopter and stowed the rifle and other gear, then stood next to Nathan to look at the map spread out on the front seat.

"You know the Swan Mountain Range?"

With a grim look on her face, Liberty nodded, her eyes fixed on the map. Unable to contain his frustration and anger, Nathan slammed his fist against the chopper. "Who in the hell would do this? What do they want with Kayla?"

With steely eyes that showed no emotion, Liberty looked Nathan straight in the eye and answered, "She was taken because of me." With no further explanation she looked back at the map and pointed. "Cassie said they were here, heading toward Granite Butte, when Kayla was taken and that their tracks led back toward the trailhead." Liberty folded the map. It was going to be dark before they reached the Swan Crest Ranger Station, where a Jeep would be waiting. From there it would be a half-hour drive to where Kayla and Cassie parked the truck.

"You want me to take her up, Nathan?"

Nathan shook his head and climbed into the pilot's seat. Liberty motioned for Jay to get in and then went around and got in the seat next to Nathan. "Let's go."

Nathan was a good pilot, and the helicopter the Sinclairs had invested in had enhanced their business by offering skiers the thrill of the high altitude basins filled with untouched powder and the challenge of skiing heart-racing peaks and fall lines. In the summer Nathan shuttled guests for overnight camping trips into northwestern Montana's high alpine lakes country.

Twenty minutes later they set down at the ranger station. Liberty grabbed the rifle and gear, then jumped out and stalked toward the jeep. After placing them into the Jeep, Liberty looked at Nathan, who had given Jay his hat and gloves and was standing a few feet away. She said, "I'll bring them both back. Be ready when I call." Then she turned to Jay and said, "This is as far as you go."

"That's not your decision to make."

Jay barely managed to get both feet in the Jeep before Liberty shoved it into first gear and spun out. She left a trail of dust and Nathan watching the tail lights as the vehicle sped down the road.

The temperature dropped considerably when the sun went down. The Jeep had a soft-top, and the heater did little to keep the chill out. Jay was thankful that she had on the warm jacket and the ski cap and gloves Nathan had given her. It wasn't long before Liberty slowed and turned off onto a dirt road wide enough for one vehicle.

A half-moon ribboned by clouds cast moving shadows. The darkened forest took on a sinister look that played on Jay's imagination. *Nobody in their right mind travels this kind of road at night. What the hell are we going to do out here in the damn dark? We won't be able to see a foot in front of us.* Jay glanced at Liberty, unable to read anything by the look on her face. *The hostage is someone Liberty is close to. A lover?*

A few miles later Liberty pulled over. She shut the lights off just as the clouds swallowed the moon. It was pitch black. Jay could hear Liberty rustling around, but could barely make out her form. A beam of light from a flashlight dimly lit the interior. Liberty smeared black shoe polish on her face, then handed the can to Jay. "Smear some of that on your face." When she was done, Liberty handed her a pair of night vision goggles. "You've had combat training. You know how to use these?"

Jay took the goggles without answering.

"Ahead about a mile is a bend. Just beyond is the trailhead where Kayla and Cassie parked the car. Cassie should be there waiting."

"And this Scalzon and the hostage? Will the hostage be alive?"

Jay's words elicited a twitch of muscle along side of Liberty's mouth. "The purpose was to get me here. She'll be there or will leave a trail that will lead me to her. Scalzon will keep the hostage alive until I get there. But if Cassie shows herself she'll be quickly killed.

"Scalzon needs Kayla alive to draw me out, and she will inflict pain on Kayla to do that. She doesn't plan to walk away from here leaving anyone alive. We're not going to walk in the front door and make it easy for her. We need to get Cassie to safety first; that's your job."

Liberty pointed to the dense area of trees across the road. "We're going to circle around and approach the parking area from behind. With those goggles, you'll be able to see the thermal heat of anyone within two hundred meters. So will Scalzon. Let's get moving."

The fall and hitting the cold water stunned Cassie. She was carried a mile or two downstream before she was able to grab onto a fallen tree and climb out. Again, she gave thanks for waterproofing. The contents of her pack were dry and her boots had fared pretty well. The rest of her was soaked, but nothing was broken, though her entire body felt like she'd been bashed against a few boulders. Grabbing her first aid kit, she cleaned the wound on her thigh where the bullet had grazed her, then applied an antibacterial ointment. The bleeding was minimal. She'd had worse.

After changing into the dry clothes she'd packed, Cassie made it to where they parked the truck and huddled under an overhanging ledge of rocks that still held the warmth of the sun. She prayed as darkness descended upon the forest. *Please, dear God, let Kayla be all right.*

In order to keep herself from making a sound, Cassie put her hands over her mouth to hold back a sob. The picture of Kayla being pistol whipped and lying on the ground with a gun pointing at her head kept running through her mind. She pressed closer to the rocks when she heard the rustling of leaves and the innocuous sound of a squirrel scrambling up a tree. *If only I hadn't lost the cell. Liberty, please hurry.*

Chapter Twenty One

Acutely aware of the sounds of the forest, Liberty stealthily made her way through the trees with Jay moving as quietly behind her. The altitude cooled the temperature at night, and their breaths were wisps of vapor. Stopping abruptly, Liberty raised her hand and motioned for Jay to get down. Ahead fifty yards the infrared light of Liberty's night goggles captured a thermal image. After zeroing in on the image with the infared riflescope, Liberty put her goggles back on and handed the rifle to Jay, motioning for Jay to cover her. Quickly slipping her goggles off, Jay looked through the scope and scanned the area as Liberty silently moved closer toward Cassie.

When Liberty was within a few feet, she tossed a pinecone and whispered, "Cassie, it's Liberty." Whimpering, Cassie crawled out from under her shelter. She couldn't see Liberty, who was standing in the dark. "Behind you."

Cassie felt the arms going around her and collapsed into them. "Shh...I'm here." Liberty motioned to Jay, then tightened her arms around Cassie to hold her up. Cassie stiffened when she heard Jay approaching. "It's all right, she's here to help." After easing Cassie back down, Liberty and Jay crouched beside her. "What happened? I tried to call."

Liberty came close to losing it as Cassie cried, safe in Liberty's arms, and told them about seeing Kayla being beaten and about her being shot. Controlling the rage that was threatening to unravel her, Liberty swallowed the lump in her throat and said, "Jay, I need you to get Cassie out of here. Get her to the Jeep and back to the ranger station. She needs medical attention. Nathan will be waiting."

Jay nodded. "Is she close?"

"Close enough. She's waiting somewhere along the trail. She knows I'm coming." *She'll want me to see what she does to Kayla.* "Tell Nathan to wait and be ready. Can you find your way back to the Jeep?"

"Yes."

"Cassie, go with Jay."

"What if you need...?"

"I'll bring Kayla home. Now go."

Liberty searched the forest with the night goggles until she was sure Jay and Cassie were not being followed. Then, for a moment longer, she crouched with her back against the rock. *Kayla, my love, I am so sorry. I was foolish to think my past didn't matter, but a past filled with death never dies. Now you're suffering because of loving me.*

She leaned her head back against the cold hardness, her heart pounding. She had little time. Scalzon knew she would come. Liberty hoped she could get into position before Scalzon knew she was there and killed Kayla.

Staying off the trail, Liberty moved silently through the forest, acutely aware of everything around her. She stopped and listened. A change in the sounds of the forest warned her that Scalzon was close. Ahead was a clearing. She carefully placed each footfall as she eased closer. What she saw made her heart lurch in her chest and dropped her to her knees. Kayla was hanging by her wrists from a tree. Her clothes were torn, and her face was nearly unrecognizable and bleeding.

Resisting the impulse to run to her, Liberty tore her gaze away and scanned the area. Scalzon was sitting a few feet behind Kayla. It was beginning to get light. If Scalzon saw her, she would go for Kayla and maim or kill her. Ripping off her goggles, Liberty raised the rifle and focused the scope on Kayla's limp body. It seemed an eternity, but eventually Kayla moved, raising her head and looking in her direction as if sensing she was there. *Dear God, she's alive. Please hang on.*

Quickly she shifted the rifle to where she'd seen Scalzon sitting, but she was gone. She froze when she heard a voice saying, "You're here. Bravo, you don't seem to have lost your skills. Good, I really didn't want it to end too easily. It's been a long time."

Changing her position, Liberty crawled along the ground. "What, nothing to say, Liberty?" Scalzon's voice went on. "Your woman is a fighter. I can understand your attraction to her. She smells good and tastes even better."

Digging her fingers into the hard ground, Liberty bit her lip until it bled to keep quiet and kept moving.

"I must insist that you join us." When Liberty raised her head, Scalzon was standing behind Kayla holding a knife against the side of her throat. "I'll cut her just enough for you to watch her bleed out."

Taking her hand off the rifle, Liberty was about to stand when a voice behind her yelled, "Don't hurt her! I'm coming out."

Liberty watched as Jay walked alongside her with her hands in the air. They were the same height and build and with the ski cap and blackened face, it would be easy to mistake Jay for her. Liberty slowly lifted the rifle and took aim, but Kayla's head blocked her shot. She took a deep breath and prayed for an opening.

Jay took a few steps to the edge of the clearing, then stopped, waiting for Liberty to take a shot.

"Where's your rifle?" Scalzon yelled.

"Back there. On the ground."

"Turn around."

Jay turned slowly, her eyes glancing down at Liberty. *Take the damn shot.*

"Very good, now throw the pistol under you jacket away and get face down." Through the scope Liberty could see Scalzon's eyes and knew she was going to cut Kayla. She took an even breath and fired. The forest went dead still. Cassie burst through the trees, running to where Kayla was hanging. Scalzon lay at Kayla's feet, a clean shot through her left eye. Liberty yelled into the phone, telling Nathan where they were, then bolted out of the trees toward Kayla.

Kayla fell into Liberty's arms as Cassie cut the ropes. Her eyes were mere slits in her swollen face, but she was breathing.

"Kayla, baby, can you hear me? You're going to be all right. I'm here." Jay and Cassie stood helplessly watching as Liberty took off her jacket, wrapped Kayla in it, then held her. "It's going to be okay. I love you, Kayla. I love you."

A short time later, Nathan was flying them out of the forest toward Kalispell Regional Medical Center.

Three Days Later

"What did she do, Kayla, use you as a punching bag?"

"I tried to run for it again when we reached the clearing. She pistoled me to the ground. I remember hearing you yelling, Cassie, and then hearing Scalzon shooting. I charged her, then everything went black. When I woke and saw you gone...I...I thought she'd killed you."

"I'm too tough to kill. Besides, I have the Olympics to train for."

Kayla reached for a tissue and carefully wiped the moisture from her swollen eyes. "Going for the Gold, are you?"

"Nothing less. Hey, you know you kind of look like a chipmunk? A road-kill one, but still a chipmunk."

Kayla winced. "Please don't make me laugh. It hurts."

"Rue said that after the stitches come out, the scars on your face will fade so you'll hardly be able to see them. She did a good job of putting your nose back where it belonged." Cassie looked at Jay, who was standing next to her and explained. "Rue is Doctor Mican. You met her. She's an old girlfriend of Kayla's."

Kayla tried to roll her eyes, but the attempt hurt. "Jay, Cassie tells me that you're flying back to California in the morning." Kayla looked down at her hands, then back at Jay. "Thank you for helping us. I wish you could stay a few more days so we could show you Lone Mountain and Montana."

"Well, uh...actually Cassie invited me back for a skiing vacation." Blushing, Jay said, "I have quite a bit of vacation coming, and...well, I'm thinking of taking her up on her offer."

Kayla noticed the way Cassie was looking at Jay. *No way!* "That would be wonderful. We'd love to have you." *Or rather Cassie would, by the way she's looking at you.*

Cassie was unusually fidgety, and Kayla took the hint. "I'm a bit tired. Why don't you two get going and stop for dinner, my treat?"

"Good idea. Jay, would you mind waiting for me in the lobby? I'll be right down."

"Sure. Kayla, it's been nice meeting you and your family. I'll see you this winter."

After Jay left and closed the door, Cassie sat beside Kayla on the bed.

"Liberty was here the first night and the next day until Rue told us you were going to be all right and should be waking up. When you started to stir, she just disappeared."

"I was doped up, but I remember her being here. I've called home, and no one answers. Have you seen her?"

"No. She hasn't been at the house or at the lodge. Jay and I checked the apartment above the Pub. It doesn't look as if she's been there either." Cassie was angry at Liberty for hurting Kayla. "Jay thinks that Liberty can't deal with what happened to you because of her."

"And because of that she's left me?"

Cassie held Kayla's hand. "I don't know."

Taking a deep breath, Kayla wiped a tear from her eye. "I don't blame her for what happened, but I can understand. What I can't understand is why she'd leave without talking to me. I love her more than I ever thought I could love anyone again. I just want her to come home."

Hugging Kayla, Cassie said, "Give her a little time. She'll come home. I know she will."

"I hope you're right. Now, don't keep Jay waiting. What's up with that? Thinking of jumping the fence, are you?"

Cassie kissed Kayla on the cheek and walked to the door then turned and smiled. "What makes you think I was on the other side of the fence to begin with? She's great, isn't she? And for your information, I'm having a hard time keeping my eyes or hands off her. And I'm not waiting until the snow flies. Good night, Kayla."

The pain pill Rue had given Kayla eased her aches, but it didn't put her to sleep. When the nurse found her awake at eleven, she'd offered her the sleeping pill that had been ordered. Refusing, Kayla lay awake thinking about Liberty. *Sweetheart, where are you? I need you. I felt you with me every moment that woman held me. I knew you'd come. Please don't leave me now.*

She was lying on her back with a cold gel pack across her cheek and forehead when she heard the door open. It was about time for rounds. When she felt the weight on the bed, her heart started to pound. Her hand was lifted off the bed and held in one she knew so well. Liberty whispered, her voice sounding hoarse like she'd been crying.

"I'm sorry. I'm so sorry, baby. I'd as soon die as see you hurt. You could have been..."

"You made me a promise that you'd never leave me again. Are you breaking that promise or are you staying?" Kayla held her breath waiting.

"I could never leave you. I'm sorry. Will you forgive me?"

Kayla removed the pack that covered her eyes and most of her face. "It looks worse than it is." She scooted over in the bed. "I love you Liberty Starr, and that's forever, as long as forever is. I can't sleep without you next to me and right now, damn it, I need you to hold me so I can."

A smile lit Liberty's face. She took her shoes off, removed her slacks and shirt, then climbed in next to Kayla, taking her in her arms. Pulling the covers over them, she whispered in Kayla's ear, "Go to sleep, my love. I'll be here when you wake up."

JP works in health care as an RN. Raised in the mining town of Butte, Montana, she now spends her time between the desert of Arizona, the beach town Carlsbad, California, and the Rocky Mountains of Montana. JP is the author of *Talon, Threads of Destiny*, and *Incommunicado*.

Contact JP at Jpmercerauthor@aol.com or visit her website at www.jpmercer.com

Other works by J.P. Mercer:

Threads of Destiny
ISBN: 978 - 0 - 9754366 - 7 - 7 (0-9754366-7-8)

Threads of Destiny embraces the coastal paradise of Santa Barbara, California, and the beautiful, romantic scenery of of its virgin wine country. It's the story of the powerful Cara Vittore Cipriano and Jacquelyn Lee Biscayne. Cara is a lawyer and Padrone of the prestigous Cipriano Vineyards and Jake, an FBI forensic pathologist, is undercoverwith the Monsoon Rain Task Force, which is closing in on the Mexican/Columbian cocaine pipeline. Twisted threads had torn their lives asunder, leaving each to follow their own path toward an undeniable, inevitable fate. Destined to cross paths again, their lives will entwine amidst a world of intrigue, cocaine, murder, and the relentless search for a ruthless killer.

Talon
ISBN: 978 - 1 - 933720 - 03 - 6 (1-933720-03-4)

Liberty Starr had just finished FBI training and believed she was doing her patriotic duty when seh agreed to join the Talons, an elite covert group formed by the President in response toan atrocious act of terrorism. The Talons and their mission are insidiously corrupted with murder for profit to further the political career and power by the President's trusted advisor, his Vice President.

Kayla Sinclair was touted as the best woman downhill skier in the world and was predicted to win more medals than any woman in the history of the Olympic Games. Kayla was at the top of her game when an avalanche crashed down on her, causing her to spiral into a liqour bottle to escape her losses.

A twist of fate brings these two emotionally damaged women together during a tumultuous time in the histroy of the country. Liberty discovers the heartbreak of betrayal and becomes the hunted. Can she find peace and absolution? Can she rekindle a small spark of humanity that still burns in a soul that is coated with the blood of those she's killed? Will Kayla overcome her demons and hatred for the mountain and allow her heart to heal and to love?

Available at your favorite bookstore.

Printed in the United States
152343LV00011B/100/P